THE ROAD TO DAMIETTA

THE ROAD TO
DAMIETTA

SCOTT O'DELL

Houghton Mifflin Company Boston 1985

Copyright © 1985 by Scott O'Dell

All rights reserved. No part of this work may be reproduced
or transmitted in any form or by any means, electronic or
mechanical, including photocopying and recording, or by
any information storage or retrieval system, except as
may be expressly permitted by the 1976 Copyright Act or in
writing from the publisher. Requests for permission
should be addressed in writing to
Houghton Mifflin Company,
2 Park Street, Boston, Massachusetts 02108.

Printed in the United States of America

Library of Congress Cataloging in Publication Data

O'Dell, Scott
The road to Damietta.

Summary: Deeply attached to the charming and
carefree Francis Bernardone, Cecilia, a young
noblewoman of Assisi, watches as he turns from his
life of wealth and privilege, takes vows of poverty,
and devotes himself to serving God by helping all
those around him.
1. Francis, of Assisi, Saint, 1182-1226—Juvenile
fiction. [1. Francis, of Assisi, Saint, 1182-1226—
Fiction. 2. Religious life—Fiction. 3. Italy—
History—476-1268—Fiction] I. Title.
PZ7.O237Ro 1985 [Fic] 85-11720
ISBN 0-395-38923-2

V 10 9 8 7 6 5 4 3 2 1

To Elizabeth

AUTHOR'S NOTE

Of the thousands upon thousands of books about Saint Francis, perhaps the best is *Francis of Assisi* by Arnaldo Fortini. A lawyer and native of Assisi, Fortini spent thirty years on this biography. It first appeared in four volumes. It is now in one volume, brilliantly translated by Helen Moak, with valuable notes of her own and a bibliography of some seven hundred and fifty items. My book leans heavily upon their portrait of the many-sided saint and his times.

For the Sufi anecdotes and parables, I have relied upon collections by Idries Shah from the Persian, Afghan, Turkish, and Arabic cultures. The scenes between Saint Francis and the Sultan of Egypt are taken from the chronicles of the Moslem mystic Fakr-al-Farasi and the Arab chroniclers Al-Zaiyat and Al-Sakhari.

The story was suggested by the life of Angelica di Rimini, a distant cousin of Perugino, the Italian painter.

THE ROAD TO DAMIETTA

ONE

W e heard the leper's bell long before we saw the leper.

The sun was up, yet frost still clung to the trees by the river. Behind us the castles of Monte Rosso, their battlements and enclosures, caught the sun. The towers rose like spears from the dark ravines and every hilltop.

The lords were at breakfast, planning their next swoop into the lowlands or against each other, which would not occur on the morrow because it was the Wednesday before Easter and all hostilities — whether close or far, whether of repayment for a death or a slight, fancied or real — were forbidden by law. By the *Treuga Dei*, the "truce of God," fighting was forbidden until dawn of the next Sunday morning, from the Passion to the Resurrection. Only a few days to plan how they would burn and destroy, maim and kill, during the next year. Yet in that brief time what these rapacious men could do!

We were moving along the road from our farm at the foot of Monte Rosso to our home in Assisi. Usually we spent part of the winter and the whole spring in the country, but my father was the *podestà*, the leader, and a member of the commune that governed Assisi, and lately, within the past month, he had been harshly criticized for living outside the city more than he lived in it, which had disturbed his sleep and didn't please him at all.

There were only four in our family now that my brother Lorenzo had been slain in the battle with Perugia — my father, Davino di Montanaro; my mother, Giacoma; my brother, Rinaldo; and myself, Cecilia Graziella Beatrice Angelica Rosanna, called Ricca, a contraction of some sort.

It was a small family, yet our caravan stretched out for nearly a league on the winding lane by the river. My father rode in front with Rinaldo. My mother sat uncomfortably in a dainty, high-wheeled wagon, sheltered from the sun by a canopy painted with scrolls and fat cupids. I came next on my white Arabian, and Raul de los Santos, the librarian and master of our scriptorium, who also tutored me in astronomy, numbers, and languages of the world, rode beside me on another Arabian.

The rest of the caravan, mostly on foot, followed after — tillers of the earth, herders of pigs, goats, and cattle, the vintner, the miller and his two assistants, the notary, a squadron of servants. Bringing up the rear were Ruffo, captain of the guards, and his men, all in full armor, riding white horses, and displaying the Montanaro pennon of crossed swords on a background of stars.

The leper's bell drew closer. When first I heard it the sound seemed to come from the far side of the river. Now it was right in front of us, on the road we were traveling, between us and the city.

My father pulled up his mount and called to one of the oxboys. "Run down until you find the creature," he said. "Get him off the road and into the bushes, where we'll not have to look at him. Do not dally with him. Use your goad freely."

My father had a great distaste for leprosy, that dread disease where noses rotted away, eyes melted in their sockets, and fingers sloughed off, one by one. As a member of the commune, it was he who had strengthened the laws against lepers.

Each new *podestà*, a month before taking office in Assisi, must now make a scrupulous search for these people. If any is living in the city or the region around, he is to be hunted out. Syndics of all villages and lords of all the castles must take care to see to this. No leper dare enter the city or walk about in it. If any does so, citizens may strike him down with impunity. No leper might eat from anything except the leper's bowl, or drink from springs, wells, or rivers, or touch the young, or go without gloves on his bare hands. In the old days they were given wooden clappers to announce their presence. My father had changed this. Now they carried bells, which could be heard for the better part of a league.

As we waited, the oxboy ran forward, brandishing his goad. After a short time he returned to announce that the leper had been driven into the bushes. My father raised his hand and motioned the caravan to continue.

The road was deserted but the bell still rang. I then saw the leper standing a short way off, warily peering out at us from a hedge. At the distance, I couldn't tell whether he was tall or short, young or old. My father let down the visor of his helmet and I turned my head away, for the sight of people falling apart truly made me ill.

At this time a lone horseman appeared in the distance. He had heard the bell and was riding cautiously. As we came upon him he stopped and greeted us with a wave of a jeweled hand. His name was Francis Bernardone and he was the son of Pietro Bernardone, the second richest merchant in the city of Assisi, my father being the first.

"Have you seen the leper?" he asked my father. "I smell him but I do not see him anywhere."

"There he is," my father said, pointing. "We chased him off the road. Proceed in safety; he'll not disturb you."

"Thank you, sir," Francis Bernardone said, speaking through a lace handkerchief he held to his mouth. "Thank you most kindly, but I think I'll take the long road. The odor burrows into my skin and stays with me for days. Nothing washes it away."

A bridge spanned the river a short distance in front of us. Touching his feathered cap to my father but smiling at me, he spurred his horse across the bridge and rode away at a fast canter.

"Poor boy," my mother said. To her any man younger than twenty years was a boy. "He's so sensitive."

"Yes, brought up by a doting mother," my father said. "She clothed him in dresses until he was five, I hear."

"True," said Rinaldo, who disliked Francis Bernardone intensely. "Sensitivity has come into fashion, so he's become quite sensitive these days."

"A result of the foolish war," Raul observed as he looked up from the scroll he was reading and turned his long, bony face in the direction of the fleeing horseman. "It was the fashion during the war to be brutal, to talk through the front teeth. Of late, like Bernardone, the young talk little, never to their elders, and when they talk to each other, they must be what we from Granada call *sensitivo*, which is the opposite of *macho*, which was stylish during the war, and which means he-goat or a spur, a square anvil, a hammer, and also, quite often, a very ignorant fellow. It's one of the small horrors of the war."

Raul was referring to the bloody struggle between the town of Perugia and the city of Assisi. It was a terrible war; we pridefully had started it over nothing much, thinking that Perugia was weak and ripe for the gathering. The war had lasted for two years and Assisi had lost its pride and thousands of its young men.

"He has a fly in his head," Rinaldo said, loath to relinquish the subject of Francis Bernardone.

"Many," my father said.

"He's a very sensitive boy," my mother called out from the carriage.

He's not a boy, I wanted to say — but I didn't. I glanced across the river and saw him raise his hand and wave. He was waving to me but I didn't dare wave back.

"Also he's very brave," Mother added, for she, like most of the Assisi women — but none of the men — adored Francis Bernardone. "He's truly the bravest of all!"

I silently agreed with her, remembering when the bulls ran on the feast day of Saint Luke the Evangelist. One of the beasts had found refuge in our courtyard, and I watched from the balcony as Francis pursued it. The problem was not simple. With his wooden sword he had to goad the bull out of the courtyard and into the street where the other bulls were running, and meanwhile he had to keep himself from getting gored.

Though the sword was made of wood, he didn't pretend that it was steel. He waved it gaily like a flag. He invited the bull to leave the courtyard, saying in a firm voice, "This is a festive game, sir, in which you play the villain. Yet we play without anger, in fun, with respect for each other, because we are friends."

The bull pawed the stones, but in a moment, to my surprise, it began to walk toward the open gate. As it passed him, Francis reached out and gave it a friendly prod with his sword. The bull paused at the gate and glanced back at him, then, as if it were glad to be under his spell no longer, lifted its tail and leaped off into the street.

That was the day I fell in love with Francis Bernardone. The very day and hour. And not because he was braver than the rest or more handsome. It was the way he spoke to the bull that pierced my heart.

We came to the river without further incident, but there we had to stop for toll. On this morning, however, Count Giuseppe di Luzzaro, having heard that we were moving from our farm in the country to our palace in the city, was at the crossing to welcome us and let us pass without paying the toll his varlets usually demanded.

The dashing count of Monte Verde was there for a reason. It was more than a rumor that he was deciding whether to marry me or not, once I had reached a reasonable age, which would be, since I was barely thirteen, at least one year from the moment. He had talked to my father on two occasions I knew about.

I had already made a quiet decision about the count and his

5

square beard and his small, pouting ruby-red lips. I had decided that I would get myself to a nunnery rather than be his bride.

"It's been scarcely a year since I've seen you," he said, running his eyes over me. "It was on this road, I remember. You were riding on a pallet then. Now you ride like a lady. My, how you've grown! And how in the mode you are, with the little peregrine perched on your wrist. The bird is called . . . ?"

"Simonetta."

"A lithesome name, but can she fly the heavens?" he asked. "She looks somewhat fragile and small of wing, but free her and let's see."

"She's not yet trained to hunt, sir."

"An apt time to train her. The skies are clear and larks are flying."

"As you can observe, we are hastening to the city," I said, determined not to unloose Simonetta and risk never seeing her again. "Besides, Father is in a hurry. He's been hurrying for a week."

The count of Monte Verde glanced at my father, who was prompt to say that he was not in a hurry and that his time belonged to the count. Like all the rich merchants in the province of Umbria, Father had set his mind upon working his way out of the merchant class and into the nobility.

The count glanced at Simonetta, alert now that she had heard her name spoken, then at me, his black beard set and challenging. I, as well as the hawk, needed training, a firm but gentle hand.

He smiled; his lips glistened. "Someday soon," he said, "I'll show you how best to handle her. We'll bring Simonetta here to the river and unloose her."

He came close and examined the hawk, running a hand over her sleek feathers and at the same time over my gloved wrist. "She has good talons, sharp and well shaped, if a trifle long, and an excellent beak. I can't see her eyes, hidden as they are by the pretty hood. What color might they be — golden?"

6

"Gold and black."

"Sharp, like yours?"

"Sharp," I said, "as bodkins. She can see in all directions."

"At once?"

"If she chooses."

"What a truly marvelous bird. I am anxious to train her," he said with a smile, turning his horse in a circle and making a bow.

The river ran low, so we lost nothing in the crossing and began the long climb to Assisi. I thought about Francis Bernardone. I wondered about him and the leper. Why had he covered his face and fled in terror? He had fought in the war, been wounded and imprisoned. He had run with the bulls. Yet the mere sight of the leper had made him tremble.

Our musicians struck up a marching tune as we passed through the Roman gate. Windows opened. People stared out at us. We made a good show with our league-long caravan and it served my father well. Now everyone would know that, forsaking the country, he had returned to live in Assisi.

It didn't matter that at dawn, before anyone was around, half of our retinue — the vintner and his assistant, the goatherds, half of our guards, and all of our farmers — would return to the country.

TWO

W eeks went by before I saw Francis Bernardone again. It was on the night Raul and I stood on the balcony above San Rufino Square, watching the skies for the serpent star.

Raul had brought a chart of the heavens when he came from Granada. Father had engaged him to teach me the history of the world and some of its languages, but Raul had a liking for astronomy, and although my father thought it pointless for females of my age or of any age, he didn't object to my spending an hour now and again gazing at the stars.

The Arabian seer who made the chart had noted that for the past three centuries a fiery apparition had appeared at regular intervals of one hundred and seven years. Raul unrolled the chart, laid it out on the balcony rail, and set a lantern beside it, and I read the Arab's notes describing the apparition as a "glowing serpent with a fiery tail, which flees across the western sky at dusk."

"We should go and tell everyone," I said, "so they can come and watch."

"Assisi, my friend, is a nervous place. If the serpent does not appear, they'll laugh at us. If it does appear then there'll be an awful scene — the populace running this way and that. Hiding under beds, in the cathedral, in the forest, in caves. As it is, if the serpent does come, few will know because few ever raise their eyes to look at the heavens. But I wish that Marsilio was with us. I sent him a letter weeks ago and invited him here to

8

witness the event, but he wrote back and called me a fool for believing in such maunderings."

The two men had exchanged letters for a long time, mostly about the shape of the earth. Marsilio, who lived in Perugia where they believed many strange things, thought that it was shaped like a pear, and Raul thought that it was more like a wheel, the various countries, islands, and oceans being the spokes in the wheel. Everyone knew the earth never moved, but both men were wrong about its shape. It was the heart of the universe, and everything else — the sun and moon and stars — moved around it in an obedient procession, like slaves. Besides, the earth was most certainly flat and hung suspended from a golden cord, like a feast-day platter, only larger.

We stood on the balcony with the map spread before us, and the serpent came soon after vespers. But somehow it lacked the tail the seer had described. In truth, it wasn't much of a serpent.

"It looks like somebody's footprint," I said.

"The street lanterns and the bonfire burning there below us hinder our view," Raul said. "On a better night, it would look much different."

"Like two footprints."

"Remember, that seer Yakub made his prediction more than a hundred years ago."

"Perhaps the serpent is worn down from all its travels. But Yakub says here in his notes that it is a good omen to wish upon."

"A voice," Raul said, "whispered to me just now, saying, 'There is no such thing as an omen for lovers to be found in the sky. Nor a voice whispering in the night.'"

From below us in San Rufino Square came a clash of cymbals and the braying of horns. A band of musicians surrounded by a motley crowd had gathered at a bonfire. One of the musicians, a youth dressed in an embroidered tunic, wearing a velvet cap with a cock's feather and a broad belt set with shimmering studs and clasps, I recognized at once.

It was impossible to hear me above the clamor, but I took a

long breath and shouted down to him, inviting him to watch the fiery serpent.

"Who is it you shout at?" Raul asked.

"The one in the velvet cap and the cock's feather — Francis Bernardone."

Raul said nothing, groaning instead.

The sound of lutes and violins drifted up on the windless air. A hush fell upon the crowd. Then Francis Bernardone was singing, softly and clearly:

> *"Put out my searching eyes!*
> *Blind me!*
> *Let me never again see thy beauty,*
> *For my heart it crucifies."*

The fire shone on his upturned face. I wondered if he saw me in my white gown with the ribbons and rosebuds, leaning above him on the balcony.

A sigh must have escaped my lips, for Raul said: "You are very prideful. He's not singing to you. Other girls also inhabit Piazza San Rufino. There's the pretty Fabrissa Filippi directly across the square. Next to her are the Barbarossas, Beatrice and Aspasia, equally favored. And let's not forget Clare di Scifi, of the noblest of all Assisi families, a girl famed for her beauty and winning disposition. If you believe that Francis Bernardone sings only to you, then, my dear, you are the possessor of an immense conceit."

Francis was singing another ballad; his words drifted up, soft as rose petals:

> *"You are mine.*
> *I am thine.*
> *In my heart*
> *You are locked forever*
> *And the golden key is lost."*

The song faded away. Silent and breathless, I leaned over the balcony.

Raul said, "You may be surprised by the question and you may not wish to answer. But if you do, answer me with the truth."

I knew the question before he had a chance to ask it. Calmly I said, as though I had said it many times before, "Francis Bernardone is my dearest love."

Raul's face was hidden, but silence betrayed his concern.

"I've loved him always," I said. "And I love him now and will forever."

"I understand, oh, how I understand," he said. "Bernardone is a charming minstrel, a singer of tender songs, a teller of fantastic tales, an acrobat whose feet never touch the ground, with whom every girl in Assisi thinks she's in love. And now it's you that joins the many. You've never met Bernardone. Never so much as spoken a word to him and yet you claim to be in love. What nonsense!"

"Must I speak to him? Isn't it enough that I have seen him in the streets, on the roads, here in our courtyard, and now below us singing in Piazza San Rufino? I have two eyes and two ears. I can see and hear."

Yet as I spoke these bold words, I was aware that eyes and ears had little to do with my love for Francis Bernardone. If I were without sight and hearing, still would I love him.

The bonfire blazed high and in the light I caught a glimpse of Raul's face. He was deciding that such an impossible thing was possible.

"Feeling as you do," he said, "I must bring you twain together. We can't invite him here because your father, to state it modestly, would not approve. But an idea hovers in my head. Bernardone is a clerk at his father's cloth shop, not far from here. I require a length of wool for a cloak and serge for a pair of breeches. So we'll visit the shop one of these days, and while I make a purchase you can observe him close at hand."

"I don't wish to observe him," I said testily. "I've observed him many times before and I have observed him tonight."

"Yes, but you haven't met him. He isn't what you judge him to be from the glimpses. A plain countenance, somewhat severe, for one thing. An unusual pair of ears — not ugly, mind you, not big, very small in fact, yet they do stand out. Not up like a rabbit's ears but straight out like those of some woodland creature. Quite charming!"

"It isn't necessary that I meet him at all. Tomorrow or ever."

"Now Princess Ricca is being wildly romantic. To her this Bernardone is a gallant knight astride a snow-white horse cantering through fields of asphodel on an April morn. Princess Ricca is afraid to meet him. She would rather dream. Which is very wise of Ricca."

Worn out with talking, we were silent for a while. Then in the silence the apparition appeared. It was a burst of blue and silver light that lasted only a breath, so brief that Raul didn't see it and no one opened a window on San Rufino Square.

"An omen," prayerfully I said to myself. "An omen of wonderful luck to come."

But nine days later the fiery omen brought heartbreak instead.

In June every year Assisi celebrated the feast of Saint Victorinus. From balconies and windows hung tapestries and pennons. Laurel wreaths adorned the doors, and everyone, save children and young girls, watched the solemn festivities and afterward frolicked through the streets to the songs and antics of the *tripudianti*, a company of dancers.

This year the leader of the *tripudianti*, as for two years past, was Francis Bernardone. The day came misty and cold, but when the church bells rang for midday he was in Piazza San Rufino with his companions, rousing the city with the call of trumpets, summoning all those who were not too old or too young to come and join him at the feast.

From my balcony, scarcely breathing, I saw him stride forth with a jaunty swing, dressed in a tunic of the finest silk and a yellow-feathered cap, holding the hand of the youth who had been chosen to play the part of Saint Victorinus. I watched as he led Victorinus to the center of the square and then disappeared in the crowd. I looked everywhere through the chanting throng for the red tunic and yellow-feathered cap.

I had seen the miracle of Saint Victorinus four times before, since I was nine years old, so I kept looking for Francis all during the play, which was no different from the other times. First, the bishop by reason of his miraculous powers causes a mute boy to speak and also brings sight to a man who is blind. Then he is brought before a magistrate, just as in the days of ancient Rome, and asked to make a sacrifice to Vulcan, the pagan god, which he calmly refuses to do.

The mob — played by those now assembled in the square — turns violently against him and demands his death, whereupon the angry magistrate commands him to place his head upon a block. The executioner wields a sword and blood gushes out — the red, red wine from Santa Lucia. Women wrap him in winding cloths and bear him away while the throng laments.

Only then did Francis Bernardone appear, striding forth in shiny black boots that reached above his knees and a sendal cloak of many colors. He cleared a place to dance and dancers formed circles, held hands, and went round and round singing, my father and brother Rinaldo among them. (Mother, who thought that dancing was a pagan sin, had left the square.)

As I watched Francis Bernardone flashing around, the wind whipping his cloak, revealing stripes of green and yellow, as I sulkily counted the days and weeks, realizing that another year would pass, another June would come, before I could dance in Piazza San Rufino, I was shocked to see him dancing in the same small circle with my closest friend, Clare di Scifi. Clare was only two years older than I, scarcely that, and yet there she was below me in her white dress trimmed with lace, floating about like a snowflake.

I fled the balcony. I closed the door tight and flung myself on the bed and stopped my ears with pillows against the sound of the brazen drums and the wild songs of the *tripudianti.*

THREE

F or weeks, for weeks, I closed my mind to every thought of Francis Bernardone.

Even when Raul brought his name up or his latest escapade was mentioned at table and no one defended him except my mother, I remained silent. If he appeared in my dreams, as he often did, sometimes as a horseman fleeing from me as he had fled from the leper, other times as a troubadour beneath my window, praising the charms of Clare di Scifi, not me, or as a clown in a parti-colored cloak leading a rout of revelers, it was not my fault.

Like lightning in a cloudless sky, these peaceful days came to an end on the first day of the feast of San Niccolò. On that day the youth of Assisi elected from their ranks a *podestà*, five judges, five counselors, and a bishop. These mock officials took over the management of Assisi and thus, by raising the lowest to the highest, the powerless to seats of power, they gave the mighty a taste of how it felt to serve and not be served and above all to learn the art of humility.

Francis Bernardone, chosen as the youthful bishop, was to take the place of Bishop Guido. Served by his companions, who were posing as acolytes, he would celebrate the evening Mass.

I never had gone to the *festa*, but on this occasion Clare di Scifi and some of the other girls who lived in Piazza San Rufino banded together against our parents and wrung from them permission to attend the Mass, provided we were accompanied by five watchful servants.

14

It was a cold night when we hurried through the streets to the cathedral, wrapped in our heavy cloaks, everyone twittering like birds, except me. The thought of Francis clad in a bishop's fine vestments, of possibly touching the hem of his robe, awakened all the old dreams. Most of the girls wished to remain in the back, where small fires in iron buckets fought the cold, but I prevailed upon them to press on until we came to the altar.

Francis appeared to the sounds of lutes, a wide smile on his face, dressed in a violet-colored robe that didn't fit, since Bishop Guido was much smaller than he was. His hair curled out from under the rim of a purple miter cocked sidewise, and in his pleasant baritone he sang the hymns and antiphons and jauntily celebrated Mass.

I watched and listened, so enthralled by every word he uttered, every movement he made, that Clare, thinking I was asleep, kept nudging my arm. And after Mass ended and Francis went tripping through the crowd, I followed him.

Before we reached the door he had disappeared, and when I saw him again, outside on the cathedral steps, he had shed his bishop's garb and was dressed in an outlandish costume, one half of which was red silk from head to toe and the other half a coarse green fabric used in the making of horse blankets.

The cathedral square was flooded with citizenry. The flood spilled over into courtyards and arcades, ran off toward other piazzas. It seemed that everyone in Assisi and the whole countryside had come to celebrate the feast of San Niccolò. Those who attended Mass were there to watch Bishop Guido squirm in his velvet chair, uncomfortable at the sight of Bishop Bernardone gaily mocking him. The thousands who remained outside were interested not in this topsy-turvy scene, but only in celebrating what was called the December Liberties, a saturnalia that had come down to us over the centuries.

Our band of five and the five watchful servants were huddled on the cathedral steps, trying to decide how best to find our way back to San Rufino, when Francis with a leap was suddenly in our midst.

"Come, young ladies," he shouted above the sounds of the swarming crowd, "and let us dance the rites of our wild forefathers — a goaty crew, I must say."

With that he seized upon fragile Amata di Renaro, flung her into the air, and caught her as she was about to strike her head on the steps. Next came crippled little Benedetta, countess of Spoleto, for whom he did a squatting dance step and whom he kissed upon the brow. Then Damiella di Malispini, whose hair he clasped in both hands and gently shook until it hung to her shoulders. He paused to glance at the crowd that had pressed around to gawk at him. With a cry he grasped Giacoma, one of the servants, and twirled her about. Then he did the same to Leonarda, Consolata, Patrizia, and blind Lucia Barbrero.

Only Clare and I were left. It was she whom he chose. Taking her hands and gazing mournfully, like a rejected lover, into her beautiful eyes, he moved her about in a circle, muttering words I didn't catch.

The crowd pressed in, leaving him little room to dance. He was out of breath. He looked at me, the very last, and with outstretched hands he silently begged me to let him rest. I smiled and turned away with a sinking heart, only to feel his hands grasp mine.

There was no place to dance. He begged the crowd for a yard of room, no more. Laughing, it took no heed. But to my delight I was suddenly moving down the step, dragged by the hand, to be gathered up by a swirl of revelers and swept round and round in dizzy circles, while I clung tight, like someone who, drowning, is about to be saved.

The piazza was a stormy sea breaking against a rocky shore. Above the roar I thought I heard Francis say words I had heard before. Yes, the ballad he had sung in San Rufino. The last words of the ballad that had drifted up to me in the night.

> *"In my heart*
> *You are locked forever*
> *And the golden key is lost."*

I tried to think of a word to say in reply. If a word had come to me, I could not have said it, yet I did not faint. I held my breath and clung with both my hands to his, moving lightly in a dream I had dreamed before.

At last the flood swept us ashore on the cathedral steps, at the feet of my four companions and the five watchful servants. I turned to thank Francis for the dance. He had disappeared, borne away by the tide of revelers.

Our little band, desperately clinging together, got back to San Rufino before the bells tolled the hour of midnight, but in a frenzy of excitement the revels went on, with only a brief pause at dawn, though the pope had issued an edict against reveling — on and on for days and ending in a pagan rout.

Drunken men, tipsy priests, women in flimsy dresses, the rich and the poor, artisans and nobles, the curds and the cream, joined hands with disorderly youth and danced in the cathedral, ate food and drank wine from its altar, which served them as a table. To the sound of castanets, horns, and cymbals, carts rumbled about the city streets, filled with half-naked women bound with leather thongs who were sold by an auctioneer.

Francis's role as the mock bishop lasted for days and ended with his riding on horseback to the bishop's palace. There he summoned Guido to the door and in a leering speech accused him of dancing drunken in the piazza, of joining the crowd eating and guzzling at the altar, and of other outrageous acts. This attended to, Francis raised his hands in a supercilious benediction; everyone had a hearty drink of wine, then all trooped off to pray.

I saw none of the orgy, it being described by my brother one night at supper, though I did hear the horrendous noise and the bacchic songs. I could easily imagine how Francis looked when he stood at the bishop's door, his black brows drawn down, a clown's smile on his face.

I didn't see Francis again until a month, a month and three long weeks, had passed. Raul fell ill and forgot about him. The Bernardone shop was not far away. I thought of going there by myself. I thought of going with my mother, but I was sure that she would talk Francis to death while I stood around in silence. I also thought of asking Clare to go with me. This would be quite silly, I decided, since she was the most beautiful girl in the city of Assisi and the province of Umbria as well. Then I decided not to go at all, thinking it much too bold if I went by myself.

Truthfully, I never decided. The decision was made for me. One night an unheard voice spoke. An unseen hand reached out in the dark and quietly took mine.

At dawn I sent a servant into the courtyard to sample the day. She came back to report an overcast sky and a north wind, so I dressed to suit the weather in what I thought might catch his eye — a blue surcoat trimmed at the cuffs and hem with gray squirrel.

The falconer brought Simonetta, my trim saker hawk, hatched in Venice and given to me by my father months ago on my birthday. I wore a blue gauntlet threaded with yellow stones on my left wrist to protect me from her talons. Simonetta wore a golden hood to protect her from the weather and from any temptations to fly away that she might encounter. White hawks were fashionable at the moment, and I had three of them, but Simonetta, jet-black with yellow legs, was my favorite.

Remembering that Francis was said to sleep late, I started off at noon, but no sooner had I reached the square than Raul, still suffering from a cold and wrapped to the eyes in a woolen surcoat, came riding up.

"You're quite bold," he croaked.

"Bold?" I asked innocently.

"You're on your way to meet Francis Bernardone, alone."

"How do you know where I am going?"

"By your favorite hawk and your pearl-encrusted shoes. Also from the look in your eye. By chance, have you told your father about all this?"

"Yes, I told him that I wished to shop for cloth and he asked where. 'At Bernardone's,' was my reply.

"'There's no other place to buy cloth in the city of Assisi, except the place owned by the scoundrel Bernardone?' Father asked.

"'Yes,' I told him."

In all of the provinces of Umbria and Tuscany, there was no place that had finer cloth in the latest weaving and colors than Bernardone's.

"'Your mother will go with you.'

"'Mother likes things that I don't like. She's a little backward in her ideas about cloth.'

"'Then you will go with a maid and a proper number of serving women. Also with guards.'"

Raul grumbled but fell in beside me. As we crossed San Rufino Square he said, though it seemed very painful for him to talk, "I heard that your idol, Francis Bernardone, stole a length of expensive cloth and some money from his father. The cloth he gave to a beggar, and the money he spent on a drunken party."

"The city of Assisi hatches rumors like summer flies," I said. "Where did you hear this one?"

"Yesterday, from your father."

"I don't believe it."

"It does sound odd. A son stealing from his own father. But Francis Bernardone is an odd one. You can expect most anything from him. And not only this. His father is angry. He's even threatened to summon Francis before the authorities."

"I still don't believe it." And I didn't believe so much as a single word of the story.

Flanked by servants and guards carrying the pennons of the House of Montanaro, we set off at a leisurely canter for the Bernardone establishment on Via Portico, which is reached by a lane lined with unpleasant stalls where animals are slaughtered. As we rode down the lane our horses trod in pools of blood.

The Via Portico itself is crowded with shops and large signs — the apothecary's cluster of gilded pills, the striped arm of the barber-surgeon, the goldsmith's unicorn. Bernardone's shop was at the far end of the street, an unlikely place for a merchant dealing in expensive cloth.

By placing trestles stacked with merchandise in front of his store from one side of the street to the other, Bernardone had made a dead end of it. This was against the law, a law my father had helped to write, which required merchants to pile their goods no closer to the center of the street than one inch, and on one side of the street only. Thus we had to dismount halfway down Via Portico and give the horses to our guards, which annoyed Raul.

"Bernardone has been fined a dozen times," he said as we threaded our way through row after row of bulging trestles. "But the fines are small; he pays them and goes right on littering the street. Like his son, Bernardone thinks himself a noble cavalier, scornful of the law."

He sent one of our guards to announce that the daughter of Davino di Montanaro was waiting, and at once boys came running out to make a path for us. A stout gentleman with a scraggly beard, wearing a shabby robe, appeared in the doorway.

"I am honored," he said, after introducing himself with a courtly bow, "to welcome a member of the Montanaro family. And please excuse the confusion. Only yesterday I received a shipment of cloth from Flanders — seven carts and seven donkeys loaded down with treasures, which we haven't had a chance to arrange on the shelves."

I made out the slim figure of his son. He was looking at me, his head cocked to one side, as I walked sedately toward him over the cobbles, my heart beating.

Raul introduced himself and me to Bernardone, who got my name wrong — Pica instead of Ricca — which was not a good beginning. Then to his son.

"I have seen you before," Francis said, smiling, "on the way to San Subasio."

"And other places," I said. "In our courtyard with the bull. And months ago when you sang in the square."

"Oh, yes, you were on the balcony, dressed in a white gown. I saw you while I was singing."

Singing to me, I desperately wanted to say, not to Clare di Scifi. Not to anyone but me. Instead, I reminded him that we had danced in the square on the night of the December Liberties.

He frowned at this and fell silent. He had changed. From the glimpses I'd had of him in the cathedral, filled as it was with candle smoke, and in the square, dense with the oily smoke of torches, I didn't have a true idea of how he looked. But now as I saw him in the daylight, I was certain that he had changed. He was no longer the smiling young man I had seen before.

He was thinner than I remembered. And his eyes, deep-set beneath their black brows, had changed. They seemed troubled. Could Raul's story be true? Was he worried about the angry threats his father had made against him? To belie this troubled mood, he was dressed in the gayest and most charming of costumes — one leg of black silk, one leg of red silk, and a tunic of three or four different colors cinched tight by a rainbow belt.

"Don't just stand there gawking," Signor Bernardone said. "Show the young lady the new damask that arrived only yesterday from Flanders. And the precious Venetian sendal, which is in short supply."

I hadn't come to buy sendal or damask, but since I couldn't say why I had come, I said nothing.

Francis disappeared into the shop, a long, narrow arcade lined with shelves, gloomy as a tomb save for the feeble glow of lanterns. He came back with two bolts of cloth, slipped into the street, and spread them out on a trestle. Draping a corner of the sendal over his arm, he held it up to catch the sunlight.

"Notice, if you will," he said, trying hard to be friendly, "the enchanted glow."

I ran my hand over the silk.

"Doesn't it remind you of a spring day," he said, "when the meadows are green and the wind blows her sweetest and God's flowers bloom?"

I nodded and strove to follow his flight of fancy.

The three bells of San Niccolò broke forth, calling workers to their churchly tasks. The sound of the bells echoed in the narrow street. Raul, who had bought a parcel of serge, stood in the doorway watching. Signor Bernardone was also watching. He darted forth, took up the bolt of sendal, pushed his son aside none too gently, and said how well the silk matched my coloring. Without a word Francis quietly slipped away.

"I'll take a piece of sendal," I said. "And my father will pay you."

"That's not necessary," Bernardone explained. "Pay when you visit us again. I'll have Moorish cloth quite soon. This coming week, perhaps, depending upon the thieves that guard the way and the cloth thieves themselves."

FOUR

T he sky had darkened, and as we left the shelter of Via Portico the wind swooped down upon us. Simonetta ruffled her feathers and took a firmer grip on my wrist. "You're very silent," Raul said. "You seem somewhat chastened. What goes on in your head?"

"Lengths of lovely cloth," I said, "that Signor Bernardone has collected from over the world. The velvets from Paris and the sendal from Venice and —"

"No," Raul said, "not the cloth, of course not. Something else. What is it?"

I spurred the horse to a canter and left him behind, but I had not gone far when I felt a sharp tug at the saddle cloth. Francis Bernardone was running along beside me. With all sorts of wild thoughts racing through my head, I reined in and waited for him to speak.

"What do you call your little hawk?" he asked, out of breath, his face clouded.

"Simonetta," I said.

"A very pretty name for a very pretty bird. But tell me, why do you keep her chained on such a wonderful day? The wind blows and there's music in the sky. Please, friend, take off the hood and let her loose to share this wondrous hour."

I looked down upon him in dismay. His dour expression had not changed. Was he mad? Raul had ridden on and was beckoning to me from the far side of the square. I was tempted to follow him and leave Francis Bernardone standing there in the bitter wind.

"You carry the falcon on your wrist because all the other rich girls do so," he said. "It's the fashion these days. But the falcon wishes to visit heaven, which is her home."

"How do you know what she wishes to do?" I asked, turning the horse round him in a circle.

"I know because I see it in her eyes."

"How can you see her eyes? You can't, because she's wearing a hood."

There was a somber tone in his voice that I had never heard before. It made me think he was speaking the truth, that he did see the falcon's eyes beneath the hood.

"Simonetta," I said, "is young. She hasn't been trained. If I free her, she will never come back. She'll starve or be hunted down."

"God will care for her, as He cares for all His creatures, even for you and me."

He looked up from under the peak of his feathered cap, fixing me with a steady glance. It was meant to make me quaver, lose my senses, free Simonetta — my father's generous gift, bought from the falconry of Filippo dei Casini, doge of Venice.

I looked at Raul, waiting impatiently on the far side of the square. I thought of a way to break the spell.

"I've heard an awful tale. It's . . . well, people are saying that you stole a piece of cloth that belonged to your father. Such terrible things. They can't possibly be true."

"But they are," he said eagerly, taking pride in the theft. "A handsome length of damask fit for a cardinal's cape. Also a fat handful of money."

"You're just dreaming up a wild story," I said, though by now I didn't know what to believe.

"I'd have taken more, two lengths of his best brocade and two handfuls of money, if I hadn't decided that this would be a sin. Here I was stealing from my father because he was greedy, and here I was, being greedy myself. But you haven't mentioned the horse. I stole a horse, too, a fine Arabian."

"You're making this up," I said, but as the words left my lips I realized that it made no difference to me whether he was a thief or not, whether he had stolen every bolt of cloth, every *soldo*, and every horse his father owned.

He began to pet Simonetta, running a hand over her shining feathers, not listening to me at all.

"When she is trained and can fend for herself," I said, "I'll think about setting her free."

Now he was talking to Simonetta, at least making sounds that caused the hawk to turn her head one way and the other.

"If you take off the hood then I can talk to her better," he said. "It is with the eyes that we talk to each other."

With misgivings, I placed Simonetta on his arm and removed the golden hood, but kept a firm grip on the chain that held her.

"She has the eyes of an odalisque," I said, to appear well read and scholarly.

He didn't know the word. "Odalisque?" he said, shaking his head.

"I mean that her eyes remind me of the melting eyes of a slave girl in a sultan's harem."

"You're familiar with harems?"

"Only through my reading," I said, embarrassed.

He held the bird at arm's length and the two gazed at each other.

"Her eyes don't melt," he said. "I am climbing a mountain in a winter storm. It is dusk as I near the top. Before me stands an icy cliff. In the face of the cliff is a small crevice and deep inside the crevice I see a fire. Her eyes are like that — fire and burning ice."

He began to talk to Simonetta, strange sounds unlike any that I had ever heard before. Then he broke off the talk and said to me, "You must have many of these pretty birds, ones to match the colors of your cloaks and gowns," he said. "You'll never miss Simonetta."

Deep within his own eyes I saw the fire and burning ice. Silently, holding my breath, I watched him unloose the chain from the falcon's leg. I watched her while she fluttered awkwardly away from us, then, gathering herself, disappeared in the stormy sky.

"She's gone," I cried.

"No longer an ornament on your wrist, but not gone," he said, pausing to gather his cloak about him. "She's in God's care. Now that you know this, you will free the others in your falconry."

Through falling snow, I saw Raul beckoning to me. My senses returned. Without a word I spurred my horse and crossed the square.

"I see that you didn't fare too badly with Bernardone," Raul said. "You only lost your favorite hawk. You're fortunate; you might have lost your purse as well as your horse and your nice silk surcoat. You might be walking homeward in your bare feet, freezing to death in your underclothes."

I didn't answer him. My eyes were upon Francis Bernardone. He was still where I had left him. Now it was snowing big flakes and he was on his knees, his hands outstretched, catching them as they fell.

The kneeling figure grew dim and disappeared in the driving snow. In all my life, I had never loved Francis Bernardone so much, so desperately.

FIVE

S now hid the walls of San Rufino. As we came to the Scifi palace, the watchman called out, inviting us to take shelter.

The bells of Santa Maria Maggiore had rung. Within the hour, my father would be sitting down to dinner. I was not anxious to explain how I had lost Simonetta. Not that he would know about it so soon — days might pass before he heard. But as a dutiful daughter, trained in the importance of truth, if challenged I must confess to an act that he would deem much more than foolish.

"It's warmer within than without," the watchman said, opening the gate. "This is an apt time to get frozen. Come, I pray you."

I asked if Signorina Clare was about. Told that she was in bed, suffering a fever, I handed over my horse and Raul rode on with the servants. Since Clare and I were good friends and often visited each other, I went by way of the back entrance, unannounced.

She lay under a blanket of fox skins, pale but beautiful in spite of her illness. "Where were you to get such a reddish nose?" she asked me.

"At Signor Bernardone's."

"What's under your arm? You're always buying something. Either that or someone is buying it for you."

I opened the package and spread the cloth on the coverlet.

"How lovely," she said. "It matches your coloring."

"Signor Bernardone told me the same thing."

"What did Francis say?"

"Nothing."

Clare and I always talked frankly to each other. But how I felt about Francis Bernardone I had kept from her, thinking that she would belittle him as so many others did.

Clare was not ill from a fever. I learned this before I ever finished the cup of broth her serving woman brought for me. She was ill from fear and anger.

"Have you heard of Rosso di Battero?" she asked me.

"He owns a castle beyond Porta di Murocuplo, in the hills," I said. "He's thin and tall and hollow in the middle, has a gray beard curled to a point, rides a gray horse, and he's always protected by six guards also riding gray horses."

She smiled wanly. "You know him better than I do. I've seen him only once. Last Easter in the cathedral, from a distance. I just found out that my family intends that I marry him."

Clare's father was a stubborn man, strict and fanatically religious. Her mother was an iron-willed woman. Her brothers were famous for their use of the sword, quick to take offense, vindictive, and cruel. I could imagine what a family command would mean to her, especially since people asked why a girl of such beauty remained unwed. Was her life doomed by some terrible disease? Had she made a pact with the Evil One, with the Devil himself? I had heard these questions and others, asked in my own home.

She was not drinking her barley broth. She lay with her hands folded tight on the coverlet, her gaze upon the window and the falling snow, a figure as remote as the cold white statue in the niche above her head. I asked her if she would marry Rosso di Battero. She picked up a heart-shaped fan and covered her face in disgust.

"No," she said, fanning herself. "No."

"If your family commands you to, you wouldn't dare refuse them."

"You'll see. At the very moment I am threatened."

28

"What will you do?" I asked, thinking of Count Luzzaro.

"I'll flee."

"Where to?"

"To Perugia. Anywhere. To Venice. I have cousins in Venice and also in Padua."

"Your brothers are fast riders. They'll come for you and bring you back," I said. Then, struck by a thought, I added, "You can hide with me. There's a big room off my tower. It was used once for weapons, a storage place. It's closed now and nobody ever goes there. You'll be safe for days."

"What a cunning thought," she said.

She tossed the coverlet aside, sat up, and glanced at me over the top of her fan. "How did Francis look?"

"Like a harlequin. Dressed up with one leg in black silk, the other in red silk, and a tunic of four or five colors."

"I mean, how did he act?"

"Sober," I said, deciding not to say a word about our meeting in San Rufino Square or about Simonetta. "Quiet."

"From the stories going around, he may have good reasons for being quiet. It's said he stole from his father, things like cloth and money, and gave them away. I don't believe it for a moment," Clare said.

She sat down at the mirror, and a woman came to dress her hair. Long and heavy and very blond, in the lamplight it looked like melting silver.

"Francis would never steal from his father," she said, "or from anyone else. It's an awful lie."

I agreed with her and we talked on until the bells rang for vespers, but nothing more was said about him.

As I hurried home I tried to think of a likely reason for freeing Simonetta. Father met me as I entered the Great Hall. He glanced at my wrist and empty glove before I had brushed the snow from my face.

"Simonetta?" he said.

I made a motion of a hawk flying away, hunting the heavens. Father was a medium-tall man who made himself look taller and more imposing by wearing thick-soled, high-heeled boots, by standing very erect with his thin shoulders thrown back, and by wearing tight collars on his cloaks and tunics.

"An untamed hawk hunts in a snowstorm?" he asked. He carried a lamp and the amber light glittered in his eyes. "Simonetta comes from a family of hawks that's centuries old, from the days of the ancient pharaohs. My falconer has sat up days and nights with this rare bird, never sleeping, walking leagues with her fastened to his fist, keeping her awake hour after hour until she no longer wishes to be free. And though her spirit remains unbroken, she's been lulled into submission. Simonetta has gone through all these stages, but she's not ready to hunt. Why did you ask for Simonetta?"

"Because she is more beautiful than the pigeon hawk or the kestrel."

"Why did the falconer give her to you?"

I shrugged, not daring to say that I had threatened the man a little when he wanted to give me the kestrel hawk. Step by step Father was leading me into a lie. Defiantly, not caring that I stumbled over the words, I blurted the truth.

"You wished to impress Francis Bernardone?"

I nodded.

"Then Bernardone is the cause of your unloosing the hawk." Father's tongue curled around the name. "A clown dancing in the street now dances his way into the household of Davino di Montanaro." He glanced at the massive door set in walls of hardest stone. "No door, no wall however strong, can keep frivolity at bay, it seems. Shall we deal with this foolishness in a different way? We shall, we shall! Come!"

I followed him through the Great Hall and into the vaulted room of the scriptorium. Two earnest young men sat at benches, pens in hand, diligently at work. Raul de los Santos watched over them.

Father said to him, "My daughter wishes to learn the arts of copying."

"Copying what?" Raul asked, pleased that I was now commanded to do what he had been trying to inveigle me into doing for more than a year.

"Since she's a religious girl," Father said, "her thoughts devoted to our Lord and His works, I suggest she start with the scriptures."

"Copying the scriptures is the surest way to heaven," Raul said. "According to Cassiodorus, 'converting the hand into an organ of speech' — thus, as it were, fighting the Archfiend with the deadly weapon of pen and ink."

"Cassiodorus was a wise man."

"When do you wish to begin?" Raul asked.

Father answered for me. "Tomorrow — early in the morning, tomorrow."

"And where in the scriptures?"

"In the Old Testament. With the first words of Genesis. It should keep Ricca occupied for months."

"For a year, signore. Perhaps two."

Listening to the storm clamoring at the windows, I thought of Francis on his knees in San Rufino Square.

SIX

I was in the scriptorium soon after breakfast, to show Father that I accepted my penance in lofty spirits and was anxious to become a proficient copyist. Raul had not arrived, so I spent my time examining the Bible, which was half my height, bound in wooden boards. Resting upon a strong oak bench, it was fixed there against thievery by a heavy chain. It was one of the two Bibles anywhere in all the provinces; the other Bible belonged to the University of Bologna. There was also part of one in Venice.

When Raul came he set me to work, not with a quill, unfortunately, but at a bench in a dark little hole at the far end of the scriptorium, making squares of lambskin into vellum by rubbing them with pumice, then treating the squares with chalk until they bore a velvety gloss. It was hard, dusty work that I didn't like.

"We don't write upon air," Raul explained maddeningly in answer to my complaint. "We write upon parchment. And with the Old Testament we write not upon ordinary parchment, but upon the prince of parchment, which is vellum. So that you may treat this princely parchment with respect, it is well to know how much labor goes into its making."

He kept me at this dreadful task for five long days before he stood me up in front of the Montanaro Bible. He handed me a freshly cut goose quill and told me to begin, following as a guide the chalked-in lines on the page of vellum set beside it.

"You have an excellent, upright hand," he said, "perfect for the combination of Gothic and Arabic styles I brought from Granada. We'll leave wide margins, and later, as you gain a surer eye and we come to the Garden of Eden, we'll add a discreet number of peacocks, apes, and serpents. Nothing flamboyant, mind you."

It was a fascinating art, exciting beyond anything I had imagined. On the first day, forgetting dinner, I worked until vespers and copied fifteen verses of the first chapter of Genesis, down to the words, "He made the stars also."

The next day I copied nine more verses of the first chapter, working slowly. The third and fourth days I did even better, down to the verse where God said, "Let the earth bring forth the living creature after his kind, cattle, and creeping thing, and beast of the earth."

The fifth day brought trouble. I had never read the Bible before, so when the words came, "And the rib which God had taken from man, made He a woman," I was shocked. I wondered why God had chosen a rib — a rib, mind you — instead of something more attractive like an arm or a thigh or even a small portion of the heart. And why shouldn't God have made a woman in the same way He had made a man?

I asked Raul about it. All he would say was, "Man has two arms and two thighs and only one heart, but dozens of ribs." Since it wasn't much of an answer, I wrote down the words reluctantly.

More trouble came on the sixth day when I began to copy, "*Vero vel et antalia eloquia apriere os non nadio* — And they were both naked, the man and his wife, and were not ashamed."

Like the rib God made into a woman, the words struck me as odd. At vespers I asked Father Giorgio of San Rufino why Adam and Eve should feel ashamed because they were naked; he blushed and said, "Would you not be ashamed, signorina?"

"No," I answered. "Why should I be ashamed of God's wonderful gifts?"

"You've been listening to the Greeks, I'm afraid."

"Others, too," I said.

Father Giorgio tried to smile. "It is Signor de los Santos's idea that you run loose in the library?"

I quoted a drinking song I had heard Francis sing:

> "*Vinum bonum et suäve,*
> *Bonis bonum, pravis prave*
> *Cunctis dulcis sapor, ave,*
> *Mundana lactitia!*"

"Does your father know that you run loose among the books?"

"He does."

To make sure that he knew, Father Giorgio told my father, who gave me a long lecture on rectitude.

On my seventh day of copying in the scriptorium, the dreadful news came. Father announced at dinner that Signor Bernardone had decided to bring his son to trial and Francis had gone into hiding. The following night he brought home the sad news that Francis had given himself up and would appear before the church authorities within a week.

"At last," Father said, "Pietro Bernardone, our esteemed merchant, respected in all of Umbria, in the cities of Milan and Venice and places as far off as Champagne, the province of France, this splendid man who has long been humiliated by his son's flagrancies at last will be rid of them."

I slept poorly that night, and the next day I began to make mistakes and had to throw away two sheets of vellum. I wrote down Italian words in place of Latin and made errors in spelling. Raul suggested that I try my hand at painting a unicorn to embellish the text. I tried hard, but the unicorn turned out to look like an ancient goat.

The morning of the trial I was up at dawn. At breakfast Father said to me, making certain that I would share in Francis's humiliation, "You will be there properly dressed with your waiting woman. And because rowdiness may be expected, with an adequate guard."

34

I put on a face to show him that I didn't wish to attend the trial. Then I smiled to show him that I willingly bent to his command. Nothing, lions or the pope's legions, could have kept me away.

Snow lay in heavy drifts across the square. The sky was clear and brilliant, but the air felt as though it might snow again. And the streets, even at this early hour, were crowded. People on foot, in carts, on horseback, were swarming through the Roman gate, pouring up from the countryside.

I stopped for Clare, so we were late and when we reached Santa Maria Maggiore there was no room to stand. We sneaked away from the serving women and the guards, sought the south side of the old cathedral, and inched our way along the wall to within a few strides of the bishop's palace, where the bishop would appear, as he always did on solemn occasions.

We tried to talk above the uproar of horns and clackers, above the sound of thousands screaming. In vain. Then bells struck three times. The crowd fell silent and the great doors of the palace swung open.

The first to appear was Bishop Guido, a short, thin man in a splendid scarlet robe. He was followed by Pietro Bernardone and, a few strides behind, his son. The three stood in the bright light on the steps of the palace, not far from us.

"Francis looks calm," Clare said.

To me he looked frightened, though he wore a rich tunic and a cloak trimmed with fur and a jaunty cap with a feather. I wanted to run up the steps and take him in my arms.

Pietro Bernardone was the first to speak. He told about the scarlet cloth stolen from his shop, a stolen horse sold in the Foligno market, and money given to the priest of San Damiano. His voice rose as he spoke. Twice, men had to come out of the shadows and keep him from throwing himself on his son.

Francis stood silent through this tirade, not looking at his father or at the crowd. His gaze was upon the sky as if he saw something in its depths that no one else saw.

Signor Bernardone read a page of accusation. A chill wind blew, but there was sweat on his brow before he finished. Drawing himself to his full height, he bowed low to the bishop, then glared at his son.

I think that he expected Francis to defend himself, at least to speak a word as evidence that he was listening, but Francis said nothing. He was still gazing at the sky, where blue shafts of light showed among the clouds.

A hush fell upon the throng, as if it were holding its breath.

SEVEN

Bishop Guido, clearing his throat and adjusting his splendid robe, broke the silence. "You have troubled your father," he said to Francis. "Give back the money you have stolen and he will be placated."

Francis turned his gaze from the sky. "Lord Bishop," he said, "not only money that I took from him do I wish to restore, with all good will, but even the clothes he has given me."

Quietly he slipped away. He was gone only a short time, then he was back standing in front of his father. He carried a small bundle. A moment passed before I realized that it was a bundle of clothes he held, his own clothes. He was naked.

A woman near me screamed and fell to the ground. A prolonged gasp came from the crowd. In the quiet that followed, Francis moved forward to where his father stood.

He held out the bundle of fancy clothes like an old, cast-off skin, and, bowing, said in a gentle voice, "Until this day I have called you my father. But now and in the days to come I can only say, 'Our Father who art in heaven.'"

Signor Bernardone glanced at the clothes, at his son standing naked before him. He tried hard to speak. Francis bowed again, raised his hands, and glanced at the lowering sky. A stray shaft of light shone full upon him as he placed the bundle of clothes at his father's feet.

I have often thought of that moment, though I remember so little of it. I do remember that the palace vanished. The silent crowd vanished. The gray clouds vanished. Everything vanished except a man and a woman who stood beside a tree in the shimmering garden of Eden. I saw, written in fire, the words I had copied so carefully from the Holy Bible, from the second chapter, twenty-fifth verse, of the book of Genesis, "And they were both naked, the man and his wife, and were not ashamed."

The earth trembled beneath my feet. Heavenly sounds came down from above, stopping my ears. The sun burst forth, blinding my eyes. Yet clearly I saw that the man, Adam, was Francis Bernardone, and his wife, Eve, was Ricca di Montanaro.

I made no movement that I remember. I said nothing to Clare nor uttered a word of what I saw or heard. Though the earth trembled, I kept my feet. But suddenly and mysteriously, as if other hands had helped me, my clothes lay upon the stones. I stood there before the bishop's palace in Santa Maria Maggiore Square, white and naked to the wind.

Francis was standing on the palace steps. He had turned from his father to face the crowd. He gazed in my direction. Doubting that he would ever find me, surrounded as I was, I took a step toward him. A hand grasped my shoulder. I heard Clare's beseeching voice as her cloak covered my nakedness.

At the same moment Bishop Guido had taken off his jeweled cloak and was throwing it around Francis Bernardone, amid the wildest of laughter. Clare pulled at the hood of her cloak and tried to cover my face. My gown, my shift, my shoes had disappeared.

"Ricca," she said — said it twice more as she led me away — "what possessed you? How could you do such a terrible thing? What will your father . . ." She choked on the words and glanced fearfully about as if she expected to see him come stalking through the crowd. Pleading with a wayward child, she shook me. "You are mad, you are mad," she cried. "Gather up your wits."

The sun disappeared. The wind grew bitterly cold. The dream faded. People were staring through Clare's thick cloak at my nakedness.

"There's one good thing," Clare said. "You are not quite a woman yet. Those who saw you might have taken you for a boy."

We hurried through the scattering crowd. Snow, driven by a chill north wind, had begun to fall. We both were freezing, she without her cloak and me naked beneath it, my feet shoeless on the slippery stones.

"I'll take you home," she said, "and give you clothes and you can wait until the storm's over. By that time your father will be less angry than he is now."

"My father's anger will not be less. It will grow. He'll be angry forever," I said, beginning to be aware of the enormity of what I had done. "It's best that I go home, but you must come, too."

Guards stood at the portal. They glanced at my bare feet as they opened the door. In the hall the serving woman looked askance as she reached for my cloak. I waved her aside.

We ran up the stairs to the tower and bolted the door behind us. But no sooner had I slipped out of the cloak into a sedate, high-necked costume than there came a series of loud raps.

I had scarcely opened the door when my father brushed past me. He crossed the room and stood stiffly at the window.

"I cannot believe what I have heard," he said, his back to me. "Not from one citizen but from twenty, and not from any enemies but from my friends as well, friends who would say nothing to cause me distress."

He turned and stared at me. I was a stranger he had never seen before.

"Is it true?" he shouted in a choked voice. "Can I believe what I have heard? Is it possible? Did you disrobe in Santa Maria Maggiore while the crowd whistled and cheered and beat on drums?"

"With all respect to you and your good friends," Clare said, "she did not disrobe for the crowd. Few saw your daughter because I threw my cloak around her."

"She did disrobe?"

His question was directed at Clare, but I answered it. "I did disrobe, but not for the crowd."

"Not for the crowd, not for the crowd," he said to mock me. "If not for them, then for whom? For the guard in the tower? The priest in the belfry who rings the hours? The serf looking down from the palace roofs? The varlet who sweeps dung from the streets? For the Devil himself? For whom does my daughter, my only daughter, Cecilia Graziella Beatrice Angelica Rosanna di Montanaro, stand naked in Piazza Santa Maria Maggiore?"

How was I to describe the vision that had overcome me at the sight of Francis Bernardone naked on the palace steps? Or ever make my father believe that for a joyful moment I was Eve, standing beside Adam among the trees and flowers of God's heavenly garden?

"Tell me!" he demanded. "What . . . Who is the cause of this?"

My head began to spin. The room moved. Father seemed to come close to me, very close, then fade away. I sat down on the bed to steady myself.

"Who?"

The word came from a far distance. It hovered in the air above me like a dark bird.

"Who?"

I lay back on the bed and closed my eyes. The bird still hovered above me, croaking the word over and over again, "Who, who, who?"

I sat up in bed. The bird had gone. I searched for my father but he was gone too. Then he was there by the window, silently pointing a finger at me, waiting.

The name came from deep inside me. It was on my lips to say and I must have said it, for my father was no longer by the window, and I heard the door softly close and steps fading away on the stairs.

I wakened to the sound of a screeching wind. White shadows moved through the room and the sun was up. Beside the bed stood Bishop Guido, in his hand a golden censer that gave off little clouds of smoke and the odor of cinnabar as he swung it to and fro. In a severe voice he was muttering about demons, commanding them to gather themselves forthwith and in the name of the Lord depart my tormented soul.

Father was standing behind the bishop, beside my mother, who was quietly weeping. There were others in the room, but I couldn't make out their faces among the sun's white shadows.

Mother quit weeping and announced that the exorcism was a wonderful success. She had seen the demons — there were three of them, two oldsters and a mean young one — leap through the window. To their deaths, she was sure.

By nightfall, completely recovered, I drank a large mug of broth and would have drunk more had not she said it would be bad for me. But in the morning when I was anxious to be up, she brought in three bearded physicians. They talked for a while, eyeing me from afar, and at last decided that I needed a bloodletting.

A bevy of serving women, those with fat white legs, were dispatched to the river to gather leeches. I had to wait in bed until noon for them to return. The river was frozen over and the ice had to be broken through. Then the women, who had to stand in the river while the leeches fastened to their bare legs, could only stay in for a short time because the water was ice-cold.

I felt no pain as the leeches ever so gently burrowed into my chest with their tiny teeth. It was only the sight of them clinging to my flesh and afterward falling off onto the sheet, stuffed red with my blood, that disturbed me.

I was in bed the rest of the day, but Mother allowed me to go downstairs for supper, which was very quiet, everyone glancing at me when they thought I wasn't looking.

EIGHT

I resumed work on the Old Testament, but Raul was instructed to see that henceforth I copied only those parts that dealt with godly thoughts and led to proper conduct.

It was three weeks and one day, exactly, before I saw Francis again.

Sister Carlota, Mother's cousin who lived in a monastery in the town of Perugia, died of dire pains in her chest, and the family rode down the mountain to her funeral. On the way back, as we neared the abandoned church at San Damiano, we were witness to an odd encounter.

Francis came out of the church, blinking in the hot sun, and fell in step beside us as we rode along. Dressed in a threadbare gown, he had a pale, half-starved look about him. He gave me a sweet smile and a bright glance, but I was appalled nonetheless.

"You're a bundle of bones," I said. "You're not eating enough."

"Enough," he answered. "Too much."

"You'll die one of these days if you don't care for yourself." I would have said more had not my father been within hearing.

At a bend in the road we passed the leper house and soon thereafter saw a young leper walking toward us. He carried a warning bell but something was wrong with it, and though he shook it with all his might the bell was silent.

I looked for Francis to take to his heels. Instead, he greeted the young man, grasped him by his bloody hands, and kissed them not once but again and again. Shocked, I remembered the day on the road to Assisi when he had quavered at the mere sight of a leper and had fled across the river to avoid a meeting.

My mother said, "Do you see the miracle? A golden light hovers above the tree where the leper is now hiding. Do you see it, Ricca?"

She frequently saw these apparitions and usually, to be a comfort, I saw them too. "A shining cloud," I said, "the same color as the mist on the river."

"Not mist, not a cloud," she cried. "It is our Lord. It is Christ Himself standing beside the tree, guised as a leper. The moment after Francis Bernardone kissed his hands, He revealed Himself." She turned to Raul, calling out to him, "Is this not so, Santos? You, too, saw the miracle!"

Raul, who was not so apt to agree with her as I, pressed a hand against his forehead and thought for a moment with closed eyes.

"A misty cloud hovered above the tree, it's true," he said.

"A glow," Mother insisted. "A light suddenly shone. Where else could the light have come from?"

"I recall," Raul said, replying with a parable, as was his custom when pressed, "a night in my childhood. One night when my nurse, carrying a lighted candle, put me to bed, I asked her where the light had come from. She blew out the candle and said, 'Tell me, my dear, where the light has gone and then I'll tell you where it comes from.'"

Mother pointed to the tree. "Look," she said triumphantly. "The leper has gone. He is nowhere to be seen. It *was* our Christ who stood there."

I didn't dispute her, though when I glanced back after we had passed, I caught a glimpse of the leper. He was lying flat against the earth, hiding until we were out of sight.

I was disturbed by this strange encounter. I dreamed about it at night. I became a leper myself and hid in the deep grass, rejected and sad. Then Francis appeared from somewhere and comforted me, kissing my hands. I thought of little else. It was on my mind when Bishop Pelagius visited the house to choose what I was to copy from the Bible.

Assisi had become a nesting place for heretics. Why I do not know, except that it was a beautiful city resting like a jewel among meadows and mountains, put there by God Himself in one of His most gracious moods. But whatever the reason, heretics were with us in great numbers.

To cleanse the city of heresy, old Bishop Guido was moved to the far north and Bishop Pelagius was brought in to take his place. Most of the heretics were Cathars, people who prayed by day and by night, yet thought that the Church's sacred cross was the symbol of Satan's victory over Christ. There were also a number of Manicheans in our midst — indeed, our master of guards was one of them — people who believed that Satan, not God, had created the world. And the Waldensians, the ones who preached that Christians should live in poverty like the apostles. And the many Donatists, Apollinarians, Sabellians, and one or two Priscillianists. In all, according to a careful count by Bishop Pelagius, there were some thirty different sects in the city.

The bishop came to supper at my father's request, bribed by a vast gift to the cathedral. He was born in Lucia, a place near Granada. A tall, pale man, he had a hawkish nose and a bulging forehead that could easily hold the world's facts and wisdom. Impressed by his high office, Mother had a sumptuous meal prepared — eels, truffles, poached trout, roast pig, and several kinds of fowl. He ate heartily, unloosing his belt as the dinner progressed, studying me from time to time with sharp gray eyes.

Afterward we went into the Great Hall, where dark shadows and the flickering light of candles surrounded us. Falling to his knees and inviting me to join him, the bishop began to pray softly in a melodious voice, asking various favors of God, one being the salvation of my errant soul.

I didn't pray and I didn't listen to him pray. As soon as he

44

had finished, I described the strange scene I had witnessed at the leper house and asked him if he knew Francis Bernardone.

"I never met the young man," he said. "I've heard of the escapade, of course. The rude treatment of his father, which struck me as barbarous. He stole money from Signor Bernardone and then mocked him in a public place."

"I am not disturbed about that, Bishop Pelagius. It's the leper that disturbs me. Why should Francis Bernardone want to kiss his hands when before he ran from lepers, holding his nose?"

"A gesture. As with the scene at Santa Maria Maggiore, a plea for praise. I understand that he has always hankered after it. And always the zealot, whether in hot pursuit of pleasure or, as now, in the hot pursuit of Christ."

"How does kissing a leper have anything to do with Christ?"

"It doesn't."

"The kisses make me shudder."

"I shudder also."

The bishop drew down his mouth and shuddered a little. He had two chins and the beginning of a third and all of them shook as he shuddered.

"It haunts me," I said. "I see Francis eagerly approaching the leper. The man shrinks away and attempts to flee, but Francis seizes him by his bloody hands and holds him back."

"So I have heard. He forced the leper to submit to an unwanted embrace, which startled and embarrassed the leper, rendered him speechless, made him run and hide. This act could have happened simply. Bernardone might have gone to a leprosarium. There are three around Assisi. You seem to be visited by a plague of lepers. God's punishment, perhaps. Bernardone might talk to the unfortunates and take them presents. Instead, he tries to play the gallant knight and makes a fool of himself."

But the scene with the leper he did not explain. Unexplained was the Francis who had treated the running bull with courtesy, who persuaded me to free my falcon. Neither of these things, as far as I could tell, was done to serve himself.

After the bishop left, while I sat at my bench copying the verses he had suggested, ones from the Bible which he thought might lead me down a more narrow path, I asked Raul how *he* would explain the scene between Francis and the leper.

"And please, not in a Sufi parable," I added. Raul's cryptic tales from the sect of Moslem mystics often irritated me.

"It can't be explained in everyday words. A parable would explain it better, but I can't think of one," Raul replied. "You know the story of Saul — how he persecuted the Christians, jailed them, and burned their houses, how on the road to Damascus he was struck down by a sudden burst of light and heard a voice speaking to him."

"I have been told this, how he regained his sight, became a Christian himself, and changed his name to Paul. Do you think that something like this happened to Francis?"

"Certainly he was converted, and it might have happened in the same way."

"But Francis was a Christian already. When he returned his clothes to his father he was a Christian. There's something else."

"How he was converted I can't explain, for there are as many ways of conversion as there are those who are converted. Bernardone's act of stopping the leper and kissing his hands can be explained, however. By embracing the lowest, the unfortunates that all his life he had shrunk from, he was surrendering himself to Christ. But he could have done so in a more modest way, without the whole populace as a witness."

"That they are a witness, that they do know about it and do talk about it, may be exactly what Francis intended. He may have wished to set an example."

"I doubt it," Raul said. "Francis is a heedless young man."

"Whether he is heedless or not, and for whatever reason he did it," I said, "the act is still there for everyone to see."

"Who knows, it may start a new fashion," Raul said sarcastically.

When Bishop Pelagius came again for supper he brought with him the most shocking news. As usual Mother had arranged a feast — two varieties of soup, one recipe from Rome and one from Venice, poached fish, a haunch of venison, and a brace of geese. The bishop ate with gusto but it was not the food that brightened his eye.

He kept the awful news until he and I were alone in the Great Hall, sitting beneath a painting of Christ, the painting my grandfather had brought home from Constantinople after the Fourth Crusade.

He pulled up his robe to warm his legs before the fire — they were white and hairless like the legs of a scholar — saying in his melodious voice, "You will not be surprised to hear about Bernardone's latest escapade."

He paused to pluck a sweet from his robe and placed it carefully on his tongue.

"Bernardone," he said, "has taken the vow of chastity. He has attired himself in a ragged gown and a rope belt and has thrown away his shoes. He's the leader of a band. They proclaim that poverty is a virtue. They go about the environs with wooden bowls, begging supper from our housewives."

Francis sworn to chastity, in a ragged robe and bare feet, begging for his supper! The ceiling spun. The marble floor heaved beneath me.

The bishop went on, his voice crackling like the logs burning in the fireplace: "Not content with begging for his own supper, he goes about the city pleading with people to give up what they own, clasp poverty to their breasts, and like him wander about with begging bowls. In time, everyone will be poor and nothing will be left to beg. What's worse, he presumes to advise the Church. He thinks that it, too, should beg for its supper."

The bishop took another sweet from the folds of his gown.

"He is a dangerous man, this new fanatic. He preaches heresy. Heresy attracts those who are bored in their faith, who find it too harsh or not harsh enough, who seek what is new and novel. And like all heretics, Bernardone will pay a price. He'll be punished."

Pelagius spoke these last words in a threatening voice, rais-

47

ing a fist and bringing it down hard on the palm of his hand. I had the feeling that he himself was anxious to deliver the punishment.

We prayed again and he left me with an admonition. "Francis Bernardone is lost to you, which is God's blessing. Accept it graciously. And do not embroil yourself in his dangerous life."

Before the door closed behind him, I made a vow and sealed it with a holy sign. Whatever happened and however long it took, with God's help I would somehow win Francis Bernardone away from the new life he had thoughtlessly chosen. With his high spirits and gentle ways, he was never meant to be a prisoner of the wild idea of poverty, the same idea that the heretical Cathars believed in.

NINE

Bishop Pelagius didn't come again for nearly a month. During that time all sorts of tales were brought home by the servants from San Rufino, from Santa Maria Maggiore, from the markets and taverns and countryside. The tales varied but a common thread ran through them: A crazy man was loose in the streets.

The bishop himself brought the latest tale. He told it with relish after a serving of skewered quail. "On my ride this morning," he said, "less than a league beyond the Roman gate, I saw Bernardone on the path a short distance beyond me. Wishing to avoid an encounter, I was turning back when the sound of his voice caught my ear. We were in an open field, only a tree or two beside the path. There was no one within sight, yet he was talking to someone, pausing to listen, then talking again. To himself, I thought.

"Curious, I got down from my horse and made a show of adjusting the bridle while I listened. The talk stopped the instant he recognized me.

"'Good morning, Bishop Pelagius. Come and join the conversation. The sparrows and I are talking,' he said, pointing to a flock of drab birds perched on a fence.

"Convinced that he was playing the fool with me, and more than a little angered at his effrontery, I said, 'What is the topic of conversation? The state of the commune's treasury now that the lords have refused to pay their taxes? Or is it the rumor of a new crusade, which reached us only yesterday?'"

" 'No, it is something of more importance,' he said. 'I asked them if they had thanked God for this beautiful day.'

" 'And what did they answer?' I asked.

" ' "Yes, yes, yes," ' they said. Now I will ask them what their wishes are for the coming day. Listen!'

"I cocked my head and listened intently. All I heard was the familiar sparrow chirp and chatter.

" 'I have trouble with their Latin,' I said. 'It's a trifle too courtly for me. Something you might hear in the pope's anteroom from the duke of Syracuse.'

" 'Yes, their Latin does have a courtly ring,' Bernardone replied.

" 'What did they say?' I asked, determined to bring him to his senses.

" 'Things more important than the lords' refusal to pay their taxes or a new crusade,' he said. 'They are asking God for a south wind, which is the best for flying, and for fields of fat worms, not too large and not too small.' "

The bishop wiped his brow and took a second helping of quail and three ladles of rich brown gravy. The anger Francis Bernardone had aroused in him was still there in his sharp eyes.

Rinaldo was off in the city somewhere. Mother was in bed suffering from a cold that had come upon her while kneeling on the chill stones of San Rufino. But my father was at table and had given the bishop his close attention.

He now cleared his throat and said to the bishop, "There are hundreds, yes, thousands, who have fewer flies in their heads than this Bernardone. It's not bad for a man to talk to the sparrows. It can't harm anyone. And it's better than talking to oneself."

"Not harmless," the bishop said. "Far from harmless. It's a symptom of a most distressing malady. It can lead him to the brink of excommunication and over the brink, shunned by the Church and all its faithful."

I sat with downcast eyes, wishing terribly to say: I have seen him talk to a bull here in our courtyard. He spoke softly to the enraged beast and it grew gentle. It must have understood what he said. It must have talked back to him, if not in words, then in some wordless way that together they had discovered.

When we left the table, the bishop and I went again to the Great Hall and prayed. After prayers, he sat in silence, thinking, no doubt, of how best to curb Francis Bernardone, to put a chain around the neck of the man he felt certain was possessed by the Devil. It was a moody silence and to me fraught with danger.

The bishop was in a better mood when he again appeared for dinner. With him he brought a stranger. Her name was Nicola Ascoli, and she was my age, a bedraggled little thing, all eyes, with a shy smile that showed two rows of pointed teeth.

The bishop had found her on his doorstep that morning. "She was there," he told us, "but fled when I approached. I sent one of my acolytes to bring her back and here she is, what's left of her."

Nicola's home, we learned, was a village in a northern province. Her mother and father, inspired by the village priest, had set off with her for Jerusalem. Across the mountain from Assisi in Ancona, which was a port on the Adriatic Sea, they found a ship bound for the Holy City. Only a day from land, the ship was driven ashore and everyone was drowned except the captain and Nicola, who found her way back to Assisi, taking months to make the journey.

Introducing Nicola into our family, I later discovered, was a plot hatched by Bishop Pelagius and my father. She was to be both an admonition and a model. Nicola had experienced weeks of the direst hardships — cold and hunger, even fears for her life — while during this time I, Ricca di Montanaro, had lived a pampered life, loved by doting parents, my smallest wish attended to. A spoiled child, in other words — selfish, indifferent to the thoughts of others, and, above all, careless of the family name.

The next day Nicola moved to the castle in her tattered dress and broken shoes, her few belongings wrapped in a soiled scarf. I welcomed her with a reserved kiss and half a smile, as the family looked on, yet I was overjoyed because she would lighten my burden. Now they would have two girls to watch in place of one.

Her father, we learned, was a baker and she had helped him bake bread. For a week or two she helped me in the scriptorium, mixing paint and cleaning brushes, but she disliked this task and asked if she might work in the kitchen.

At home her father had never allowed her to make pastries but she had watched and learned. So this is what she did in our bakery, making confections in all shapes and colors and tastes, especially those that sparkled like diamonds and tasted of cinnamon — which was rare and cost as much for a handful as a plot of good farm land.

Father liked her pastries. And Mother, adoring Nicola as a tragic young thing, was determined to make her forget. She encouraged her to become a girl with no past, only a bright future. To that end she had me copy on parchment a set of rules of etiquette compiled by the fashionable poet Robert of Blois, and read them aloud to Nicola, who could not read.

My mother tried to guide Nicola in other ways. She thought of her as a doll and dressed her in that fashion, in the finest of beribboned underclothes, shoes of the softest leather and thinnest soles, and velvet tunics with fluffy sleeves laced to the elbows.

Nicola liked her clothes, but when my mother suggested that she learn to play the lute and when Rinaldo requested the pleasure of guiding her through the labyrinths of chess, she smiled her diffident smile and refused them both.

She was excited, however, by the two mammoth ovens, so huge you could walk into them without ducking your head. The ovens baked ten dozen loaves of bread every day, sometimes more, and could roast a whole cow and two pigs at the same time. She was fascinated by the three leather tanks where long-legged frogs and squirming eels and various kinds of fish were kept ready for the frying pot, and by the sides of beef and pork stacked in huge pickling tanks to keep them from spoiling. The row of condiments above the working table interested her, too: sage and parsley, marjoram and mint, and strange spices — peppercorns, saffron, nutmeg, the priceless cinnamon.

Nicola was just as excited about the cathedral and its glittering angels. She went there every day, often at matins and vespers both. Sometimes she listened to Francis Bernardone give one of his speeches on the street. I always knew when she had listened to him, for her eyes would be shining with tears.

One day as the bells of the cathedral rang for vespers, she came running to the scriptorium. She stood, covered with flour, in the doorway and shouted, "He's here. He's here!"

I was at my bench, printing an initial for the twenty-third chapter of Exodus. It's a delicate task that takes a steady hand. I put down my brush.

"Who's here?" I asked, though I knew.

"Francis Bernardone. And he needs stones. He's gathering stones to build a church."

I took my time with the brushes. I cleaned them and put them carefully side by side in their enameled box.

There were reasons why I should not let Francis Bernardone gather stones in the courtyard. Rinaldo and my father were away, but they would learn about it when they returned. I would be blamed for giving away things that didn't belong to me. There were stronger reasons, too. I was struck by the awful thought that he had seen me standing beside the palace steps, my clothes in a heap. If not, he would certainly have heard, for, if my brother was truthful, it was talked about not only in Assisi but also among thousands in the smug city of Perugia.

My heart beat wildly; then it seemed not to beat at all. "Tell the guards," I said, "to tell Francis Bernardone that my father is away and he's to come back another time and ask for permission to gather stones."

Nicola grumbled something that sounded rude, then said,

"But he's here. And there are dozens of stones lying in the courtyard. Against the wall, back where an old pillar has fallen down. They're covered with moss and of no use." Tossing her blond curls, she grumbled again.

"Apparently," I said, "you have forgotten the 'Rules for Girls of Gentle Breeding' my mother lovingly had me prepare for you."

"I haven't. I know them by heart. Sometimes they seem silly. As they do now."

"You've forgotten the very first one."

Nicola smiled. "The one that says that a girl of the gentle class should not raise her voice in anger or act impatiently. But I am not angry or impatient. I am only saying that a young man who wishes a few stones for a ruined church is out there waiting in the cold."

A chill thought seized me. The man waiting in the cold was the one who had turned his back upon me, who had deserted Ricca di Montanaro for the life of a barefooted mendicant.

"Go," I said, "and deliver a message to the beggar. Say that I have no authority to give him stones for a church."

Nicola wheeled about and ran down the hall, sniffling, but before she ever reached the courtyard I overtook her.

TEN

T he last of the sun lay on the summit of Mount Subasio in the distance. The gate to our courtyard was open, and just inside it stood a hooded man.

"There he is," Nicola said. "Francis Bernardone."

"It's not Francis Bernardone," I said.

"I've seen him before. I saw him begging in the street. It was yesterday, when I went to pray in the cathedral."

"It can't be!"

Yet the moment I spoke these words I realized that it *was* Francis, the new Francis, barefooted, wrapped in a tattered robe held together by a rope like those used to tether oxen. My heart sank.

Skipping along like a dancer, he came toward me and stopped but a stride from me. "Praise the Lord for this beautiful day," he said. "Praise Brother Sun for the task he has just completed. Praise Sister Night who is about to visit us again. And praise the stars also, the first of which I see there beyond the mountaintop and shy as a maiden rising from sleep."

His words issued from the hood that nearly hid his face, words from the depths of a cavern.

"Lest I frighten you," he said, "I am the Francis Bernardone who, you may remember, has been in this courtyard before, on the day of the bulls. Who has sung beneath your window. Who has sold you cloth. A length of sendal, or was it samite? I can't recall."

"Sendal," I said.

"Yes, sendal becomes you more than samite."

"The cloth faded the first time it was cleaned," I said.

"Then please return it to Signor Bernardone. He has a good name, which he wishes to keep, I am certain."

"The cloth was given to a servant," I said, angered at the pain that had pierced my heart. "You also persuaded me to free my hunting bird, who is dead by now, an act for which my father has severely punished me."

"Your bird is in God's care. It is safer than on your wrist."

The bird story that Bishop Pelagius had told me quickly came to mind. "You seem to know all about God and what He does. Does He speak to you as you speak to the sparrows?"

"Yes, and how fortunate for me, humble sparrow that I am."

In the failing light I couldn't see his face, hidden as it was by the heavy folds of his hood, yet I felt that he was serious. Yes, Francis Bernardone spoke directly to God in the voice of a sparrow. Perhaps he talked to God in the voice of the poor little donkey that was now waiting beside the gate.

Impatient with talk, he began to dance quite gracefully — a joyous little dance, one foot to the side, then the other foot forward. "We are gathering stones," he said, pointing to the donkey, including the beast in the task. "We gather them for the church of San Damiano, which is in a perilous state, weedgrown and close to falling down."

"I've seen it. It has already fallen down. Why waste time with it? There are many beautiful churches in Assisi, and a new cathedral and an old one, too."

"I've had a shining vision. In the night the Lord appeared and asked me to put back the stones of San Damiano that people have taken away to build houses and barns for themselves." He gestured toward the far wall of the courtyard. "I see a pile of stones over there."

"They weren't stolen from San Damiano, not a single one of them," I said. "They all came from a small temple that stood there once. It was dedicated to Venus. As you may know, Venus was the goddess of love."

A muffled sound came from the cavern of his hood. The word Venus seemed to have disturbed him.

"Since Venus was a pagan," I continued, "the stones are not suitable for a Christian church."

"God created the stones, as He created you. They are His, as everything is His. Stones, like people, can be put to many uses, and like people they may be redeemed, though with people redemption is far more difficult than with stones."

Dusk changed to night and the guardians of the gate lit torches. From San Rufino Square came the sound of watchmen setting off on their rounds of the dangerous streets.

"One stone," Francis said, "will bring one blessing. Two stones and the giver is doubly blessed. Three and he's —"

"My father has built two churches in his lifetime," I said. "Both of them bigger than San Damiano. By now he must be blessed a thousand times over. He's in no need of further blessing."

"There are never enough blessings," Francis said. "A thousand are not enough. And those who give, though rich, are not called upon to pass through the eye of the needle."

"Come when my father is home," I said. "Let him decide about the stones and if he is in need of more blessings."

"When is he home? He travels much."

"Perhaps tonight. Perhaps tomorrow."

A chill wind had come up. Francis wrapped the tattered robe around himself and tightened the rope around his waist. In the darkness he seemed to change. He loomed larger against the dark walls. His dark robe turned black. The heavy folds that hid his face took on a forbidding shape. A cold finger ran down my back. I was seized by an impulse to flee. But as I turned away from the silent figure, Nicola came running with a torch.

Francis took the beast's tether and for a moment I thought that he meant to leave and not come back.

"Your friend Clare di Scifi," he said, "sent word that she has a stone for me, a small one she's been using for a doorstop, which she wishes to give to our little church. I'll go to get it tomorrow; then I'll come here and talk to your father."

Clare offering her doorstop to Francis Bernardone? He must be lying. It wasn't just an ordinary stone. I had often noticed it, a piece of precious jade, sea-green and shaped like a monkey's head, which her mother had brought from the Holy Land. She would never give it up. Or would she? Painfully, I remembered how she had defended Francis against my father. Was it true? Was she secretly in love with him?

"Signor Montanaro is a very Christian man. He will surely forgive us," Nicola said, grabbing Francis by the arm and leading him across the courtyard.

I watched the torchlight flickering among the temple stones, hoping that my father would return at that moment and find the two pilferers in his courtyard.

They were not gone long. They came back, Nicola carrying a piece that looked like the hand of a goddess, Francis Bernardone with a heavy square stone from a fluted pedestal.

"Your cart is full already," I said to him. "Your poor beast will founder long before it reaches San Damiano."

He asked Nicola to put the piece of marble in the cart and kept the heavy one balanced on his shoulder.

"Thank you," he said.

I thought he was talking to me. Instead he was talking to the donkey.

"Thank you for all that you have done this day and for what I will ask of you before we reach San Damiano. I swear that I will not burden you further with another stone, large or small. Thank you, dear brother."

The beast did not answer; at least, I did not hear him answer. Then Bernardone spoke to me. "And thank you, dear friend. God will bless you doubly for these generous gifts."

"The stones you are taking away are not gifts," I said. "They are stolen."

He was silent. I seized the torch and angrily shone it in his face, to confound him, to make him aware that I, Ricca di Montanaro, was standing in front of him.

The light penetrated the cavernous hood. It revealed the same face I had seen on the morning he had knelt on the palace steps. It was the face of Adam, the face that had haunted me every hour of every day since the moment I stood before him among the trees in the Garden of Eden.

"I am the Lord's thief," he said, "but I'll return the stones, if you wish."

It was the voice of Adam speaking to me again, the same gentle voice I had heard before, long ago in God's beautiful garden. "No," I said impulsively, "take all the stones you need."

"The cart is full," he said.

"Then come tomorrow with an empty cart."

"I am in need of a thousand stones, but let others give us stones. Thus they too may receive God's blessings. Blessings shared by many are far better than those shared by only one. They are like rain to the desert rose."

Tilting under the weight of the cumbersome stone balanced on his shoulder, he asked the donkey to leave the courtyard, if possible. Obligingly, with groans and grunts, the beast pulled the cart into the street and I followed, walking at Francis's side as he staggered along, Nicola at my heels.

He would soon grow sick of gathering stones for a ruined church, of wandering about from house to house holding a begging bowl, starving himself, listening to insults, being pelted with rocks and offal. It was a game he was at, different from the game he played as a troubadour, different and novel and tiring. All I needed to do was wait with patience and quiet understanding.

We crossed San Rufino Square, which was deserted save for a watchman and a slinking dog.

"Let's go down the hill," Nicola said, "and help Francis with the stones."

"Let's," I said, reluctant to leave him.

"To San Damiano?"

"Yes."

But before we reached the far side of the square we heard the clatter of hoofs on the cobbles. I pulled Nicola into the shadows behind the fountain and we waited for the horsemen to pass. There were six men, Rinaldo, my father, and Giuseppe di Luzzaro among them. By this time Francis was on the road that led out of the city. I could barely see him trudging along and hear the creaking of the cart.

"He has a long way to go," Nicola said.

I was sorely tempted to run after him, to lift the stone from his shoulders, but the consequences of such rashness held me back. Only my heart followed him down the long road to San Damiano.

ELEVEN

We hid in the shadows and watched until Father and his companions reached the square and turned toward home. Then we followed them at a distance. Two doors opened into our palace — the big main door that faced the square, and just around the corner near the courtyard gate a second door, an arched break in the wall, called the Door of the Dead. My two baby brothers were carried through this door in their little white coffins covered with flowers. Also my brother Lorenzo, after he was killed on the battlefield in Perugia.

We slipped by the guard and down the long passageway, no one seeing us. Nicola scurried to the kitchen to finish making her tarts and I to the scriptorium. When my father came in a few minutes later I was seated at the bench, busily at work on the initial for the twenty-third chapter of Genesis.

He glanced over my shoulder, complimented me upon the progress I had made in the art of illumination, and as he left gave me an affectionate pat on the head. Since my hair was still damp from the night air, it would have given me an anxious moment had he not been wearing leather gloves. I worked hard until the trumpet announced supper, though I made a mistake and had to paint the initial a second time.

At supper I was seated across the board from Giuseppe di Luzzaro. He was in a good humor, flushed ruddy by the sun, quite handsome in his fur-trimmed tunic, with his black curls nicely arranged across his forehead. He took off his garnet thumb-rings and washed his fingers carefully in the bowl of scented water, and then instead of passing the bowl to his right, as was the custom, he smilingly passed it to me.

This was the first time I had encountered Luzzaro since the day I disrobed in Santa Maria Maggiore Square. If he had not seen me, then surely he had heard about what I had done. When I sat down to supper I kept my eyes to myself, expecting to find a hostile light in his. But if anything, his smile was warmer than usual; there was no hint that he was upset with me. Suspicions lingered. Was his passing the finger bowl to me and not around the board a gesture of defiance? Was he not flaunting his forgiveness of an act that had repelled everyone else?

Yet everyone was in a festive mood. The men had hunted in the country from early dawn and returned with strings of meadowlarks. The birds were brought on after a serving of lentil soup, roasted in their feathers and pinned in a row on pine branches. I had eaten larks before, stuffed with small gobbets of fat, bread crumbs, and pine nuts, and had found them delicious, but on this night, with Francis Bernardone in my thoughts, the sight of them turned my stomach.

We were entertained by a pair of wandering minstrels, man and wife, who presented the sad story of Tristan and Iseult, the husband reciting while his wife played the zither. At the moment when Tristan pierced the monster's heart with one thrust of his sword, I cheered. And at the end, as Iseult lay down beside her dead lover and died of grief, I thought of my own love for Francis and hot tears rolled down my cheeks.

After supper I hurried to the scriptorium and closed and bolted the doors. I had decided during the meal to write a letter to him. He would never again sell cloth in his father's store. Nor would he return to our courtyard to gather stones. Nor would I be apt to meet him on the street. And if by some odd chance I did meet him, what would I say? We had talked in San Rufino Square and in our courtyard. Yet in all that time I had not been able even to hint at the passion that was consuming me. And worse still, most of what I did say was coldly said, to embarrass him.

As I sat on the bench smoothing out the sheet of parchment I had chosen to write upon, wondering whether to write a long letter or just a note, how to begin and how to end, and what should lie between, a wild thought struck me. If I addressed him in a graceful phrase, then copied bits of the Song of Solomon, which by chance I had stumbled upon, then closed the letter with a brief salutation, would he think me overly bold?

I need not explain why I was writing to him. If he wished to take it as such, it could be a love letter. And if he didn't, if he wished to believe that the Song of Solomon was about love for the Church only and not about earthly love, as Bishop Pelagius believed, then at least he would have to admire my devotion to holy things.

I began at once and wrote rapidly, not taking time to illuminate the first letter of each verse, choosing the verses not in order but as they appealed to me:

As the apple tree among the trees of the wood, so is my beloved among the sons. I sat down under his shadow with great delight, and his fruit was sweet to my taste.

O my dove, that art in the clefts of the rock, in the secret places of the stairs, let me see thy countenance, let me hear thy voice; for sweet is thy voice, and thy countenance is comely.

Behold thou art fair, my love; behold thou art fair; thou hast dove's eyes within thy locks; thy hair is as a flock of goats, that appear from Mount Gilead.

Thy teeth are like a flock of sheep that are even shorn which came up from the washing.

Thy lips are like a thread of scarlet, and thy speech is comely; thy temples are like a piece of pomegranate within thy locks.

Thy neck is like the tower of David builded for an

*armoury, whereon there hang a thousand bucklers, all
shields of mighty men.*

*The voice of my beloved! Behold, he cometh leap-
ing upon the mountains, skipping upon the hills.*

*I have compared thee, O my love, to a company of
horses in Pharaoh's chariots.*

I was turning to another page of the Bible when a voice
sounded in the hallway and a loud knock echoed through the
room. I spread out the Bible to conceal the parchment I had
written upon, hurried to the door, and slid the bolt. Count
Luzzaro stood in the doorway, puffing out his cheeks in an
expansive grin.

"I have heard you were a scholar," he said in a sober voice,
though he had consumed a flagon of wine at supper, "but I
could scarcely believe this to be true, since you're such a lighthearted miss."

"Not a scholar," I said. "A copyist. I write what scholars have
already written. I have never had a thought in my life worth
writing down."

"How charming!" he said. "How fortunate! Girls should
never, never think. Their minds should waft gaily hither and
yon on a summer's breeze, in tune with lithesome dreams. They
can think in times to come, when they are women and have
more to think about and more need to think. Youth is far too
brief a time to squander."

He glanced over my shoulder at the narrow room and the
shelves crowded with books and reams of parchment.

"There's a quiet room in Castello Catanio that would be just
right for a library," he said. "You've seen it. You have danced
there. Remember?"

"No," I said, though I did remember, vividly.

"You are cramped here. You can't move without running into
yourself," he observed, choosing to ignore my cold reply. "Papers strewn about like a raging snowstorm."

He shivered and hugged himself, as if an icy blast had struck

64

him, and playfully pushed past me into the room. His gaze fastened upon the bench where I had been working, the Bible that lay on the table, and the sheet of parchment half-filled with words from the Song of Solomon.

"Your pen moves like a spider spinning a web," he said, taking a light from the table to hold close to the parchment. "It's all circles and curlicues and spidery lines wandering up and down. Beautiful to behold, but most difficult to read."

Difficult for you, most powerful count of the Assisi commune, because your Latin is not very good, I said to myself. He had told me once that he'd read the whole story of Abelard and Heloise, but this I doubted. Most likely he had heard it from a troop of wandering players.

"Song of Solomon," he said, rolling the three round words on his tongue, casting his green eyes lightly upon me. "Well, well."

"So, well, well," I said to have him understand that I was not embarrassed. "From the Bible, the Old Testament." I added the fiery warning Bishop Pelagius had flung from his high loft in San Rufino on Palm Sunday months ago: "Freezing hail and devouring fire await those who mock the Lord, those who use this song for a worldly purpose."

"Ho! Protect us against devastating hail and devouring fire — *Grando nec ignis edax peprimat hos nec mala pestis,*" his lordship exclaimed in halting Latin. Shining his candle on the open page, he gave me a daring, conspiratorial glance and began to read:

" 'By night on my bed I sought him whom my soul loveth. The joints of thy thighs are like jewels, the work of the hands of a cunning workman. Thy navel is like a round goblet, which wanteth not liquor. Thy two breasts are like two young roes that are twins. His legs are as pillars of marble. His locks are bushy and black as a raven. I sought him, but I could not find him. I called him, but he gave no answer. The watchmen that went about the city found me, they smote me. I charge, O daughters of Jerusalem, if ye find my beloved, that ye tell him that I am sick with love.' "

His lordship straightened himself and said, "Wheeeew! Whence comes this torrent? 'Thy navel is like a goblet, which wanteth not liquor.'"

"Round goblet," I corrected him.

"'His legs are like pillars.'"

"Pillars of marble, your lordship."

"'His locks are bushy and black.'"

"Black as a raven."

"But tell me, who speaks these ravenous words?"

"The Rose of Sharon, the Shulamite."

"To whom does she speak them?"

"To her beloved, of course."

He was silent for a moment or two, turning the ring on his left thumb round and round. "Taking note," he said, "of a pen on the bench beside an open ink jug, inkstains on your fingers, and a parchment sheet peering out from beneath the Bible on which are visible several words freshly written, I hope that you are composing a copy of the Song of Solomon in your beautiful spidery hand and that you will sign it prettily 'The Rose of Sharon,' and then, and then, send it off to me by the fastest of messengers."

I closed the Bible and hid the letter I was writing to Francis Bernardone beneath it. My silence encouraged him. When I looked up, he had cocked his curly head to one side and his lips had broken into what he must have meant as a fetching smile. To me it held the faintest shadow of a leer.

I didn't blame him. A girl who shed her clothes on the steps of the Santa Maria Maggiore palace before a gaping crowd. A girl who wrote down verses from the Song of Solomon. What was a warm-blooded man to think, though he was a lord and a gentlemanly knight?

He glanced the full length of my figure, at my neck, my bosom, my waist. His glance fastened upon my golden slippers, sewn with rubies, the ones my father had brought home from France for my birthday, which were gossamer-thin and made my feet look smaller than they really were.

66

He brushed the curls from his eyes to see me better. Having decided that Ricca di Montanaro was a wanton, he was now pondering what to do and what to say. He struggled. His forehead grew damp. Words came to his lips and stood poised there. One slipped out — "Please" — and another, "believe," then still another, "me."

He would have finished the sentence, I am certain, had not a rout of huntsmen come singing down the Hall. Choking, clearing his throat, he bowed himself through the door and disappeared.

I closed the door and was sliding the bolt when Raul announced himself with one of his secret knocks — three quick taps, a pause, then three more taps.

"What happened to Luzzaro?" he said as I let him in. "I just passed the count stumbling along as if chased by the Furies."

"Not all of the Furies, only one," I said.

Raul picked up Solomon's poem. "Your father never gave you permission to copy this. What's it for?"

"Why do you ask when you know it's for Francis Bernardone?"

"You mean Brother Francis; Francis Bernardone is dead."

"Not dead to me."

"You are walking a path beset with trouble. Trouble for you and for all the family. All of us together. You do recall that Aga Akil brought her small unruly son to the wise Mulla Nasrudin's school?"

"Yes."

" 'He is badly behaved, your honor,' she said. 'Our family has tried most everything but nothing has availed us and him.'

" 'Have you scared the boy?' the Mulla asked.

" 'No.'

" 'Then I will.'

"Whereupon he waved his arms and ran screaming from the schoolroom. The woman fell in a faint. The Mulla returned and revived her.

" 'You frightened *me*, not the boy,' she complained bitterly.

" 'But did you not observe,' replied Mulla Nasrudin, 'that I was also frightened. Always when danger threatens, it threatens everyone alike.'"

Raul held the poem toward the candle flame. "Do you understand?"

Having heard this parable several times, the first time when I was eight years old, when I held my breath because I couldn't have a piece of cinnamon cake and got black in the face while the family stood around wringing their hands, I snatched the poem from his hand.

TWELVE

I copied no more of Solomon's Song until the next evening and finished it two days later. I was then overcome by a week of indecision. Should I address him as "Dear Friend" or plain "Francis," or formally as "Esteemed Francis Bernardone"? Certainly not as "Brother Francis." I decided upon "Dear Esteemed Friend."

A problem followed. Should I become a weasel and ask him if he thought the song was about a young man beloved by the Rose of Sharon or if the young man was meant to be the Church in disguise, as Bishop Pelagius believed? And if it were a young man and not the Church, did he think that such great love could exist upon this earth? I even thought of tearing the poem into very small pieces and throwing it away.

Finally, at week's end, I signed all of my six names and affixed a seal of hot red wax into which I pressed the intaglio ring I wore on the little finger of my left hand, leaving the imprint of an angel holding a lamb in her arms. I wore other rings, but this was the most apt to please him.

At first I thought of sending the letter by one of the guards, but not fully trusting any of them I decided upon Nicola. I was certain of her loyalty and confident that wherever Francis Bernardone might be — wandering through the countryside or in the city streets — she would find him.

On the morning she was to start off with the letter Nicola fell ill with a fever of some sort. Hard upon this, at noon of that day, came something far more upsetting.

Clare di Scifi appeared while I sat in the courtyard. I was turning the pages of the *Collected Letters of Heloise*, an unwieldy bundle of parchment as large as a pile of hay, which had just arrived from Paris.

She rode in through the courtyard gate, sitting sidesaddle on a fractious black mare and accompanied by an escort of two men in light armor and carrying halberds. I recognized her from afar, the heavy, braided hair swinging to the motion of the horse, ashine like coils of honey in the sun. But when she slipped down from her mount and ran toward me, I saw that a vast change had come upon her. Though less than a month had passed since we were together, in that brief time she had changed. Always a beauty — nobles and serfs alike called her the most beautiful girl in Assisi — she was no longer a girl. She was now a woman and more beautiful than ever.

As we threw our arms around each other and the first words were spoken, I felt the change. It was in her face, as we embraced, silently holding each other at arm's length, that I saw the difference.

Clare's beauty had been the kind that I loved in some of the statues the Greeks made. It reminded me of a statue we had in one of the niches in the Hall — a head of Princess Ariadne, giver of the golden skein that led Theseus to safety. In white, unveined marble, a faint, dusky glow beneath the white, all of its features are harmonious, as if the artist had used a perfect mold, one made from the face of Venus herself. Such had been Clare's beauty, white and perfect and cold.

It was her eyes that had changed, only her gray eyes. But they had utterly transformed the face that I was so familiar with. The icy mask had vanished and in its place was radiance.

A varlet came to lead the horse into the shade. She stopped him, and when I offered her food and drink she refused them.

"I mustn't stay," she said. "I wanted to see you again, if only for a minute. To say goodbye before I go."

"Go where?"

I conjured up the Holy Land. Her mother, Ortolana, had

gone there with my mother and some Assisi women soon after peace was signed with Saladin, sultan of Egyptian infidels. They crossed the Mediterranean Sea, reaching Damietta in Egypt by galley. From there they traveled, often on foot, through the desert, where robbers were numerous and water was scarce. Once they followed lion tracks to find a spring. They came to Gaza and the fallen city of Jerusalem. Clare, as devout as her mother, had spoken to me about this pilgrimage, which had made a great impression upon her. She had asked me if I would make the same pilgrimage, just the two of us, and I had shuddered at the thought.

"Clare, where *are* you bound? Not to the Holy Land, I hope. Not on a pilgrimage!"

"Yes, in a way of speaking, it's a pilgrimage."

I waited, holding my breath, still struck by the light that suffused her face.

"You've heard about Francis," she said. "He's getting together a band of men. They'll call themselves Friars Minor. He's going around right now picking up stones for a church."

"He came here asking for stones," I said. Suddenly I felt the sharp thorn of suspicion. "How do you know so much about Francis and what he's doing?"

The sun was overhead, beating down upon the stones. Sweat showed on Clare's forehead. She asked for a drink of water, but when it came she still didn't answer. I asked her again about Francis.

"I know because we have talked," she said stiffly, as if I had accused her of some indiscretion. "Months ago. We talked about an order for women, single women. Provided he receives permission to preach."

"Heavens!" I exclaimed. "I thought your heart was set on a fine marriage. Not to the one your family has picked out but to someone worthy. Fifty young nobles are breathlessly waiting for a chance to win your hand."

She smiled. For a moment I thought that she might be playing a game. Clare loved games and had fooled me before.

Once she had packed her carrying bags while we were in her room talking, and when I asked her where she was bound, she had said, "To Jerusalem; do you want to come?" She left the next day with an escort but only went to see her aunt who lived in Siena, a few short leagues away.

"The marriage you wish to hustle me into is not the dream you envision so sweetly," she said. "Your mother and my mother, both of them, have lost children in childbirth. And some of the children who didn't die died soon after. On this very square of San Rufino, in the past year, two of our friends have died giving birth. It's not an inviting picture, is it?"

"No, but children do live and grow up, by the thousands."

"You're younger than I, some two years and more. Besides, you've lived a sheltered life in a quiet family. Mine spreads over the whole countryside — fierce uncles, baleful aunts, shoals of arrogant cousins, and cruel brothers. I've learned much about marriage from them, mostly against my will."

"I am not the innocent you take me for," I said, standing up for myself. Clare was strong-willed. She could run over you like a hay cart filled with flowers, so softly that sometimes you didn't notice until many days later. "I have read about people a lot — Caesar and Nero, Plato, Sophocles, Alexander the Great, Ulysses, Cleopatra, Sappho, Eleanor of Aquitaine, Heloise . . . I've read the Bible from 'In the beginning God created the heaven and the earth' to 'Christ be with you all. Amen.'"

"You've read a lot, dear Ricca. So much that you're developing a squint."

"I never met Heloise or Eleanor of Aquitaine, not in real life. But reading about them I've lived their lives. I myself have lived one life only, just one, but I have been many people in that time — a dozen, fifty, a hundred. So I am not so innocent as you make me out."

"Reading," she said, "is not living. It's life secondhand."

"That sounds like Francis Bernardone," I said.

"It is."

72

A sharp thorn of suspicion was still there in my breast. Had Clare fallen in love with Francis Bernardone? How else could a beautiful girl, raised in a noble family, even dream of dressing herself in sackcloth with a rope belt and tramping barefoot through the streets, begging for stones!

"This nuptial couch," she said, "which you wish to hustle me into, can be a bed of sorrows. I think of my cousin, Amalia Sciprione. At fourteen she married a widowed nobleman who on her wedding night took full possession of her in the dining hall before their drunken guests. On some of our farms, to this day, my own father claims the ancient right and beds with the bride before the bridegroom does."

Clare nodded to one of her escorts, who ran forward to help her into the saddle. She brushed the hair from her forehead and frowned.

"Besides all that," she said, "parents choosing partners for their children at age twelve and thirteen, the brutalities my cousin suffered, the awful deaths in childbirth, the sad deaths afterward — there are other indignities. A woman loses all her possessions the moment the marriage vows are spoken. And worse yet, she comes a slave to her husband."

She took up the reins. Her face changed. It was radiant again as she looked down upon me.

"I haven't told my family," she said. "When that is settled, I'll come for you. We'll be Friars Minor together, by the side of Francis Bernardone."

She didn't wait for an answer. Raising her hand in farewell, she passed quickly through the gate. The sound of hoofs died away as my heart ceased to beat.

She had lied to me. From the very beginning, before I disrobed on the church steps, long before that, during the running of the bulls and the wild dances of the *tripudianti*, on the feast of San Niccolò, on the day youth took over the city and Francis had strutted around in the robes of a bishop leading a licentious rout, during the nights he sang ballads in San Rufino Square — that long ago, she was in love with Francis Bernardone. And she had kept it to herself. Carefully and secretly, pretending otherwise.

I fell to my knees and pressed my brow against the stones. "Please, God," I prayed aloud, "don't let Clare win him away! Prevent this with Your might!"

THIRTEEN

The letter to Francis Bernardone I recopied twice, added to it five songs, took out three, made the capitals more ornate, changed the colors to a darker shade of red lined with blue, and in place of the intaglio used my Florentine ring, whch was carved in the semblance of an apostle preaching to the multitudes, while doves hovered overhead. The barefooted figure dressed in sackcloth, his hands raised in benediction, I hoped would remind Francis of himself.

I swore Nicola to secrecy and sent her out every afternoon, sun or rain, to the places where he might be. But the month of April passed, and half of May, before she caught a glimpse of him as he entered the cathedral of San Rufino.

"I didn't follow him," Nicola said when she came to the scriptorium to report the happening. "I didn't want to disturb him during devotions, so I waited on the steps until he came out. But when he came out he was with your friend, Clare, and they were talking. I decided it was not a good time to hand him your letter. It might have been, I don't know. Perhaps I should have. What do you think?"

I caught my breath. It took me a moment to quiet my anger. Nicola didn't help by casting sympathetic glances at me beneath her lowered lashes.

"You were wrong," I said. "I don't blame you, but you should have paid no attention to Clare di Scifi. It's none of her business."

"She's such a beautiful girl and dressed so elegantly with a fur mantle and all, I was scared. Besides, they were busy talking."

"About what?"

"She said she hadn't told her family and he asked her if it would help if he told them."

"What did she say to that?"

"'No, oh, no, it will only cause a terrible fight. Every one of my brothers and uncles would lift their swords against you, sir.'"

"What then?"

"Then they parted, right at the door, and he said, 'Peace be with you,' and she repeated his words, saying something else I couldn't hear. He went down the road to San Damiano, skipping along barefooted with his ragged gown aflap. I had a notion to run after him . . ."

"Why didn't you, ninny?"

"He was running too fast."

Three days later Francis went off to preach in the dusty little villages on the long road to Florence, and not until he returned at the end of summer did he receive my letter. When he did, it was from my hands.

I was busy in the scriptorium, working on the thirty-sixth chapter of Genesis. I had just finished writing down, "And Husham died, and Hadad the son of Bedad, who smote Midian in the field of Moab, reigned in his stead," when the door opened and my father beckoned to me.

Holding my arm, he walked to the door and flung it open. The morning sun poured in upon us.

"You've been a faithful daughter," he said. "I'm proud of the work you have done and proud of your comportment while you were attending to it. May the Lord now give you peace and guide your hand."

I didn't go back into the scriptorium. The first thing I did was to call for horses. With Nicola riding beside me, I took the road to San Damiano, where, word had it, Francis Bernardone was to preach that day. In my purse was the letter that had taken so long to write and so long to deliver.

So that we would not be conspicuous among the country people who would be there, Nicola had suggested that we borrow clothes from the servants.

"We'll wear our best," I said. "There's no reason for us to look like peasants fresh from slopping the pigs."

As we rode down the mountain, I repeated to myself what had by now become a litany. Francis had once aspired to be a knight. He had attired himself in the costliest of armor and ridden off to Perugia to make his name as a warrior. Failing in that, he had become a poet, a troubadour, and on many occasions a resplendent rakehell. He had changed again. Now he was following Christ's thorny path. Failing in this, he would surely change again. He was a human weather vane. When he did change, I would be there, as I was at this moment, riding to hear him preach, as I had been on the cathedral steps, on the nights he had sung in San Rufino Square, and countless times before, in my dreams as well. It was more than a litany — it was a prayer.

Rising out of a briar patch, gray and moss-grown, San Damiano looked like something left over from the Roman days. Only a few carts and horses stood outside, but within the narrow aisles were crowded. Light from a small, bleak window fell upon a young man — he turned out to be a Brother Giles — speaking in a barely audible voice.

Nicola and I found a place to stand against the wall in the back of the church.

Giles was saying, "Blessed is he who loves and does not therefore desire to be loved. Blessed is he who fears and does not therefore desire to be feared. Blessed is he who serves and does not therefore desire to be served. Blessed is he who treats others well and does not desire that others treat him well."

Francis Bernardone stood behind him, to one side of the

altar. His head was bowed and I could not see his face. But when Giles finished his homily and Francis came forward to take his place, a shaft of sun fell upon him. My heart leaped with joy.

I hadn't heard Francis speak at church. His voice was different from the voice he had when we conversed. It was livelier and more tuneful, more like the voice he used when he sang ballads in the square.

"No one of us can be deemed truly gallant unless lighthearted," he said. "And humility is happiness, for the injuries that hurt us the most, that we keep most secret, are those that injure our pride."

He glanced over the heads of the people, in my direction — at me, or so it seemed.

"As Brother Giles has told you, 'If a man were to live a thousand years and not have anything to do outside himself, still he would have enough to do within, in his own heart.'"

Barely had he spoken than a crested bird flew into the church, down the aisle, and fluttered at the bleak window, seeking a way to escape. Then it circled the altar and at last came to rest upon his shoulder.

Taking the bird in his hand, he said, "My little friend, you owe much to God your Creator because He has given you freedom to fly anywhere. Also He has given you colorful and pretty clothing. He preserved your race in Noah's Ark so that it did not disappear from the earth. And you are also indebted to Him for the realm of the air, which He assigned to you. Therefore you should praise your Creator."

Nicola whispered in my ear that distinctly she had heard the creature answer him, saying, "Praise be to the Lord." Whether it did say these words or not, Francis opened his hands and the bird took flight. No longer lost, it flew past me and out the portal.

He began a sermon on the true meaning of happiness, which lasted for a long time and had nothing to do, as far as I could tell, with the kind of happiness that was written out in the letter hidden in my cloak.

While I stood half listening to the sermon, I searched the crowd for Clare. I was certain that she was in the church, though I had seen no sign of her escort when we arrived. It was always a large one — four or five grizzled men in red and gold livery, carrying pennons that displayed the crouching lion of the Scifis.

After the sermon was over and most of the people had left, I ran down the aisle, clutching my letter. Between me and the altar, the women of the Scifi family were gathered — Clare, her sisters, Agnes, Beatrice, and Caterina, and their mother, Ortolana — dressed in their fine jewels and furs, chattering away. I hurried around them without pausing to speak and handed the letter to Francis.

"How beautiful!" he said, turning it over to look at both sides of the vellum. "The ribbon and the wax and the scholarly script. It is too beautiful to open. I will take it home and observe it during gloomy moments."

"Open it now," I said, foreseeing that he would put it away on a shelf and forget it.

He untied the ribbon and slipped it inside his ragged gown. Then he broke the seal. He read quickly, skimming the words, but he saw enough.

"In praise," he said. "Verses written by a great poet."

"In praise of the man she loved?" I asked him.

He tightened the rope around his waist. Did I see a flush of color beneath his dark skin?

"Oh, no. In praise of the Church."

"How," I said, though my knees threatened to fail me, "how can the Church have locks as 'bushy and black as a raven'? It could have legs that are 'pillars of marble,' I can see this. But not a navel that resembles a 'round goblet.' The Song may be an allegory about the Church, as you say, but even so Solomon uses physical love as a metaphor. So it can't be all that bad!"

79

Francis touched his forehead as if he were about to make the sign of the cross, then paused. "You're the daughter of Davino di Montanaro, are you not? Yes, I recognize you. You're the giver of stones."

"Yes, and my name is Cecilia Graziella Beatrice Angelica Rosanna. My friends call me Ricca."

"Ricca," he said, testing the name on his tongue. "The name Angelica suits you better."

Angelica? Was he having fun with me?

He finished making the sign of the cross. Again he tightened the rope around his waist. He was dismissing the Old Testament poem and Rose, the Shulamite. I made no effort to stop him. Enthralled, speechless at the sound of my name on his lips, I sought desperately for something else I could ask.

A question about his advice to the bird occurred to me, but at the moment Brother Giles came sidling up, his toenails scratching on the floor. He was followed by the Scifi family, all except Clare, who stood off by herself, wrapped in a dream. I spoke to her as I went up the aisle. She didn't hear me.

FOURTEEN

T he homeward ride was a joy. High above, the icy ridges
of Monte Subasio glittered; the house that clustered at
its feet, the smoke rising lazily from the chimneys —
all glittered. The streets that had seemed ominous hours before,
the city itself, glittered and glowed like a jewel. Everything
was changed. I was breathless with love.

Nicola mistook my silence. "You were disappointed with our
Francis?"

"No," I said, "oh, no!" I restrained myself and added in a
churchlike voice, "He was quite sympathetic, though he spoke
but little."

"No wonder. He preaches so hard he hasn't many words
left over when he stops. Did you see as he held the bird in his
hands that a light shone around him, a wonderful shining halo?"

Nicola was like my mother — she saw halos everywhere. I
believe that they both really saw halos. Yet did it make any
difference whether the halos were there or not, so long as they
saw them? For myself, I had come to believe that the power
Francis had with birds was the same power he had over me.

Nicola was riding astride, showing her trim ankles and pretty
shoes. A man called down from a window, remarking on their
beauty, and she called back in the rough language of her mountain home, complimenting him on his vision.

"What was the letter about?" she asked.

"Love poems."

"Love? Poems? From where? I would like to hear them."

"They're in the Bible."

"I can't read."

"I forgot. I'll read them to you."

"Tonight?"

"Soon."

"After supper?"

"The bishop is coming for supper, remember? You were planning to make tarts for him. The pink ones shaped like a bishop's hat."

"When he leaves?"

"He never leaves before midnight."

"After midnight, then?"

"Perhaps. If I'm awake. Sometimes he puts me to sleep with his talk."

The bishop left early, however, soon after he had eaten sparingly, which was unusual, prayed hastily, and heard my brief confession, which I mostly made up since I had nothing interesting to confess. Father and I saw him to the door and we both kissed the handsome amethyst ring on his finger. I went back to the scriptorium while the men stayed talking at the door.

They were there only a short time when I heard Francis Bernardone's name mentioned and the bishop raise his voice. I left my bench and ran through a back passageway and into a room near the door where the men were standing.

They had lowered their voices, but I clearly heard the bishop say, "A list of his heresies has been assembled. It's a matter now of putting them in a letter. They will surprise the pope. He doesn't realize how cunning these heretics are. How they flourish in our midst, right here under our noses."

"When does the letter go?"

"As soon as it is written. At the moment my scrivener is ill and I write a wretched hand."

"Ricca will be pleased to write it for you," my father said. "Thus we'll catch two birds in a single trap. She writes an elegant hand, which should please the pope. And while writing the letter she may ponder the sins she herself has committed."

"And is committing," the bishop added.

"How close she's been to the sin of heresy."

"And how close she is. For I see no sign that she has changed toward him," the bishop said.

There was a short silence. I heard nothing but the sound of the wind gusting through the open door. If I were given the letter, I would carefully write down the list, all the facts the bishop had gathered, one after the other, but at the end I would say, "All these charges, your honor, I am pleased to report, are only rumors hatched by troublemakers."

I was shaking my head, doubting that such a wild scheme would ever work, when the bishop said, "With respect to your daughter, I am reluctant to burden her with the letter."

"It is not a burden," Father said. "She will be glad to write it."

They were parting as I left the room and hurried back to the scriptorium. I was busy with my brushes when Father walked down the hall and bade me goodnight.

On Friday the bishop came at midday and during dinner informed my father that the scrivener, having regained his health, would have the letter ready by Sunday morning.

"I'll read it carefully and be ready to send it to Rome on Monday," he said. "When I was here on Monday last you promised me horses."

"As many as you wish," Father said.

"A dozen," the bishop suggested. "And I'll see that they're equipped in the brightest of bishopric colors. I have found that guards and clerks and the pope himself are impressed by numbers and pennons. And he must be impressed, because the matter is urgent. Even urgent matters lie around in Rome, sometimes for a year."

Bishop Pelagius lived in a grand palace attached to the far end of the south transept in the old cathedral of Santa Maria

Maggiore. After vespers every Sunday and sometimes on feast days, he gave a reception for prominent citizens of Assisi. I had been there and liked them because of the multitude of pretty confections served on gold salvers by an army of handsome knights. There was always music, too, by the commune's orchestra of seven pieces — three viols, three lutes, and a drum.

Sunday came slowly. Long before vespers, Nicola and I were in the cathedral, down in front on the left side, where we would be seen by the bishop as he stood at the lectern. And we were the first at his door afterward.

While Nicola admired the confections, I joined those who were wandering through the palace, gazing at the bishop's fine tapestries, and sitting in the priceless chairs that had come from Egypt and Constantinople. When I had been there before, I hadn't strayed farther than the salon where food was being served.

There were six rooms downstairs. I went through each of them and saw nothing that looked like a desk. A winding stair led to a landing, then to a second floor of two big rooms that contained nothing of interest. On the third floor I went through two smaller rooms, and off a third one I found what looked as if it was the bishop's study. In the middle of the room sat a writing desk, an immense one with brass scrolls around the edges and, for feet, colored glass balls shaped like lion's claws.

The desk was cluttered with quills, sharpened and unsharpened, inkwells, stacks of vellum, and a half-eaten pear turning brown, which showed marks like those the bishop might make with his big, broad teeth. There was no sign of a letter anywhere in the rubble.

I sat down at the desk and went through the drawers, four of them on each side of me, but found nothing. Then as I stood up I noticed a small desk in a far corner of the room. On it, in clear sight, was a scroll addressed to Pope Innocent III, sealed with a blob of purple wax which was stamped with the bishop's ring. I put the letter inside my dress and strolled down the stairs. The salon teemed with guests, including my family. I slipped away, not speaking to anyone, took a short cut through the cathedral, and ran down the winding street to our house. There was time to rewrite the letter — not a lot, but enough if I hurried.

Standing at my bench in the scriptorium, I carefully lifted the bishop's seal with a sharp knife used in the making of vellum. The letter, longer than I expected it to be and written in the diminutive Gothic so popular in the province of Granada, was in reply to a letter from the pope in which His Eminence had asked Bishop Pelagius to examine rumors that had reached him, rumors that pictured Assisi as a hatchery for heretics and Francis Bernardone as its leader.

Hurriedly I wrote a new letter, shorter than the bishop's, copying the Granadian Gothic as best I could. I said that the rumors had been duly investigated and found to be false, especially the rumor that Bernardone was posing as a priest, hearing confessions and conducting rites over the dead. While he was a little off in the head, I wrote, he was not a heretic.

I placed the bishop's seal on the new letter, attaching it with hot wax so that no one could tell it had been tampered with. The only suspicious thing was the paper, which was not of as good a quality as the bishop's and lacked its faint purplish tinge.

When I got back to the palace, the salon was so crowded that it was impossible to tell one person from another. I glided through the room quietly, an eel through the grass, and had one slippered foot on the stairs when from nowhere the bishop reached out, took my hand in his, and gave it a lingering squeeze.

"We have missed you," he said. "I saw you leave. You looked pale. You look pale now. I hope nothing is amiss."

"Nothing," I said, "except a small pain, which I have attended to."

The bishop hesitated a moment before saying, "What a handsome girl you are!"

"Woman," I corrected him.

"I envision glorious days for you, now that again you have your pretty head on straight."

Then Nicola appeared and saved me from what could have been a lecture. She stood on tiptoe in her pink boots and stuffed a tart into the bishop's mouth. While this took place, I wandered away and up the stairs. As I reached the second floor I tucked up my skirts and ran.

The passage on the next landing was deserted, but as I approached the door to the bishop's study I heard voices at the end of the passage, men quietly discussing church affairs. I turned about and went down to the second landing and seated myself on a bench, placed there no doubt for those who grew faint on the endless stairs.

I sat for a short time, then climbed the stairs once more. The door to the bishop's study was closed. I put an ear against the door and listened but heard no sound. I took hold of the brass knob, which felt stiff and cold in my hand and would not move. I used both my hands and wrenched at it. With a startling noise it flew open.

I was about to put the letter on the table in the same place I had found the bishop's letter when I heard steps in the passageway. There was no reason for me to be in the bishop's study. The only place to hide was behind a tapestry that covered all of one wall. I slipped behind it as someone, a light-footed girl, came in sneezing and, between sneezes, humming to herself.

The girl swept the fringes of the tapestry, went out, and brought back something that made a noise as she placed it on the table; then she left.

I put the letter on the desk, beside the bowl of fruit the girl had placed there, closed the door quietly, and fled down the stairs. As I reached the second landing, my sleeve swept a bust of Pope Innocent from its niche. It did not break but it tumbled along the marble floor, making a loud racket, which fortunately the din from below drowned out.

My father and Bishop Pelagius stood at the bottom of the stairs, Father's hand placed deferentially upon the bishop's arm. They were deciding on the number of horses required to carry the bishop's letter to Rome, what color the beasts should be, what the riders should wear, and whether or not drums and a flute were adequate for the occasion.

While I listened and said nothing, a robed man came down the stairs, holding the letter I had just left on the bishop's desk. The blob of wax that sealed it sparkled in the candlelight. Since it was well known in Assisi that the bishop had made a list of heretics and was sending it to Rome, the eyes of everyone present were fixed upon it.

I turned away, expecting that the letter would be given to Pelagius. I tried to think of something to say if I were accused, but the man went on, sauntering through the room, stopping here and there to talk, and finally disappeared.

I lived in dread for two days, until the third day in midmorning, at the hour when the streets were crowded, the caravan left the palace, resplendent with the bishop's flags, led by twelve men in scarlet dress on proud white horses, to the sound of lutes and drums.

Somewhere in their midst was the letter I had written to Pope Innocent III.

FIFTEEN

The letter I had given to Francis, so carefully written on fine vellum, illuminated by small birds and beasts (I knew that he loved them all dearly), had caught his eye. The poem itself had aroused his interest and brought a flush to his cheeks, and words, though they were not what I wished, to his lips.

On the whole, deeming the letter a success, and more than a success, somewhat of a triumph, I sought another subject for a letter, one not based on the Bible. At last I settled upon the lives of Abelard and Heloise and that night read copies of the letters they had written to each other.

The circumstances of their lives were wholly different from those of mine and Francis's. And they themselves were wholly different. Abelard was a brilliant philosopher and Heloise his brightest student. Francis now was unlike Abelard in every way, modest and self-effacing where Abelard arrogantly courted fame. But there was a tie between Heloise and me. I had a warm feeling for her and suffered deeply at her misfortunes.

In the morning I sat down an hour before I was to start work on the Bible and wrote the letter. What I was to say was vague in my mind, but my purpose was very clear. If Abelard, the most famous philosopher in all of the countries of Europe, could break his priestly vows, then Francis Bernardone, a lowly preacher, could break his.

Francis was not a scholar. I had even heard him say that he

read the Bible and nothing else. He had never read the story of the two lovers, therefore, and if he had heard the story he would not know the details to be found only in their letters.

At first there were nine questions I wished to ask him. These I reduced to eight, to six, and finally the six to four, the four designed to show Francis how Abelard had erred in his treatment of Heloise and, as I have said, to encourage him to ponder his own life and his friendship with me.

The four questions read in this order and these words:

You will remember, sir, that Abelard was master of the Cloister School at Notre-Dame in Paris, nearly a hundred years ago. He met and fell in love with Heloise and persuaded her uncle to accept him as a boarder. In return for his board, he took on the duties of tutoring Heloise in philosophy.

My questions, sir, are these:

In view of the fact that Abelard arranged the bargain with her uncle, Canon Fulbert, with the hope of seducing Heloise, as he later admitted, and since he did indeed seduce her, does the fault for the tragic events that followed lie with him alone? Or does it lie with Canon Fulbert for bringing the two together under one roof, especially since he resolutely thought that by currying favor with Abelard he would further his own churchly ambitions?

There are other questions that I wish you to answer, sir, and may I be so bold as to refresh your memory, for what is a living story to me can only be, considering all your holy concerns, vague shadows of a worldly past.

When Canon Fulbert, you will recall, discovered that the two were lovers, he at once and in a towering rage banished Abelard from the house. Soon afterward, Heloise became heavy with child. One night when Fulbert was away, Abelard secretly had her taken, disguised as a nun, to her sister's home in Brittany, where she gave birth to a son.

Abelard, as time passed, grew ashamed of the treacherous way he had treated Canon Fulbert. In the end he went to see the canon and excused his treachery by saying that great men, like himself, and since the days of Adam, had suffered the fatal wiles of women. Further, he promised the canon that he would marry Heloise, provided the marriage was kept secret. Canon Fulbert, as you will further recall, was so elated that he embraced Abelard and sealed the promise with a kiss.

My question is this, sir: Was it wrong for Abelard to insist that his plan be kept secret, based as it was upon the fear that marriage might hinder his future with the Church?

But the uncle, against his promise, disclosed the marriage. Feeling bound by love to protect Abelard, Heloise denied on oath that they were married. The denial enraged Canon Fulbert and he fell upon her with sticks and curses. He felt that Abelard had broken their pledge. In revenge he thought up an inhuman plan and brutally carried it out.

"Violently angry," Abelard reports in one of his works, "Fulbert and his kinsmen . . . One night when I was fast asleep in an inner room of my lodgings, they bribed a servant and punished me by means of a most barbarous and shameful revenge — one that was heard of by all with utter amazement — namely they deprived me of that part of my body with which I had committed the deeds of which they complained."

At this place in their tragic lives, I begin to wonder, sir, about many things, especially if God did not act in the guise of Canon Fulbert. And I wonder also *if, at the end when, it is said, the body of Heloise was laid at her husband's side and he reached out his arms to her, it was not to ask forgiveness.*

I copied the story and the questions that I hoped would catch his attention, all in a fine Gothic script. I showed them to Raul, for he was the one who had told me their tragic story when he first feared that I was possessed. And later he had sent to Paris, to the cloister of Notre-Dame, and purchased a copy of the letters, using money from the library funds to meet the cost, which was the price of a good parcel of land and tight dwellings.

Work in the scriptorium was finished for the week. The copyists had gone and I had put away my pens and brushes. It was a warm day with a wind from Subasio gusting across the rooftops. But Raul was wrapped in a mantle, his fur cap pulled down; only his black eyes showed. He glanced down at the letter and shook his head.

"You're aware that I give advice sparingly," he said, "and that I often call upon history, believing that what has happened in the past may happen again. For this reason I told you about Abelard and Heloise and suggested you read their letters. However, you continue to tread the same steps as Heloise. You're stumbling like a sleepwalker toward an abyss, the same abyss that she stumbled into."

Raul had been talking through the folds of his mantle. He now freed his mouth.

"I have watched this affair with dread. Still I refrain from giving you advice, other than to beg you to read her letters again — not with the idea of propounding questions for Bernardone to answer, but for you yourself to answer. The letter you sent and this one that you plan to send are only a ruse to gain favor with a man whose life is as devoted to himself as was Abelard's."

"Francis Bernardone is not Abelard," I said, keeping anger from my voice. "Abelard was ambitious, aspired to be the very best, the best lecturer at Notre-Dame, the best philosopher in the world, the best everything. Francis is different. He doesn't wish to be the best, to be rich or famous, an abbot or a cardinal. He only wishes to be the humblest, to serve the poor, those that are dispossessed and those that sorrow."

"Your Francis Bernardone and all his perfections remind me of a story they tell in Seville. In the Street of the Serpents there was a beautiful black, silky Nubian goat, famous in the city and the countryside for the prodigious amounts of milk she gave. The curious came for miles to pat her velvety sides. Buyers flocked there with fabulous offers. The city council passed resolutions in her honor. But the owner was very quiet, silent about the beast's one bad habit, which he had never been able to cure. Once the milk jug was full, the goat kicked it over."

"Another of your Sufis," I said. "What does it mean?"

"I quote parables to you on the theory that what we can't see in bright sunlight, we can see in the shadows. If you wish to see an object clearly — for instance, a man standing under a tree on a distant hill — you don't widen your eyes; you narrow them, you squint."

"I am squinting and still I don't see."

"Keep squinting," Raul said.

He had not come to quote parables — that I saw by the tight line around his lips and the jut of his beard.

In a moment he said, "I bring news that may interest you. Bernardone, as you know, has been traveling about Assisi, acting like an ordained priest, and preaching, collecting money, which he uses as he sees fit. His antics displeased Bishop Pelagius, so the bishop wrote a fiery letter to the pope, accusing him of heresy."

I listened as though I were hearing about the letter for the very first time.

"Well, Bernardone got wind of the letter somehow and hied himself off to Rome, where the pope greeted him civilly, but, shocked by his rags and bare feet, politely dismissed him. That evening — and mind you, I am repeating rumors that strike me as somewhat ridiculous — the pope repaired to the altar of the great church, the altar beneath which lay the most sacred relics of Israel: the rod of Moses, given him by God, the Tables of the Law, the Ark of the Covenant. He knelt and prayed, then out of the sky, out of nowhere, there suddenly came a shattering sound. The roof pitched. Candelabra swung in violent arcs. The alabaster columns cracked and swayed. A terrible wind howled through the resplendent aisles.

"For an awful instant the pope thought that the church would be swept away. Then he opened his eyes and saw that the structure was whole once again, supported upon the broad shoulders of the ragged beggar of Assisi.

"Innocent awoke from his dream and called his cardinals together and said to them, 'This is truly the man who, by example, will uphold the Church of Christ.'"

Raul picked up the letter I had written and handed it to me.

"I impart this news as a final admonition," he said. "The pope has blessed Bernardone and given him the authority to preach churchly doctrines. He is lost to you at this hour and forever."

Not forever, I said to myself.

Raul turned to the bench where a candelabrum stood and selected the largest of the candles. "Destroy the letter," he said, "lest it add fuel to this awful fire."

I shook my head and, thinking that he would burn the letter himself, hid it away.

SIXTEEN

I waited for Palm Sunday to give Francis the letter, knowing that on that day he would be at San Rufino. I carefully rewrote it. The Gothic script I changed to Carolingian, it being more feminine and easier to read. The capitals I repainted in blue and gold, and instead of mere decorations I showed Christ entering the city of Jerusalem in a bower of olive branches.

I counted the hours, the days, the long nights, until that holy celebration. They moved maddeningly slowly. I could have gone looking for Francis in the countryside, but Palm Sunday seemed the best time to see him again, less bold than if I went to search him out.

There was conflict in Assisi, as usual, between the rich and the poor, merchants and nobles. Rumors spread that there would be strife on the holy Sunday. Our enemies in Perugia even threatened to disrupt the day. I lived in fear that warfare would break out and close the cathedral.

My fears proved groundless, but something I had not foreseen did upset me greatly.

The day dawned peaceful and clear. By midmorning the streets were crowded with worshipers, bright in velvet mantles and silver corselets, on foot and on horseback, on their way to the cathedral of San Rufino, the poor and the noble. Hidden beneath my mantle I carried the letter to Francis Bernardone.

The portals were decked with olive branches, pine boughs, and sheaves of early flowers, so thick that it was difficult to pass through them.

Nicola said, "It's like walking through a forest."

And so it was, but inside the cathedral clouds of incense obscured the nave and the kneeling worshipers. Far off through the clouds there was a glimmer of candles. Bishop Pelagius was praying in his golden voice: "Oh God, who by an olive branch commanded the dove to proclaim peace to the world, sanctify, we beseech Thee, by Thy heavenly benediction, these olive branches, that they may be serviceable to all Thy people unto salvation."

I stood on tiptoe while the bishop prayed, craning my neck to find some sign of Francis amidst the restless crowd. I searched until my eyes stung, but to no avail.

Echoes of the bishop's elegant voice were dying away when Clare appeared out of the clouds of incense and clasped me in her arms. She was all in white. She wore a diadem in her coiled hair and gleaming pearls at her throat.

"You look like a bride-to-be," I said. "But where is the shining knight who will take your hand in his?"

She raised a jeweled finger and pointed toward the window at the far end of the cathedral, where a patch of blue sky showed. "There," she said. "There! Don't you see?"

Clare's mother and her three sisters, a gathering of aunts, uncles, and cousins, and the seven knights of the family, resplendent in their shining breastplates, stood nearby.

"But when do you wed?" I asked, thinking she was making a joke.

"Soon," she said.

"Will I be your closest friend and stand beside you, my arms full of pretty flowers, and support you if your legs grow weak? And how, please tell me, does he look? Is he tall? Is he knightly? Is he —"

Clare frowned and interrupted me, saying a word that I lost in the triumphal chorus of "Holy, holy, holy, Lord God of hosts" that went roaring through the church. Her frown passed quickly, but it proved to be the foreshadowing of events to come, events that between dusk and dawn were to shake Assisi.

The first sign came when everyone, including myself and Nicola and all the Scifis and their cousins the Favarones, went to the altar and received the blessed branches from the hands of the bishop. Clare stayed behind. When I returned she was still standing at the portal, but now her eyes were downcast and a trance had come upon her.

A strange thing then took place. Quiet fell upon the kneeling crowd as Bishop Pelagius walked down the altar steps, carrying a sacred olive branch. The crowd started. What was this powerful, arrogant, short-tempered bishop about to do? He might do anything. The hush deepened. All eyes were upon him as he stopped in front of Clare and handed her the sacred branch.

I was startled. What did the gift of the sacred symbol mean? Surely it marked the sealing of a pact. But what pact could it be? There was no sign from Clare as she accepted the gift. Curtsying to the bishop, she waited calmly until he had turned and started down the aisle. Then she grasped my arm.

"Come," she whispered and dragged me through the portal and down the long flight of steps, Nicola running along behind us.

"Let's go before the family comes," she said. Her face was drained of color.

"Go where?"

"Anywhere."

"Why, for heaven's sake?"

The first of a long procession began to file down the steps and into the square.

"I must hide," Clare said. "Now, somewhere."

"Hide from what?" I asked, annoyed with her.

She didn't answer. In the procession filing out of the church I caught a glimpse of her mother and her two sisters and behind them the seven knights of the family, towering over all in their feathered caps and shining armor.

I shook her by the arms, not gently. "You're acting like a child. Whatever is wrong? What are you hiding from?"

She seemed puzzled that I didn't know. "From my family,

of course," she said. "They've been suspicious for weeks that something is about to happen. The bishop's gift only increases their suspicions. If I go home now, they'll gather round and question me. There'll be a terrible fight. The fight will end with the doors closed and bolted and me a prisoner. There's nothing I can do except hide until the vows are taken."

"What vows?" I stammered. My head reeled at the sound of the word, although from the day we had stood together beside the palace steps and watched Francis renounce his father, from that day to this moment, I should have known. I raised my voice. "Vows, what vows?"

"The vows of the Friars Minor."

"You're taking vows? Where?"

"At Porziuncola. In the chapel."

"When?"

"The day after tomorrow, at vespers."

The bells of San Rufino, high against the heavens, began to toll the hour. The procession had broken up and the crowd milled around us.

"Hide me," Clare said. "Please, until the morning comes."

Clare, the beautiful Clare di Scifi, was taking the vows, thinking to run errands for Francis Bernardone, to collect stones for him and beg for bread, to be close to him, to breathe the same air he breathed. What a little hypocrite!

The gaze of Manaldo Scifi, the tallest of the seven knights, was moving back and forth over the silent crowd. I was tempted to shout, "Lord Manaldo, your sister Clare is here. Look, she is here!"

"If you hide in our home," I said to her, "and they come for you, what does my father say? Does he lie? The Scifis are vengeful men. You do not lie to them or to their cousins, the Favarones, who are with them."

Clare made a sound. It was like the noise a stricken animal makes when caught in a trap. Turning away from me, she fled through the square. She was fleeing toward the poorest part of the city, where she could find someone willing to hide her.

97

I ran wildly through the crowd. When I caught her, there were tears in her eyes.

"Hurry!" I said, taking her hand.

A crossbowman was on guard at the Door of the Dead, astride his bench. He opened the door, and the three of us, Nicola and Clare and I, slipped in and took the steep stairs to my tower.

The letter I had written to Francis was still hidden in my cloak. Tomorrow he would be at Porziuncola, waiting for Clare. I would deliver it, place it in his hand with a curtsy and a discreet smile.

Meanwhile, as Clare watched San Rufino Square from the balcony, I wrote another missive, a short one, to Ortolana di Scifi, informing her that her daughter was on the way to Porziuncola, there to take the Franciscan vows. I signed it "Pacifica Primavera, a friend," and gave it to a servant to deliver the next day as the San Rufino bells rang out for tierce.

Barely an hour after I had given these instructions, Nicola reported that horsemen were on the street. I hurried to the balcony. The big, tuneful bells of San Rufino rang, followed by the booming bells of Santa Maria Maggiore. Watchmen's lanterns showed in the square. People were scurrying home, for the law prohibited loitering in the streets after dark, even on Palm Sunday.

The horsemen stopped at our gate and I heard them arguing with the guards.

"I'll send them away," Nicola said. She ran to the balcony and shouted down to them, "Varlets, be off!"

Shouts came back, a torrent of them. As I left the room and hastened down the stairs, I heard the rasping voice of Manaldo. I opened the door in his face. Taken aback, he bowed and muttered an apology.

He loomed in the doorway, a tall man, his corselets worn tight to reveal bands of bulging muscle. He moved his mouth in an unfriendly smile to let me know that he knew that I would answer him with a lie.

I hesitated, sorely tempted to tell him that Clare was hiding in the tower and thus bring the escapade to an end. But I clung to the belief that by hiding her, by taking her to Porziuncola myself, by giving her over into the hands of Francis Bernardone, I would gain immense favor in Francis's eyes.

"May I ask," Manaldo said, "have you seen my sister since you were together in Piazza San Rufino?"

I said, meeting his gaze, "No, I have not."

He showed no sign of believing me. He tarried on the doorstep, fingering the hilt of his sword, hoping no doubt that my father would appear. I thanked him for his brotherly concern, saying that I was sorry that my father was not at home, which was the truth, bade him a polite good evening, closed the door, and at once sent Nicola to the stables to order three horses to be saddled and ready at dawn. For whom she was not to say.

SEVENTEEN

The night went slowly. Clare slept fitfully; when awake, she whispered words that no one could understand. I lay fitful also, overwrought by fears of the portentous day to come. It dawned to the sound of rain and a clamorous south wind.

Horses were waiting, saddled and beribboned, but the stable-master was reluctant to send us off. "Where do you go?" he asked, scanning the wind-driven rain.

"To a wedding below Porta della Buona Madre," I said. Buona Madre was in the opposite direction from Porziuncola. "If the Scifi family comes looking, tell them this. And to my family, should they ask, which is not likely since they seldom rise before noon."

"There's a river to cross," he said. "You had best wait until the storm passes."

Clare answered him by climbing into the saddle. Nicola and I did likewise.

"When do you return?" he asked.

"Before noon," I said.

"It's best that you wait until then. Better yet, signorina, wait until tomorrow."

I told him that the wedding wouldn't wait and thanked him for his advice. We rode quickly out of the courtyard, quicker yet as we passed the Scifi castle. Not until we reached the Roman wall did we settle down to an even gait.

Clare, riding in the lead, head bared to the rain, happy as a bride on the way to her wedding, only stopped talking long enough to fling glances over her shoulder to make sure that we were not being followed. We had hours before my note to her mother would be delivered, before her seven brothers — armed, with black pennons flying and trumpets sounding — would take to the road.

By midmorning we were within sight of Porziuncola and heard the hour being tinkled out by its small, cracked bell, which would have fitted a cow much better than it did a belfry. Unfortunately, between us and the church was the river, running swiftly between its high banks.

I was faced with a crucial choice. The one way we could cross the river was to ride on for a league and a half to the bridge. Then, having crossed the river, we would have to ride the long distance back, which meant that unless I left Clare to make the rest of the journey alone, I would never reach home before noon. But if I turned back, the favor I hoped to gain with Francis by bringing Clare to him would be lost. I decided to go on to the bridge, though now the wind and rain had increased, and I would be late getting home.

Night was falling as we saw the lights of Porziuncola, and a procession of men — a dozen or more, carrying torches — came out of the dark to meet us. We got off our horses and together went down a long aisle through the pines.

The portals of the church were decked with pine boughs. As soon as I had tied my horse I ran inside, not waiting for the others. Candles burned on the altar and Francis stood in their glow. I had made up a flowery speech as we rode along to give when I arrived. Suddenly it flew from my mind.

"Clare's outside," I said.

"Bring her in where it's warm," Francis said.

"She's nearly drowned. She's fixing her hair. We have been riding since dawn in a bad storm. I am nearly drowned also."

My face, dripping rain, bespoke the ordeal. Francis took a

cloth from his robe and gave it to me. I wiped my face but didn't give it back. He thanked me, seemingly impressed by what I had done, by how devoted I was to Clare.

"We had word this morning that Clare's family isn't pleased about her taking the vow. They're out searching for her, we heard," Francis said.

"Yes, her brother Manaldo came to our door last night and asked if I had seen her. I told him that I hadn't, though she was hiding in the tower, not a hundred steps away."

"Was he distressed?"

"Angry, not distressed."

"If they're angry and searching for her, they'll certainly come here. We had planned the ceremony for tomorrow, but perhaps it would be wise to hear the vows tonight."

"They'll come," I said, "but only after they have turned Assisi upside down and begun to comb the countryside."

Hours ago Clare's mother had received my note informing the family where Clare could be found. By now the brothers would be on the road to Porziuncola and, since they rode fast horses, nearing the bridge. They might be nearer yet. Reckless as they were, they might ford the flooded river, in which case they would be less than an hour away.

"It's safe to wait until tomorrow," I said. Now that I had begun to lie, lies came easily. "Clare has had a frightful day. She needs to dry her clothes and sleep."

The letter I had written to him was in my cloak, wrapped up and dry, but I decided that this was not the time to deliver it.

"I'll bring her," I said and ran outside.

From the church steps there was a clear view of the field between me and the river. The seven brothers would be traveling with torches. I saw none; the fields lay in half-darkness, wanly lit by a quartering moon. They might not arrive until morning. During that time, possibly longer, I must do everything in my power to prevent the ceremony.

Nicola and I helped Clare straighten her rumpled dress. She was silent and stiff, like a doll children were fussing over, and her hands were cold when I touched them. It suddenly came to me that she was questioning the fearsome step that loomed before her.

If she changed her mind, I was not to blame. I had harbored her for a night, risking my father's wrath. I had braved a storm and brought her safely to Porziuncola. If she turned back now, if her love for Francis Bernardone was overshadowed by her love for her family and she refused to join his barefooted rabble, she would lose him forever. And Francis could not blame me if this should happen. He would know that I had done my part and more.

I chafed her cold hands. "Dear Clare," I said, secretly crossing myself, "it is not too late to turn back. If you must take the vow, you can join the Benedictines. It's an order that accepts only girls from rich families, those who can furnish handsome dowries. I know this because my mother's aunt is a Benedictine prioress in the city of Venice. Her name is Sister Sofia, and she was a beautiful girl. Not so beautiful as you, Clare — no one is."

Silent and rigid, Clare's gaze was fixed on the open doors of the church, from which the altar's light shone forth.

"Your family is humiliated," I said. "They are stricken. Manaldo, all your brothers, search for you. And they'll find you wherever you hide. They'll harm Francis if he stands in their way. They'll snatch you from the arms of the church itself. They would much rather see you dead than tramping about barefooted with a begging bowl. They are brutal men, your brothers. They live to defy the law. They know nothing else. They will not rest or be appeased until you are back with the family."

Clare trembled as a chant poured forth from the church. A moan came from deep inside her.

"Please," I said, "we'll go home together and wait until things are calm once more." I gripped her arm lest she seek out the chanting voices. "Until we are forgiven."

Nicola spoke up to say that she saw a line of horsemen with torches moving away to the south of us. It was possible that the seven brothers were at the river, trying to force their steeds across the flood. If so, if they succeeded, they would soon reach the church.

The chanting stopped and Francis appeared in the doorway. He ran down the steps. He stood gazing at Clare, at her white face, judging her, her downcast eyes. His own eyes were like caverns where flames leaped. My heart leaped too. Silently I prayed that he would find her wanting.

He looked toward the river. The lights had vanished.

"The horsemen have moved on," I said, to deceive him. At any moment, I thought, the brothers will be riding out of the trees to take Clare in their arms and bear her off. "They're on their way to the bridge. They can't be here much before dawn."

"It's best that we not wait," Francis said, taking Clare's hand. "Come."

I followed them into the church and down the aisle, desperately trying to think of a ruse, some way I could delay the ceremony, give the hurrying brothers more time. I thought of seizing one of the candles and lighting the straw that covered the floor. I could fall where I stood and let out the scream that was choking me.

Before I could do either, Clare had taken off her pearl necklace, the rings on her fingers, the jeweled girdle that bound her waist, and had thrown them into a heap at the foot of the altar. Francis handed her a gray habit and she held it in her arms as she knelt.

A man came forward out of the shadows with a lithe step, carrying something that glittered — a pair of shears. Clare unloosed her hair; it fell to below her waist. The shears were sharp. They made only a small sound in the quiet church. They took no longer at their task than the length of my breath.

Clare rose from her knees and glanced at the coils lying on the stones. To me they looked like the coils of the golden snake that wound itself around the apple tree in the Garden of Eden. Then she turned away and went outside to put on sandals that they had fashioned for her and to change her white jeweled gown for a gray robe.

The moon had set. The night was cloudy with a gray mist hanging over the river. It would be difficult now for Nicola and me to return to Assisi, and dangerous as well, for the country was inhabited at this hour by roving bands who would gladly kill you for the shoes you wore.

There was something else. Though Clare's hair was shorn, I clung to the hope that Manaldo and his knights would descend at any moment, wrest her from the hands of Francis Bernardone and his men. Or, if this did not occur, then God Himself might in some mysterious way interfere in my behalf.

While Clare traded her shimmering dress for a woolen robe, Francis held counsel with his men. They decided to take her to San Paolo, a Benedictine monastery a league distant, where they thought she would be safer than at Porziuncola.

I was disappointed to learn this, but when I was asked to tell the nuns at San Paolo that Clare was coming, I agreed to go, stubbornly clinging to the hope that something would happen on the way, either by chance or by God's intervention.

Nicola and I rode off at once for San Paolo, Francis Bernardone and Clare following us on foot. As we came within sight of the monastery, Nicola, who had not spoken since we left, stirred herself to say that while she was riding along she had given thought to taking the vow herself.

"Do you think your family would be displeased?" she asked.

"I can't answer for my father, but Mother would give her consent. For myself, I wonder that your awful experiences have not soured you on another pilgrimage. And that's exactly what this one is — a pilgrimage in a ragged robe and sandaled feet."

"But, Ricca, a pilgrimage with a man who is like one of the apostles. I often think of him as an apostle and sometimes I even think of him as Christ Himself. Do you have this feeling, too? You must. I saw you watching him tonight when he stood at the altar. You scarcely breathed. Your face glowed with love, heavenly love."

"You were deceived. It was the candles that glowed," I said, "not my face."

EIGHTEEN

L ike a fortress, the gray stone walls of San Paolo showed
through the mist.

Two lanterns burned at the gate, above a bell, which I
rang and rang and rang until a sleepy nun appeared. I asked
for Mother Sibilia in the name of Francis Bernardone, as I had
been told to do. The nun led us to a barren room furnished
with one chair, a guttering candle in a niche, and above a dusty
window a picture of Christ.

We waited for Mother Sibilia a long time, until a streak of
light showed in the east. She strode in with a firm step, her
thick soles resounding on the stones. A tall, thin-faced woman,
immaculate in white coif and robe, she darted a glance at
Nicola, who, struck by her regal appearance, was watching
with an open mouth.

"What is of such importance that I am called upon at this
hour to meet Signor Bernardone?" the abbess said, speaking
rapidly, her words tumbling along like pebbles in a stream.

As I started to answer, she interrupted me.

"I've encountered this man before," she said in a frosty voice.
"He came to our gate with a begging bowl, the poor asking food
from the poor. Excusing himself by pontificating, by saying that
he came at the command of Christ our Lord."

I had seen Mother Sibilia at San Rufino and had met her
once through Bishop Pelagius. Something about her thin mouth
and cold gray eyes had always repelled me.

"I think, however, that he came not for food," she said, "but to accuse us here at San Paolo delle Ancelle di Dio of living in luxury. To shame and admonish us. Such bravado! Such insolence! Such stupidity!"

A cold draft of air snuffed out the candle and she went to the niche, talking to herself, and lit it again.

"What is it now?" she asked. "Has he sent you here to beg? Where is your bowl? Perhaps you're here with a larger request. Perhaps it's money you want?"

Before I could answer she started for the door. I thought that she was about to leave, but she turned to fix me again with her cold eyes.

"Who are you, anyway?" she said. "You can't be one of his new recruits, dressed as you are. What's your name, young lady?"

"Ricca di Montanaro," I said, determined not to be cowed. "We met once, last year. I was with Bishop Pelagius. My father is Davino di Montanaro."

The names — my name, my father's name, the bishop's name — seemed not to impress her.

"Ricca di Montanaro," she said, shaking her head at me. "Then you're the one who disrobed in Piazza San Rufino on the occasion of the quarrel between the Bernardones, father and son. How unusual! I've sometimes thought of removing my habit and running wild through the spring grass. But never in Piazza San Rufino. There are many versions of this occasion: You disrobed and looked like a newborn newt. You disrobed only halfway, showing only the nether parts. You disrobed halfway, showing the upper parts. Or, you didn't disrobe at all. What did you do and why? I am curious."

"Next Sunday I'll return to San Paolo and tell you everything. There's a mystery lurking somewhere in all of it which troubles me. I'll treasure your advice."

Wasting not a moment, fearing that Clare would come before I finished, I explained my mission. The abbess walked back and forth, keeping her eyes on me, but when I came to the part about Clare she stopped and called to a nun who was standing outside the door.

"Lock the gate," she said. "And do not open it to anyone who rings between now and dawn, whoever they may be and whatever they want."

The nun scurried off. I heard the gate shut and an iron bolt slide into place.

"Is it possible," the abbess said, "that Clare di Scifi . . ." She paused. "This is the daughter of Ortolana di Scifi? You're certain?"

"Yes, the daughter."

"I had no idea that she ever thought of taking the veil," the abbess said. "We would have welcomed her here with songs and bells ringing without cease for days and nights. Now, now we have the spectacle of a lovely girl, nobly born, bound in vassalage to a mad schemer and his uncouth band. You were there at Porziuncola. What was the pledge she took?"

"None, so far as I know."

"The Franciscans — they call themselves Friars Minor but I call them Franciscans — take a vow of poverty, I understand. Anyone can join the order just by asking. Was her hair shorn?"

"Yes. But this might be a gesture."

"Not with the Benedictines. With the Franciscans, who knows? They are coming for what reason?"

"For protection."

"Against what?"

"The Scifi family, who are furious. The brothers, whom you must know, are out searching for her now. They were on the river near Porziuncola last night. And others of the family will follow them when she's found. The Scifis will come by the dozens to take her home."

Mother Sibilia went to the window, wiped the dust away with her sleeve, and glanced out. Dawn had broken. Calling for a second nun, a pretty one, she gave instructions to unlock the gate, wake the sisters, see to it that all wore fresh smiles and habiliments. She was unlocking the gate, opening her arms, I gathered, because she hoped to take Clare into the Benedictine fold. I sat quietly and waited, but through my mind raced a prayer that Mother Sibilia would succeed.

With the sun, the sisters in their winged coifs, laundered robes, and shining black shoes were standing at the gate. When Clare and Francis Bernardone came into view they began to sing in their birdlike voices, "Deliver me from my enemies, O Lord; to Thee I have fled."

The Scifis appeared soon after the pilgrims had been welcomed and fed. First came Manaldo, dashing up with his brothers, demanding to be let in, and when the gate was not opened, he gave it a sharp blow with his sword. He then complained in a loud voice and his brothers joined him. The abbess ignored the clamor.

"My advice about this Manaldo di Scifi, who bangs with his sword and shouts," I said, fearful that she might drive him away, "my advice, though you have not asked for it, is to open the gate lest he break it down, which he would much prefer to do."

Fingering her beads, the abbess reflected upon my words, went to the window and glanced out, then motioned me to follow her. At the gate she said in the gentlest of tones, but clenching her hands at the same time, "Who are you that clamors at the walls of San Paolo delle Ancelle di Dio?"

Manaldo gave his name, not humbly, adding names, six of them, none that I had ever heard before.

"I am Abbess Sibilia," she said and added a few names of her own to let him know that she, too, came from noble stock. "May I ask what you so ardently desire that you beat upon the gate and raise your voice like a varlet?"

"I come for Clare di Scifi," he said, "who is now behind your walls."

"For what reason?"

"Because she's a runaway. And I, her brother, am here to take her home. She left her family to follow a ragged group of misfits, led by the wastrel Bernardone. You have heard of him?"

"I have," the abbess said, "and favorably."

To my relief, in answer to my prayers, she then slid the bolt and opened the gate, and Manaldo swaggered in, followed soon by the other Scifis, dozens of them, dressed in fur-trimmed velvet. A baby in its nurse's arms clutched a rattle encrusted with pearls.

It took Manaldo some time to quiet the Scifis, to caution them to obey the rules of the monastery, to curb their tongues, to display none of the fury they so rightfully felt. When at last he herded them to the chapel, they stood silent and tight-lipped but with blazing eyes.

The abbess produced Clare, leading her down the aisle like a shepherd leading a lamb. The family stirred. Someone coughed. The baby began to cry.

As Clare and Mother Sibilia reached the altar and the candlelight fell full upon them, as the family saw for the first time the girl they adored fully revealed in gray robe and sandals, a loud gasp — everyone must have gasped at once — seemed to suck up all the air.

Clare knelt and prayed and everyone was quiet. But when she rose and took off the white cloth that bound her head, when it was revealed that her golden hair had been shorn to a stubble, a prolonged cry rose from every throat.

The family descended upon her, all talking at the same time. Ortolana spoke of the great love she felt for her daughter, of the grief and dishonor she had suffered because of Clare's madness. The two sisters reminded her of all the favors, the happy hours, the bountiful life she was renouncing. Everyone had words to say. But she responded to no one, to none of the questions and pleas.

An uneasy silence came over the family. The silence deepened. Someone called upon God in a frightened voice. Some began to mutter. Suddenly a furious storm broke loose. Clare was encircled by a shouting pack who plucked at her, heaped abuse upon her and upon Francis Bernardone, the madman who had ensnared her. The culprit who had defied the rich, the ancient nobles, the very heart of Assisi itself — he was attempting to dethrone the powerful, to make a laughing stock of their daughters. *Vilitas*, gross vulgarity, base ignorance, villainy! they shouted. Manaldo clutched at the hem of Clare's skirt. She pulled away.

A cloth, symbolizing the sheet that had concealed Christ's body, covered the altar. In one swift moment, Clare reached out and grasped one corner of the holy cloth. By this symbolic act she received the protection of the Church. Now no one dared touch her, save those who would scorn its wrath.

Manaldo stared, torn between violence and fear.

"Your presence here is a sacrilege," the abbess said to him. "In the name of Christ our Lord, leave us in peace."

Manaldo glanced toward his brothers, who stood against the wall, hands on their swords. He sized up the Franciscans gathered nearby, a burly lot, who carried clubs and were watching. He glanced at Francis Bernardone, who stood among them, holding a cross. He appeared to be comparing one side against the other. But it was not, judging from the awkward way Manaldo bowed to the abbess, from his shaking voice as he answered her, the fear of bloody battle that held him back. Instead, it was the fear of God's punishment.

Mumbling an apology, he strode up the aisle, followed quickly by the other Scifis. Not until they were outside the gate did they utter a sound. Frustrated, enraged, they then raised knotted fists and swore revenge upon those who had held them up to scorn.

From the steps of the monastery we watched the Scifis go. My spirits sank, for I had prayed that somehow, if even by violence, they would take Clare away with them.

The abbess said, "She is safe now from the Scifis and also from that wretched Bernardone."

"How can that be?" I said.

"Clare was brought to San Paolo for our protection. And we shall protect her. We shall not give her up to one or the other. She shall live with us and worship God in the proper way."

"But how can you ever protect her? How?"

"The walls of San Paolo are strong. And so are my beliefs. With patience and a little of God's help — He sometimes seems a bit contrary — we will find a way."

The abbess stood with her feet apart, holding her coif against the morning breeze; she seemed as formidable as San Paolo's fortress walls.

Nicola, whose awe of Mother Sibilia had tied her tongue, managed to say, "Is it true that you must have a dowry to come and be a Benedictine? I have heard this."

"It is a custom, long established," the abbess said. "But for you, your pretty smile and dancing eyes are dowry enough. We have a plenitude of ill-favored faces."

Nicola blushed. The abbess smiled and gave her a quick hug, at the same time glancing toward a group who had come out from the chapel. It was Francis Bernardone and his men with their knotty clubs.

He was close. I could have reached out and touched his robe, given him the letter, but my hand was shaking so much I held back.

"You will protect her?" he asked Mother Sibilia.

The abbess smiled bleakly and replied in her frosty voice, "We shall indeed. Meanwhile, since she has grown pale and thin unto death, we'll see that she has food and that she eats it."

"Likewise," Francis said, "give her counsel. Her youthful ears have been filled with blasphemy and untruth and threats. It is a dangerous time for her. She could be tempted to flee San Paolo and return to her family."

I might have said something at that moment to shock them both. It was in my mind and on my tongue to say, I have known Clare di Scifi since childhood and I know that she has never been religious nor is she now. The truth is, she's infatuated.

She has fallen under your spell, Francis Bernardone. Someday, all too late, she will regret it.

"Clare is safe. We'll protect her against the rabble," the abbess said, glancing at Francis and his men. "If she is unhappy with us, we'll relinquish her. Unhappy nuns are an offense. Especially to God, who has enough troubles without them."

The abbess had more to say, but Francis smiled and came blithely out the gate. As he was about to pass me, I handed him the letter.

Without looking at it, he put it away and gave me a small nod of his head in the way of thanks, went on walking, and began to sing in the same stirring voice that had enthralled me on the nights in Piazza San Rufino. It was not the words of a love ballad that drifted back to me now, yet a ballad nonetheless, one that bespoke the change that had overtaken him:

> "All praise be Yours, my Lord,
> Through Sister Moon and Stars;
> In the heavens You have made them,
> Bright and precious and fair."

With beating heart, I watched him take the road to Porziuncola, breasting the wind that he loved, through trees streaked by sun and shadows.

NINETEEN

The wind shifted as we rode homeward, and the rain changed to a light fall of snow that melted as it fell.

"What is it that we say to your family?" Nicola asked. "I can't think of a single excuse, not one."

"There are no excuses for what's been done," I said.

"But we've been gone for days."

"Only a day and a night."

"We'll be outcasts — at least I'll be. Shall I get on my knees and beg to be pardoned?"

"Stand on your feet," I said bravely, sounding much braver than I felt. "You are not a serf, so don't act like one."

As we approached the Roman wall, horsemen burst forth from San Rufino Square. They rode at a gallop and carried the blue and gold pennons of the house of Davino di Montanaro. Without a word, without so much as a smile, I passed them by, nor did I move faster when they turned about and followed us.

The family was not at home. Where they had gone, a servant who had not gone with them would not chance a guess. From her uneasy look, I knew that everyone was abroad, searching for me in the streets.

The family came at suppertime and sat down at the table and began to talk in a cheerful way. But they talked among themselves, not to me, as though I were not there, as though nothing had happened. I did notice, however, that my father's hands shook when he washed them, my mother's eyes were red from weeping, and Rinaldo's voice had an angry edge to it. Only Raul spoke to me that evening and then not in their presence.

After I had eaten — alone, despite all appearances — I went to the scriptorium and began a letter to Francis Bernardone. This one was symbolic like the others, dealing again with the unhappy love between Abelard and Heloise, which continued to disturb me.

Raul came in cautiously, afraid, I presumed, that I might fly at him. He spoke about the flowers that were blooming in the snow.

"I think they are lilies," he said. "But I am not certain. Lilies with little scarlet waves around their rims. Do you know their name?"

I did, but I shook my head and didn't look up.

"Spring in Assisi is a laggard," he said. "Spring in Granada comes soon."

I went on with my letter, calmly awaiting the lecture that was sure to come, presuming that my father, too outraged to trust himself, thinking of his futile lectures in the past, had chosen Raul to speak for him.

To my surprise, Raul went on with his observations about the flowers of Granada and Assisi. He recited a funny parable that had nothing to do with my escapade or much of anything else. He concealed the discomfort he must have felt and bade me goodnight with his warmest smile.

The family masquerade — the ordeal by silence, of pretending that I had not gone to Porziuncola ever, and that although I was visibly among them I really wasn't there — lasted for a week, or perhaps twice that long or longer. It ended abruptly just as I had begun to think that I didn't exist and if I did exist I had gone insane and would have to be exorcised again.

We were at supper. A special supper — Bishop Pelagius was there in his regal trappings. The table steamed. Flush-faced servants raced back and forth, keeping it filled with platters of turbot, roast goose, dove and duck, spring lamb racked in beds of minted jelly, beef raw and lean, stacks of hot breads, and bowls of brown gizzard gravy. It went on and on; first my father talked about business, then the bishop, mopping the perspiration from his domed brow, talked about souls and such. In the midst of all, while I sat enmeshed in silence and all that could be heard was the crunching of teeth, driven to desperation I rose from the table and fell upon my knees. In a halting voice I begged forgiveness for all the unforgivable sins I had committed, those of late and those of long ago when I was a child, since that day when I pinched my baby brother (who now was dead), causing him to scream at the top of his lungs, and then myself denying all knowledge of why he had screamed.

Scarcely had the words left my lips when my father said in his gentle voice, a small frown between his eyes, "We have made plans for you to go on a journey. You're to leave us and travel north to Venice, to the monastery of San Andreas, where the prioress is your Aunt Sofia, whom you know of but have never met."

I gasped.

"And so blithely dishonor," Rinaldo added.

He was the angry one. The others were only humiliated. He gladly would have hunted Francis Bernardone down and run him through, had it not been for the dire consequences — banishment from the city for a year, at least.

"You will be happy there with Aunt Sofia," Mother said. "She loves you very much and will look after you as she would her own daughter. Mother Sibilia says that the sisters there will love you and you will love them."

Did the abbess have a voice in the decision to send me off to Venice, as far from Francis Bernardone as possible? If so, it was cruel of her! Had Bishop Pelagius also lent his voice?

I presumed he had and was certain of it when he wiped the web of perspiration that had gathered on his forehead and gave me a careful smile, as much as to say, You see, dear signorina, that the prophecies I made some months ago have now, alas, come true. But do not despair. I will pray for you and God will hear the words I speak in your behalf.

Reaching out, Father gave me a gentle pat. "You'll have time to gather a number of things for the journey," he said. "Modest oddments and such things as brushes, pens, ink, colors, things that pertain to copying — an art that I hope you'll pursue in Venice as diligently as you have pursued it here. You'll not be leaving tomorrow or the day after. You'll have time, therefore, to gather your things and yourself as well."

Anger suddenly took the place of my long hours of humility. Defiantly, I rose from my knees and glared at him. "I'll leave at this moment," I cried. "I'll change clothes, but that is all, and leave this house tonight."

"You will not leave this house tonight," he said.

"Then at dawn."

"Nor at dawn. And when you do go, it will not be alone. I am assembling an escort. You will have guards. Serving women will accompany you, as will Raul de los Santos, who has visited the north on several occasions and knows the roads to travel and the most likely places to stay the night."

Not trusting myself to say more, I mumbled an excuse and fled. Safe in the tower, I flung myself on the bed and wept, not the inconsolable tears of grief, but the salty tears of frustration.

Before dawn, while the household slept, I locked myself in the scriptorium and wrote to Francis Bernardone. It was a long, confused letter penned in Gothic, using gold bordered with bright meadow-green, in celebration of spring, which was everywhere except in my thoughts. Of all that I wrote as the sun rose that morning, I remember this part especially, for it came burning from my heart:

In the last message, which I placed in your hands at San Paolo, I questioned you about Heloise's rapturous love for Abelard and their unhappy fate. Since, as I have said already, I leave soon for Venice and will have no chance to talk to you before I go, and

since we are not apt to meet for some time to come,
unless by rare good fortune your mission brings you
to that far-off city, and since messages get lost and
are poor at best, I wish to confess, as though you
were my father confessor, a priest and not a member
of a brotherhood that does not hear confessions. I
confess that my letters to you are only attempts to
gain your attention. And I confess that from the day
I saw you first, the day of the running bulls, from
the morning you stopped to embrace the leper, from
the nights you sang in San Rufino Square, from the
hour when you removed your clothes and gave them
back to your father, since then and before then, I
confess on my knees that I have loved you always.

I sealed the message with wax, marked it with a finger ring
that showed a circlet of hearts, and before the house was awake,
sent it off by messenger to Porziuncola.

TWENTY

Rains, followed by weeks of black fog that crept up from the lowlands and shrouded the city so that day was turned into night, delayed our journey. A rash of robberies on the road to Venice delayed it further.

During this month and more I continued work on the Old Testament. I also wrote three missives to Francis, none of which I sent, for the reason that not a word in all those long days came back in answer to the last message I had sent him.

My father owned a large warehouse in Venice, which gathered paintings, manuscripts, and tapestries from various countries around the Mediterranean Sea, even those with whom the Church was at war, and from places as far off as Mongolia. These things were sold in cities to the north — such as Milan, Florence, Bologna — and to princes and kings, including the pope in Rome. The most profitable part of the enterprise, however, was comestibles that only the very rich could afford.

The merchandise was distributed by a caravan that made the trip between these various cities three times during the year. Since it passed through Assisi on the way to Venice, my father changed his mind about sending me north in fashionable style and decided that I should accompany the caravan. He then had to change his mind once more when the caravan was lost while crossing the river Arno.

At last, after more than a month of delays, Raul brought word that we were to leave the next morning. He would lead the group.

It was toward evening when he came to the scriptorium. I was working on the fourteenth chapter of Exodus, drawing decorations for the twenty-sixth verse, where the Lord commands Moses to stretch out his hands over the sea, that the water may come back upon the Egyptians. He stood looking over my shoulder at the decorations, complimenting me on how real the sea waves looked.

"Are you ready to go?" he asked.

"I've been ready for weeks. All packed, except for my brushes," I said.

"You seem anxious to go, which surprises me, considering that you're going to a strange city, far from home, for a year at least, perhaps longer."

"Not anxious. I just want to put all of it, everything that's happened, behind me."

"You are not religious, though you do have stray Christian thoughts now and again and when in trouble you call upon God or Christ. But you don't realize how rigorous life in the monastery may be. The prioress is a relative, but your father has given her instructions to treat you like the rest of her flock."

The copyists had left for the day and we were alone in the scriptorium. I was baffled by his words. He was advising me to disobey my father, to not go to Venice. Why? Suddenly, as he put a warm hand on my shoulder, I sensed the answer.

For months now, after dinner when I had my hair done on top of my head in a coronet and wore a gown that displayed my budding figure, I had been aware of his glances. He never uttered one word of praise at these times or later. But he didn't need to. His glances spoke boldly for themselves.

"You'll be a prisoner in Venice," he said.

"I'm a prisoner here."

"You need not be," he said, his hand heavy now on my shoulder. "Tomorrow, as soon as we come to Perugia, we'll take the road that leads to Granada. To my family. They will like you and you will like them."

He went on about the work we would do together, how we would be married in the beautiful mosque and travel to Fez in Morocco and visit the great library there.

After he had finished with his dream and I had washed out my brushes and put them in their box, I said, "You have been the finest of teachers. Since I was seven, you have crammed my head with more knowledge than it could possibly hold. You have put up with my sulks and tantrums. You are a loyal friend, the dearest I have or will ever have. Yet . . ."

Raul said nothing.

We rode out of the courtyard at dawn. We went at an early hour because Father deemed it best that we leave unnoticed, while the city still was asleep. Before we left Piazza San Rufino, however, people were staring down from their windows, and a gaggle of boys and a small spotted dog were following at our heels.

Accompanying us were six men, four of them armed guards, a cook and his helpers, three serving girls, an older woman, Constanza, with sharp eyes, and a brace of strong varlets. Though I carried a crested peregrine on my wrist, it was not an impressive train, nothing to compare with the one we passed soon after we left Assisi: a Roman princess traveling north to Paris, there to wed a prince in the basilica of Notre-Dame. By Raul's count, her entourage presented nine ladies-in-waiting, a male secretary with pen and paper at hand, two elderly chaplains, an assortment of varlets, servants, cooks, two tailors carrying a pennon of crossed needles, a reader of books who was reading to the princess as they moved along, thirty muleteers, one cardinal, and two bishops — all in fur-trimmed robes though the day was warm — plus one hundred and three soldiers, two Spanish clowns, and fifteen trumpeters with jeweled trumpets.

We wound down the mountainside, held to a turtle's pace by farmers and their carts on the way to market. At the first bridge over the river, where the road branches, one branch trending west toward Porziuncola and the other north toward Venice, a brief argument took place when I suggested that we go by way of Porziuncola and there pray to God for a safe journey.

"But it's a full hour out of our way," Raul objected. "There are shrines along the road where we can pray."

"Dozens of them," said Costanza, the sharp-eyed one. "And I have already spoken to God."

Since they knew why I was determined on Porziuncola and both were opposed to it, I suggested that they travel ahead. "I have a good horse and I'll catch up with you by noon." With this and a small apology, I rode off before they could say more.

The church doors were open, bedecked with twists of wild flowers freshly picked, and from inside came the sound of a voice, either preaching or in prayer, which I recognized at once as that of Francis Bernardone.

After a long pause, I was surprised to hear the hesitant voice of Clare di Scifi raised in song, the words Francis had written in celebration of spring, that I had heard him recite in the cathedral:

"Praise be to Thee my Lord for Brother Wind
For air and clouds
Clear skies and all the weathers
Through which Thou sustaineth all Thy creatures
For the time of spring and flowers."

I was shocked. The anger of the seven Scifi brothers had cooled somewhat since Clare had taken the vow — this I had heard. But I was certain that she was still where I had left her, behind the stout walls of San Paolo delle Ancelle di Dio, in the protecting arms of Mother Sibilia.

She was not only in Porziuncola and not behind the monastery walls with the nuns of San Paolo, she was with Francis. Beside him, exulting in his presence, singing words he had written about God's creatures and spring.

I had come here to ask him about the letters that I had written and that he had not answered — and to free the peregrine perched on my wrist. It was the last of the hawks. The rest I had already freed, beginning on the day after I had freed the first in San Rufino Square. They were unloosed over a period of months — secretly, so as not to arouse my father's ire.

The one on my wrist I intended to free in front of Francis, after I had spoken of the letters. At the moment I left him, I would let the falcon loose. In his eyes, it would surely be a graceful act, but more, much more, it would be the proof of my undying love.

I was thinking about riding away when lanky Brother Giles appeared. He strode toward me, shouting. I would have run him down had the horse not reared.

"We've been talking about you," he said. "We knew you were coming. Francis had a vision two nights ago that you would come to Porziuncola. And here you are." He grasped my gloved hand and kissed it. "The Lord has sent you. Praise the Lord!"

As I sought to quiet the peregrine, uncomfortable at this onslaught, Clare came out of the church.

"Sister Clare," Brother Giles shouted. "She's here. Look, the angel is here."

I got down from the horse and we embraced. She smelled of sweat and hard work.

"I know what you have endured," she said, clinging to me, tears in her eyes. "I have never thanked you, dear Ricca, for all you have done. I know that you are being sent away because of the help you gave and the great sacrifice you made for me."

A twinge of conscience, sharp as a bodkin, ran through me.

"I am sorry that I never thanked you," she said.

"But the Lord has," Brother Giles said. "In His divine thoughtfulness He has brought you to Porziuncola. To loving care and rest and heavenly peace."

He kissed my hand again. He pointed to the flowers that bedecked the church door.

"Everything," he said, "awaits the wedding. Even the flowers.

See how they nod their pretty heads in sweet anticipation. With your permission, I'll impart the wonderful news to Brother Francis. He'll be delighted. His vision has been fulfilled. Praise the Lord!"

I looked at Clare. In the harsh light of day, with her golden hair shorn, her ears revealed, the delicate bones in her head clearly seen through a thin layer of fuzz, her figure hidden by a coarse gray robe too big for her, there was nothing left of the woman she had been. She looked like an innocent, a young, awkward boy.

She was silent until Brother Giles had gone. Then she said, "He's a little enthusiastic. Does he frighten you? I hope not.'

Her tone had changed. It was no longer the tender voice she had used a few moments ago. It reminded me now of her religious mother.

"With the help of Brother Francis," she said, "I have started a sisterhood. We take the same vows of poverty. We are Friars Minor together, brothers and sisters, following in the footsteps of our Lord." She paused and said softly, "Francis had a vision where you appeared — Brother Giles just spoke about it. In the vision you came to Porziuncola and joined us."

Seeing the clear outlines of a trap, I said, "Your sisterhood takes the vow of poverty. Does it also take the vow of chastity?"

"Oh, yes, of course."

She spoke with fervor, with a touch of the arrogant tone of the Scifis. Francis might love her soul, hidden beneath the ugly gray garb, but never, never, could he love the woman.

"I'm not ready to leave the world," I said.

"You won't leave it at all. On the contrary, you'll enter the world. The world of true love."

Francis was watching us from the church steps. He made a cross with his arms and asked Clare if she would tend the altar candles, saying to me, as he eyed the falcon on my wrist, "In the vision I had of you I did not see the falcon. I thought you set all of them free."

"All but Black Prince," I said.

"Why do you hold to the Prince?"

"I came here to set him free."

"And to join Clare and her new sisterhood, I hope."

"Until today, only a few minutes ago, I had never heard of Clare's sisterhood."

He smiled and, to hide his disappointment, spoke to the falcon, not in words but in bird sounds, which caused it to ruffle its feathers and chirr. Forgetting me, fascinated with the hawk, he began to praise its barred plumage, its amber eyes, its cruel, scimitar beak, and finally he plucked it from my fist. Black Prince had never suffered a stranger to touch it, but now it settled upon his bare hand like a sparrow on an olive branch.

Bold enough to intrude, I said, "I've written two letters to you, sir, and neither have you answered."

"I've meant to."

"Have you read them?"

"Yes. What artful pictures you draw and what a beautiful hand you write. It flows like, like . . ."

"Honey?"

"Not honey. The questions you ask are bitter. Beyond your age, perhaps. Which do you wish me to answer?"

"If you must answer only one, tell me, please, why Abelard had a child by Heloise, to whom he gave the endearing name Alcete — as you know, Alcete means Light of the World. And then, swearing her to secrecy, aware that his career in the Church would be harmed if it were known that he had fathered a child, he secretly married Heloise. Only to force her, as he grew tired of her, into a nunnery."

"What you have just said is what you said before. What is the question?"

"In his place, would you have done the same?"

"I am not certain. But I can say that at one time in my life I was fully capable of being Abelard."

"At one time in your life, but not now."

Francis made a cross of his arms, raised his eyes to the heavens, and was silent.

I didn't press him for an answer. "Is the Song of Solomon," I asked, "a poem about two lovers, the Rose of Sharon and Solomon, or a love poem between Solomon and the Church?"

"It can be one or the other. Or both."

"Which do you prefer?"

He was silent, smiling to himself, perhaps at some memory.

"When you were younger," I said to remind him, "running about at night from tavern to tavern, singing under windows, which did you prefer?"

"In those days, I hadn't heard of the Song. If I had, then surely, surely, I would have made up a pretty tune about it."

"And sung it under my window?"

"Yes, to the sounds of lutes and violins."

He was an agile young man, slippery as the eels that glided around in our leather tank at home.

I waited, thinking that he might bring up, without being reminded, the last message I had sent him, the one in which I had openly confessed my love.

"I wrote you a letter weeks ago," I said, "and sent it by armed messenger to be certain you received it."

"Oh, yes, it came," he said. There was an odd look on his face. Was it pain or puzzlement?

"Perhaps you think that it was brazen of me, but once you sang love songs beneath my window, like this one:

> 'Put out my eyes!
> Blind me!
> Let me never again gaze upon thy beauty
> For my heart it crucifies.'

"Do you remember?" I asked.

"Of course, dear friend. Memory is a moon that never sets. But now, by the grace of God I sing under the window of the Virgin Mary."

I wanted to shout, You are fickle, Francis Bernardone; you're a mad changeling! But instead I quietly said, "At San Rufino you urged your listeners to remain unmarried. What would happen if they all were to take your advice? How long, sir, would the world last?"

"I don't expect everyone to follow my preachings. Only the few. Only the chosen."

"The chosen? Who is the chooser? God?"

"No, each man chooses for himself."

"And each women chooses for herself?"

"Yes."

"But Clare di Scifi didn't have a chance to choose. She fell in love with you and head over heels was swept away into a sisterhood."

"Away, that is so," Francis said, a strong note in his voice. "Away, to the arms of Christ. And only to Christ, our Lord."

He was answering the rumor, abroad in the city for weeks now, that the two were secretly lovers. People believed this; the Scifis and all of my family believed it. And until this very moment, I, too, had believed it.

"You're not in your fancy clothes, your furs and jewels," he said. "You are dressed for travel. Where do you go?"

"North to Venice, as I wrote you in my letter."

"Oh, yes," he said, pretending the letter meant nothing to him. "Why do you go to Venice? It's an oriental city, rife with corruption."

"I go because I am being sent there."

"Why are you sent?"

I hesitated. I glanced at the trees bending to the gusting wind, at the portals with their spring flowers, finally at him.

"Why?" he asked again.

"Because of you, signore."

He quit fondling the hawk. Baffled and silent, he looked at me. Color rose to his cheeks.

I took the hawk from his hand and launched it on the air. It flew as high as the trees, then wheeled back and hovered above us, beating its wings, torn between us and the sky.

I didn't wait for the bird to disappear. I put heels to the

horse, and when I came to the clearing I glanced back. Francis was watching from the church steps. Boyish Clare di Scifi, fuzzy-headed in her ugly woolen sack tied by a cord around her middle, who would tramp the streets, begging for pork rinds and stale bread, stood behind him.

"Patience, patience, patience," I said to the thud of the horse's hoofs, remembering the moment I had told him why I was being sent to Venice. Remembering his silence, the color that rose suddenly to his pale cheeks, as he struggled with memories of happier times. As he thought of the letters I had written to him, the last one.

The hawk I had freed was a symbol and a pledge. I had prevailed over Clare di Scifi. I would prevail over his latest love.

TWENTY-ONE

Past noon I overtook the caravan, resting in a shady grove. Before I got down from the horse, Raul was at my side, babbling away.

"We'll soon come to the crossroads where we turn west on the road that leads to the coast and on to Granada," he said. "I can see that you've already made a decision. A wise one, I trust. I see it in your face. It speaks out from your radiant eyes and smile."

Bluntly I told him that he was mistaken about my eyes and face and smile, that I was happy thinking of my new life in the carnival city of Venice. Without further comment we went northward, past the crossroads where we could have taken the road to Granada, traveling until dusk.

At nightfall of the third day, while we were camped in a meadow beside a slow-moving brook, Tommaso, the captain of the guards, a windy oldster, heard the sound of hoofs behind us in a wooded ravine we had just passed through.

"It can be one horseman or many," he said, speaking quietly to allay our fears. "But this is a favorite haunt of cutthroats, and the time of day they usually emerge. I suggest, therefore, that all the women repair to their tents. When last I rode through here I met with five of the scum. Of that band, however, there's now only one, and he with a missing leg. Be calm, have faith in my strong right hand."

The cook asked him if we should pray, but before Captain Tommaso could answer, the rider appeared at the mouth of the

ravine, crossed the brook, and dismounted. To my great aston-
ishment, it was Nicola Ascoli.

During the past three days I had thought of her. Of all the
family, all of them except my father, she was saddest to see
me go. She had followed me into the street, clinging to the
horse's mane, until I found the courage to ride away.

Joyful cries of "Thanks be to God" rose from the camp,
now that we were confronted not by a brigand but by a pretty
girl with a travel-stained face.

Nicola had chosen a wrong turn in the road or she would have
overtaken us sooner. "I went to the left instead of the right," she
said. "Then I was in a forest for a long time, hiding from a
band of men. They were cut-purses, for while I watched they
held up a man and a woman traveling in a cart. Then this
morning I had to hide again . . ."

Full of the day's wild adventures, she would have rattled on
had I let her. My delight at seeing Nicola was short-lived. She
brought a problem. I would be protected by the prioress,
Mother Sofia, a handsome gift for my board and keep having
been given in advance. But what of Nicola Ascoli, unsponsored,
without a *soldo* to her name?

She had eaten two eggs, she told me, stolen from a farmyard
the night before, and nothing since, though in a basket tied to
the saddle she had a rooster hidden away, which she wished to
present us for supper. But the rooster, thin and bedraggled,
stretched his neck and challenged us with a crow, so defiant
and yet so appealing that we took a vote on whether to have
him stewed for supper. The men voted to place him in the
pot, but the women prevailed, so we kept him and gave him
the name Cerberus, the watchful keeper. And keeper he proved
to be.

Sleeping for the most part at well-guarded inns, we made
our journey without incident until we approached the town of
Padua. Here, pitching our tents midst scattered trees in open
country, we were awakened late in the night by the frantic
flapping of wings and prolonged cries of distress.

The guards bounded out of their tents — all were asleep at the time — to confront a number of brigands in the act of running off with our horses. If successful, the raid would have left us stranded leagues from the nearest help. Afterward Cerberus became our pampered guide and, with the help of Captain Tommaso, brought us safely to the fabulous city of Venice.

The city, as everyone knows, is paved with seawater and not with stones. Twice each day the tides of the Adriatic Sea flow in, sweep up the streets, and flow out again.

You do not, therefore, ride gaily into Venice, nor do you walk. At the edge of the salt meadow where the land ends and the sea begins, boats of all descriptions wait to take you to this island city — double-ended gondolas, mostly painted black, each rowed by a single oarsman; small, shallow-draft boats of all colors; the floating palaces called *bruchielli*; and, if fishing is poor, the fisherman's skiffs.

We left our retainers in the meadow, including Cerberus, and hired a gondola to take Raul and Nicola and me to Piazza San Marco. From there it was a short walking distance to the monastery.

My aunt was at prayer when we arrived, so we had a long wait in a bare room lit by a small window and a row of candles beside a crucifix and a picture of Christ, like the room where I first met the prioress of San Paolo, Mother Sibilia.

The two women were also alike. Indeed, when Aunt Sofia came striding into the room, a candle clutched in one hand, shielding it with the other, she gave me a start. Like Mother Sibilia's, her pale skin was stretched tight over sharp bones and deep hollows. It was a face that comes from hidden heat. For a terrifying moment I saw myself standing here in this same room, holding a candle in my hand — it could be three years from now, perhaps longer — pale, hollow-cheeked, like this woman.

I expected her to remark on how I had grown since she had seen me — I was a baby in arms at the time. But instead she asked if the long journey had fatigued me, then complimented me on the fine work I had done as a copyist and said she hoped that I would continue the art while I was at the monastery.

At this time Raul mentioned the six manuscripts he had brought from our library.

"We are lacking in books," my aunt said, greatly pleased. "Since the fire last April that left our library in ashes, we have had few. Only the books that were in our rooms escaped. Those who tend our fires, which I think they often set themselves, did more damage with their buckets of water than was done by the flames."

We had heard in Assisi about the fire soon after it happened. It is my belief that arrangements for my residence at the monastery, between my father and my aunt, were based upon the trade of valuable books for her willingness to take me under her wing.

In any event, our porter carried in from the street a large bundle from home. Raul opened it and made a little speech expressing my father's pleasure at this chance to start a new library at the monastery.

"Here are the seeds that will sprout and come to flower," he said. "The Book of Daniel and the Books of Hosea and Amos, complete. Incomplete is the Book of Genesis, copied only to the first verse of the third chapter."

He gave this fragment to Aunt Sofia, the three sheets I had copied in bold Gothic and gold capitals, down to the place where Adam and Eve stand shamelessly naked in the Garden of Eden as the serpent appears.

"What an exquisite hand. Whose work can this be?" Mother Sofia said, knowing full well that it was mine. Aware of the disrobing scene in San Rufino Square, aware that it came from the Bible, aware of everything, because my father had told her. "The capitals are so proud and stately, yet withal so sensitive. Who is the artist?"

Raul pointed to me.

Holding the candle on high to see me better, Sofia smiled.

"How fortunate we are," she said, "to be given such a treasure."

Her white robe blended with the white wall behind her. All I could make out were the bony face and the hollow cheeks, her dark eyes studying me, the incorrigible Ricca di Montanaro from the city of Assisi.

"And here, the New Testament, which comes from the hands of the finest copyist in Spain," Raul said, holding out my father's Bible, "which will be copied for you."

My aunt crossed herself and said, "How long will it take to complete the enormous task?"

"Two years at least," I said. Then, fortunately remembering Nicola, I added, "If I work with my assistant, I can finish the task in one year, perhaps less." I glanced about for my friend, who had disappeared, apparently to inspect the monastery, as she had at San Paolo. "She prepares the vellum, mixes colors and ink, attends to the dozens of details that lessen the labor of a copyist. I brought her from Assisi — her name is Nicola Ascoli — in the hope that you may find a place for her."

I cast a look at Raul, who had turned his back when I mentioned Nicola as my assistant. He was musing, no doubt, on my ability to dissemble.

"Nicola is also very religious," I said. "With her father and mother she tried to reach the Holy Land and had many terrible experiences."

Aunt Sofia was sympathetic. "The poor child," she murmured. "How sad. We are crowded here but I'll find a place for her. And if you're in need of apprentices, there are many sisters who would love to help you. Some among them are quite adept at Latin."

Suddenly I saw myself training a flock of sisters, forgotten in a Benedictine monastery, hundreds of leagues from Porziuncola, copying books for weeks, for months, for years. The thought gave me a terrified chill.

"Thank you, Aunt Sofia," I said, looking straight into her eyes, "but I'll not need help."

TWENTY-TWO

M y aunt was unpleasantly surprised when Raul, having placed me on her doorstep, informed her that he wished to show me some of the places he had come to know during his visits to Venice.

"We'll return before nightfall," he said, "and I will then be on my way to report the tidings to Signor Montanaro, who is anxiously waiting. To inform him that I left his daughter in safekeeping, protected by the warmest of familial affection."

Listening to his speech, Mother Sofia looked anything but familial. She frowned and her brows fluttered with disapproval. Before she could object Raul had me out the door.

He led me down a narrow lane that twisted snake-like through arcades, across squares and bridges, and at last into a sunless *piazzale*. All sides of this little square, he pointed out, were a warehouse that belonged to my father. The sign over the wide doorway read: DAVINO DI MONTANARO AND SONS.

The sons the sign referred to were my two baby brothers, who died before there was a chance to give them names, my brother Lorenzo, who was killed on the battlefield at Perugia, and my brother Rinaldo, who was much more interested in playing the lute and writing poetry than he was in business. Indeed, Rinaldo had never set foot in Venice.

The warehouse was a dim-lit cavern stocked with barrels and crates of merchandise that had come from far places in the world — from as far away as Samarkand and beyond. The smell was not a single smell but many, all mixed up, so that oil from Spain and dates from Africa and saffron from India and the dried flat fish from Beirut and skeins of yellow wool from England all combined into one powerful smell, which was both pleasant and strong, so overpowering that I tasted it on my tongue.

An army of bare-chested men toiled away in the cavern, creating an awful din. In an enclosure beside a main gate, which opened onto a wide canal where ships were moored, I met Simon Gregorio.

"Signor Gregorio," Raul said, "is in charge of the warehouse. He has many responsibilities, but as far as you are concerned, only one — he is a dispenser of money. What from time to time you receive from your father will come through Signor Gregorio."

Gregorio, who had wary eyes and a head as round as a melon, took a step backward, spread his hands wide, and made what I came to know as a Venetian bow.

"If meanwhile," he said, "you look into your purse by chance and find fewer coins than you had presumed were there, kindly let me know and I will respond at once."

"Thank you," I said, glancing into my purse. "I find that I have at this very moment little or nothing."

Signor Gregorio ducked into a counting room where clerks, quill in hand, using Arabian abacuses, were making notations. He came back with a handful of money, which he emptied into my purse.

"Your father has instructed me to be generous with you," he said. "And so I shall be. There are many fine adornments to be found in Venice. The most elegant of gowns, oddments to suit any fancy. Do call upon me whenever it pleases you."

"Thank you, sir, thank you," I said.

He ducked back into the counting room and came out with a second handful of coins.

My purse bulged, so I thanked him again. He proved to be generous with me, and also with himself.

Through a maze of dog paths, winding lanes, arcades both covered and uncovered, small bridges, large bridges, Raul guided me back to Piazza San Marco, a vast square bordered by palaces of the Venetian rich. It was a mild afternoon fading into dusk but the square was filled with agitation. Bands of strollers were conversing in loud voices, and more with their hands than their mouths — in Assisi it was bad manners to make gestures while talking; only varlets and serfs did so. The agitation was about the new crusade against the infidels announced by Pope Innocent.

Repeating the words I had overheard, I asked Raul if he planned to heed the pope's call for a million men to confront the sultan and his barbarians, to end at last and for all time their hold upon the Holy Sepulcher.

"The pope's plea falls upon my ears like a stone," Raul said. "It leaves me deaf. It wearies me. And judging from your tone, it wearies you as well. Since you aren't worried about me, the scholar, or about your father, who is too old, or your brother Rinaldo, who would rather dream of violence than participate in it, you're worried about Bernardone."

It was the first time he had mentioned Francis since the moment of my return from Porziuncola. "Will he join the crusade, do you think?"

"How do I know what goes on in his head?"

"You must have a thought about it."

"A very small one."

"What is it?"

"The crusade, the fifth now, after four silly failures in a hundred years, reminds me of the tale about Nasrudin the philosopher, who was walking around his house, tossing pieces of bread here and there.

"'What are you doing?' someone asked him.

"'Keeping the tigers away.'

"'But there are no tigers around.'

"'Exactly. The bread's a good idea, isn't it?'"

A flock of pigeons was pattering along behind us, begging for food. Raul bought a twist of barley and gave me a handful, and we walked along and fed them, a few grains at a time.

Dusk found us in front of the cathedral. We were beneath the golden horses that had been stolen during the sack of Constantinople and were now high up in the loggia.

"The new crusaders," Raul said, "the ones who aren't killed, who fortunately return, will steal more treasures from those they call barbarians to stuff their coffers and adorn their churches."

I didn't give up. "Will Francis go?"

Raul shrugged one shoulder.

"He fought in the war with Perugia," I said.

"Was dehorsed and thrown into prison for a year. He may recall those uncomfortable days and wisely stay home. This I doubt, however. He has a restless soul, part warrior, part troubadour, part clown — he's being called God's fool. I rather think he likes that name. There's no telling what will occur to him next. For your sake, I trust that he sails to the Holy Land and finds a war to his liking."

We went into the church. I knelt on the cold tiles and asked God to counsel Francis against heeding the pope's call for a new crusade.

When we came out, night had fallen. Boats lit with lanterns and torches were moving along the Grand Canal, throwing colored shadows across the square and on the faces of the nobles' palaces. From a distance came the sound of lutes and singing voices. All this, with the night air that smelled of the sea and of far-off places, could have tempted Raul into another declaration of love. It didn't.

He drew his cloak around his shoulders. I took his hand and we crossed the square and went along the winding street, over the four bridges that led to the monastery. Church bells rang in the night.

"We're late," he said, giving me a tug. "Your aunt will be waiting, angry and waiting."

She was both. Standing at the portal, which she held half open to exclude him, she snatched me in. It was a very poor beginning.

TWENTY-THREE

After bowls of cold mush, Nicola and I were taken by two young nuns to an immense bare room furnished with a bed, a painting, and a bench. A small window looked out upon the rooftops toward Piazza San Marco, where torches were burning, and beyond to the Grand Canal and the Mare Adriaticus.

Aunt Sophia came, bringing with her a list of rules. Her mood had improved. She even attempted a smile when Nicola said she liked our room better than the ones at San Paolo delle Ancelle di Dio.

"It would be un-Christian and also unfair to our sisters," she said to us, "to those who live ordered lives, for you to live as the spirit impels you. I demand, therefore, strict obedience to the rules set down by Saint Benedict and honored by thousands of women for more than six hundred years."

Aunt Sofia shook out a scroll, which reached the floor, and held it to the light. It was frighteningly long. Fortunately, she read only that part of the rules dealing with the times for prayer.

"Matins," she said, "lasts but a short time. Lauds, which foretells dawn, lasts twice as long as matins. Prime follows lauds and ends just before daybreak. Tierce comes next; then sext welcomes workers to the midday meal, which often includes olives and bread and fruit in season. Nones takes up the middle of the afternoon. Vespers occurs at sunset, the time for supper, which must be finished before dark and is less bountiful than the midday meal, although we often serve a bowl or two of raisins. Complin follows soon after dark, and at that time everyone, everyone, is in bed. As you two will be, promptly after I leave this room."

Her words dashed all hope of favors to come. Whether it was her own idea or my father's, I was to be treated to the common lot. I was now in a monastery, a Benedictine monastery at that, famous for its piety. Had I known what the summer held, I would have risen as soon as Aunt Sofia said goodnight, risen quickly to my feet, gathered my clothes, and fled.

Besides the prayers there was hard work — cleaning, scrubbing, clothes to wash and iron, a garden to weed, dishes to wash. Afterward there were the sick to care for and poor people in the city whom the monastery shared its meager things with. And toward the end of the day, sewing if you had the strength and the wits to attempt it.

I marveled at these women, old and young, most of them frail. They slept little and on hard pallets. They went poorly clad, with stomachs that were never full. They tended the sick and raised their thin voices to God, asking little for themselves. How starkly they stood out from all the nobles and knights, my own brother. The ones who were never hungry, whose throats were never dry, who swung big swords and set hot fires and killed the innocent as well as the evil. Those who lived for praise and were called heroes.

I marveled at these women and blamed myself that I lacked their courage.

It was an unhappy year, made worse by Nicola's happiness. She loved to rise in the middle of the night and pray. She got up at dawn and prayed. She loved the kitchen, though she missed the cinnamon and saffron and the jugs of treacle she'd had in Assisi. We never fought, but seldom a day passed that she didn't fray my nerves.

This unhappy time ended suddenly; at least it seemed sudden to me, though I later learned that my father and Aunt Sofia had planned the event for months. Even before I arrived in Venice.

Her library didn't compare with the thirty libraries of Baghdad or the library in Cairo that housed two thousand one hundred and ninety-seven copies of the Koran, but before the fire it was a large and growing one.

Modestly ambitious, yet hoping to surpass the Benedictine library at Padua, she had accepted me with the understanding that I was to work in the scriptorium. When Raul had deposited me and an armful of scrolls on her doorstep, I had assumed that I would begin on them at once. Instead, following my father's request, Aunt Sofia had sentenced me to the life of a novice, a harsh probation meant to last a year.

Before long, however, feeling it was a waste of my talents, she took matters into her own hands. She set me to work restoring her copy of the New Testament, which had been badly damaged in the fire the previous year.

The task began slowly. Though Venice was the third largest city in Europe — after Paris and Bruges — paper of quality was scarce. The common variety was available in any amount, since the Venice wharves teemed with trade. But why commit the Great Book to paper that would become dog-eared with a few readings?

After searching Bologna, Milan, and Padua, we found a cache of the finest vellum not a league distant from Venice, on the island of Burano, hidden away by some thoughtful monk during the sack of Venice by the Saracens.

The first week of December, having spent nine hours of each day at our benches, work on the New Testament was finished. One hundred and fifty-three pages of manuscript were taken to the bindery, where artisans fashioned hardwood boards, secured the pages between them, and bound the boards in the richest of Cordovan leather. I printed the words NEW TESTAMENT on the cover in Florentine letters limned in sea-blue and sunrise-gold and presented the book to Aunt Sofia.

Overwhelmed, she clasped the Bible to her breast as if it were a child long lost and said to me tearfully, "I knew from the moment I saw you that God had sent us one of His most precious beings, an angel in disguise."

A celebration was held at San Marco. The bishop blessed me as I knelt at the altar, and a procession was formed that wound through the piazza, my aunt walking in the lead with the Bible cradled in her arms. But no word was forthcoming about my return to Assisi. In fact, that night at supper, she gave me the task of copying the rest of the materials Raul had given her.

"On the best of vellum," she suggested, "limned in the elegant Florentine script I so admire, though it's a trifle gaudy. How long do you think this task will take you? A year, perhaps?"

I nodded, overwhelmed by the prospect of more long months in Saint Benedict's monastery in the city of Venice.

"We can find a dozen sisters who will be glad to help you," she said. "Everyone is fascinated with the work you're doing. Such beautiful work!"

"They would only be in the way," I said churlishly. Then, realizing that I might ease myself out of all future work and Venice itself, I apologized, saying that I would be very happy to train two of the sisters.

Alas, soon after the New Year, Raul brought us more scrolls. I spied him as he came up from the Grand Canal, as he glanced up to see me standing at my window, the window where I often stood, which faced southward toward home and Porziuncola. I hurried into the street.

"How wonderful to see you," I cried, clasping him in my arms. "Did you have a good journey? You look well. Are you tired? Is the family well?"

He brought out a note in my father's writing, which I put away to read later. I waited, all but tapping my feet.

"Be patient," Raul said. "I am about to recite a parable."

"Don't," I said. "Please don't."

"It concerns the barefooted one."

"No; the news without the parable."

"Well, you'll not be surprised to hear that men by the hundreds, young and old, fat and lean, knights and merchants, have flocked to Porziuncola to shed their clothes, array themselves in sackcloth, and take to the byways, preaching poverty. Girls and women flock there also, to trade their fair raiment for sackcloth, to join Clare di Scifi and her Franciscans. She calls them the Poor Clares. Even her sisters, Agnes and Beatrice, have joined. And there are rumors that Ortolana will be the next of the Scifi women. I wonder what the Scifi men will do? Perhaps give a word of thanks."

I waited, my face a mask, my heart beating.

"There's a miracle also," he said. "It was reported from Gubbio, just before I left. It seems that the town had been bedeviled by a wolf, a large and ferocious beast that roamed the surrounding country, killing everything it saw, even humans. People were afraid of taking a step beyond the town walls lest they be slain by the monster.

"Francis, hearing of their plight, went to Gubbio and talked to them about taking the wolf to task. The townspeople were horrified. They told him that of a certainty he would be killed. But Francis and a companion, while the people climbed on the town wall and watched in horror, strode into the countryside and called to the wolf. Even before he called, the beast was already running toward him, jaws agape, flecked with foam."

Raul was enjoying himself with the story, but we were blocking the narrow street, so I suggested that we move on to a wider place.

"To the consternation of the townspeople," he continued, now dramatizing his words, making wild movements with his hands, "Francis Bernardone gave the sign of the cross and the wolf came to a halt.

" 'Come here, Brother Wolf,' Francis said, speaking sternly. 'Come here and lie down beside me.'

"When the beast obeyed his command, Francis read it a lecture. 'You have done a lot of damage around here, Brother Wolf. You have murdered God's creatures and human beings who are made in God's image. You deserve to be punished as a robber and a murderer. But I want to bring peace between you and the people of Gubbio. Therefore you will be forgiven your evil deeds, and from now on neither people nor dogs are to persecute you.'

"He made everyone promise to feed the beast every day, since it was only from hunger, he told them, that it did evil things. From then on, it is said, peace reigned between the townspeople and Brother Wolf."

Raul gave me a sidelong glance, gauging the effect of the story he had told in his mocking voice.

"What do you find so strange about Francis and the wolf?" I asked him.

"Everything!"

"Have you forgotten that Buddha, one of your favorites, has said, 'While dwelling on the mountain top, I drew lions and tigers to me through the power of friendship. Surrounded by lions and tigers, by panthers, bears and wolves, by antelope and deer, and wild boar, I live in the forest. No creature is frightened of me, and I have no fear of any living thing'?"

"That was a thousand years ago, my dear Ricca, and it was Buddha speaking. Bernardone is not the Buddha Siddhartha."

"The men are related," I said, seeing clearly and for the first time the thoughts that bound the two together. "They both are drawing water from the same well. They're trying to reconcile animals and men. And also man and man."

"You must think that Bernardone is another Christ."

"Nothing of the kind."

"But the veil of adoration still covers your lovely eyes."

"How poetic!"

"And truthful."

We walked on to the monastery, but Raul, who felt uncomfortable in Aunt Sofia's presence, who in turn felt uncomfortable in his, refused to go farther. Opening his portmanteau, he laid out on the steps a bulging armload of scrolls.

"The Confessions of Saint Augustine," he announced.

"You brought all this for me to copy?" I asked, appalled by the towering pile. "It will take months. Years. How long is this supposed to go on, the rest of my life? Until I am blind and old?"

"Until you are over your infatuation," Raul said, sounding like my father, and with his mouth drawn in, looking like him.

"Who is to be the judge of all this? Mother Sofia? Davino di Montanaro? Raul de los Santos? Who? Who is to say when the infatuation, as you call it, has come to an end?"

"You alone will be the judge," he said, "since you're the only one who will know whether it's ended or not. When and if it ends. Now. This year. Or next year, or never."

"Never!" I said.

I asked about the new crusade. "Has it been abandoned? We hear little of it here in the monastery, only that kings and nobles are busy fighting among themselves and give no thought to the infidels."

"Delayed but not abandoned," Raul said. "Your friend Bishop Pelagius has been summoned to Rome by the pope. It appears that as a young man he showed unusual talents as a warrior. It is said that he fought for Perugia against Assisi. Invented the strategy that won the war. There's talk of his being put in command of the new Christian army, which is supposed to land in Damietta and attack the sultan of Egypt."

I didn't ask him again if he thought Francis might join the crusade, though it weighed heavily upon me, for thousands upon thousands had been killed in the other four crusades and thousands would be killed in a new one.

That night I wrote a letter to my family, putting down everything that I did on a usual day in the monastery — a long list without complaint, hoping that if I seemed to be industrious and happy, then contrarily my father would ask me to return. Raul took the letter with him when he left.

TWENTY-FOUR

L ong months passed yet the *Confessions* went much more
quickly than I had foreseen, once I had solved the copyist's quirks in the matter of Latin verbs and had accus-
tomed myself to Augustine's odd notions about women and
at last to Saint Augustine himself. I was repelled by his belief
that women were thorns in man's flesh, ungodly distractions on
his tortuous path to salvation.

It isn't necessary for a copyist to believe in what is being
copied, or to resist the temptation — powerful, with me — to
change an ill-advised word here and there. For instance, early
in the *Confessions*, where the saint wrote that he "should not
believe many things concerning himself on the authority of
feeble women," I removed the word "feeble."

I also straightened out several other things that I found
belittling. And I overcame my anger about the author's taking
a beautiful serf girl as his mistress and then, after she bore him
a child, whom he ecstatically called "The Gift of God," brazenly
abandoning her, much in the arrogant way Abelard abandoned
Heloise.

Still, the work irritated me. I got tired of the endless talk
about salvation. I longed for the saint to report another meeting with a sloe-eyed serf, another theft of fruit from a pear tree.
But I was to be disappointed. The saint remained a saint and
the *Confessions* became a drudgery. Had I not had the services
of two of the sisters and Nicola, I would have given up.

Toward the end of the book, Augustine says, after much of

the same, "And I called it formless, not that it lacked form, but because it had such as, did it appear, my mind would turn from, as unwonted and incongruous, and at which human weakness would be disturbed. But even that which I did conceive was formless, not by the privation of all form, but in comparison of more beautiful forms; and true reason persuaded me that I ought altogether to remove from it all remnants of any form whatever, if I wished to conceive matter wholly without form; and I not. For sooner could I imagine that that which should be deprived of all form was not at all, than conceive anything between form and nothing — neither formed, nor nothing, formless, nearly nothing . . ." Writing this down laboriously, understanding little, I stopped in the middle of the paragraph.

Music — the sound of a thousand lutes and trumpets — was pouring through the window. San Marco Square blazed with torches. Their light streamed across the copy I was making. I got up and closed the window.

I had missed one of the *festas*, the masquerades when everyone in Venice, the doge himself, everyone except the nuns, and even some of the church dignitaries, dressed in costumes and masks. Fishermen forsook their skiffs and became armored knights. Lowly clerks washed the ink from their fingers and became the merchants they slaved for. Scrubwomen rose from their calloused knees and in a breath took on the fair mark of princesses. Knights became paupers. And there were quiet souls who chose to be demonic, leaping imps of hell. Everyone, it seemed, wished to be somebody else, for a brief night at least.

I opened the shutters and looked down upon the arcaded square, at the Grand Canal in the distance where lanterns showed on drifting gondolas.

"Nicola," I said, "we have never gone to a *festa*. Here is one on our doorstep. Let's dress up and go."

"We have nothing to dress up in," she complained.

"There's a shop this side of the Rialto bridge where they sell all kinds of masks, whatever you want."

She went on with what she was doing and never looked up.

"Hurry," I said. "It's getting late and the shop is a long walk. The masks will be picked over if we don't go now."

"What will Mother Sofia say?"

"That we can't go. We'll have to recite a hundred Hail Marys just because we asked."

"Then we shouldn't ask."

Nicola took all the monastery rules as law. She had grown as strict about them as the nuns were.

"Tell me," I said, "are you going or not?"

She looked up from the bowl of color she was mixing. "I'm afraid."

"Then don't go. You won't have much fun at the *festa* if you're frightened every minute."

"You're right. I won't."

I went softly down the stairs. I saw no one, for the nuns were all in bed, it being well after complin. I was up only because I had Aunt Sofia's permission to work on the *Confessions*. The big door was bolted. Quietly I slid the bolt, let myself out, and ran.

There was a dwindling crowd at the shop, and I found in a pile of pawed-over masks only one that was not broken, the face of a bright young man with a commanding mouth, a long, straight nose, rather dark in complexion, possibly a Spaniard; though painted on cardboard, it was quite arresting and lifelike. Could I pass as a man? Did I wish to? And why not!

Not until I came within sight of the torches burning in San Marco did I realize that my slippers showed below the hem of my cloak. There was nothing to do about this. I put it out of my mind and joined the maskers, who were moving through the square like a rainbow river — disappearing, forming rivulets, appearing again to form a river of many colors.

Caught up in the flood, unable to move in any direction except the way it was flowing, waving my arms, making silly noises, singing off-key, thinking only of Francis Bernardone, only of him and all the delights we would share if he were here, I flung myself, exhausted, into an opening between two shops.

A mask showed out of the half-darkness, lit by a candle shielded in a paper cone. A hairy hand held the light that revealed the mask of a pretty girl with blond curls and a spot of red paint on either cheek.

"Do you mind if I share this haven with you?" said a manly voice. "My feet have given out. For the moment at least."

Pressed so close that I could feel the candle's heat, I couldn't very well refuse him.

"It would be better if they held the *festa* outside Venice in the *campagna*," I said, "where there's grass instead of stones."

"Yes, it's the stones but chiefly the holes between the stones that do you in. However, if this *festa* had been held in the meadows, as you suggest, then we would never have met."

"Have we met?"

"Like two pieces of driftwood on the shore." My companion, attempting a bow, was restrained by the walls on three sides of us. "My name, despite the mask, is Filippo."

The voice was aristocratic.

"Filippo di Viterbo. And yours? I note that your hands are the slender hands of a woman. Is it Celesta or Margherita — that's my sister's name — or Asparia or Angelita? Kindly tell me."

"Ricca."

"Ricca what?"

"Just Ricca."

"A pretty name," he said, "sufficient for the moment."

The candle was hot on my cardboard mask.

"Sufficient," he said in his drawling, aristocratic voice, "for the night is long."

His arm began to press against my breast.

"How fortunate that we have found each other," he drawled. "Now, when I go away crusading I'll have someone to grace my dreams."

"When do you go?" I asked, to buy time while I waited for a chance to leap into the stream passing down the narrow byway.

"Soon. Tomorrow. Next month. Who can say? But I, Filippo di Viterbo, will go whenever it is that the fleet sails."

He asked me to hold the candle, which I did, and turning sideways he drew forth from his cloak a flask of wine that sparkled ruby-red in the candlelight. He wiped the mouth of the flask with a handkerchief.

"Wine from our vineyards on the river Po," he said, holding the flask before me.

"I've already had too much to drink. My stomach is about to rebel."

"This will settle your stomach. It's an excellent wine, not sweet, a trifle dry. You'll like it. Most girls do."

I put the flask to my lips but didn't drink. I thanked him and passed the wine back, and he drank what was left. He edged himself between me and the opening that led to the street. His breath came hot through the slits in his mask.

If I screamed, no one would hear my voice. He dropped the empty flask on the stones at my feet. It made no sound that I could hear in the maelstrom of sounds that swept the street.

I moved enough to get one hand free, and raising it, I ripped the mask from his face. The movement touched the paper cone that was shielding the candle and set it on fire. In the spurt of light, I saw before me an old man with a stained white beard and a painted mouth.

The wretched, leering face gave me the strength to push his body against the wall, far enough to free myself and run. After twice round San Marco Square, I managed to find a way out of the singing mob and reached the monstery near the hour of midnight. The big door was closed. I sat huddled on the steps until the bells rang at dawn and Aunt Sofia let me in.

She didn't smile, but she said in the gentlest words I had heard from her, "I don't blame you. Once, when I was your age, long ago, I confess that I did the same. I never regretted it, and don't you. Did you enjoy the *festa*?"

"No," I said. "Not at all!"

TWENTY-FIVE

A ugustine's *Confessions*, as difficult as they were, I would
have copied before winter came had not Nicola been
swept away by a children's crusade. I was left to work
alone.

The crusade had begun in some country to the north of us
by a boy preacher who roused the children of his village into
a frenzied desire to march on Jerusalem and win back the
Holy Sepulcher. The frenzy spread over all of Europe and
children by the thousands took to the road, hundreds of them
marching south through Venice. They came singing, with banners and small wooden crosses decked out with flowers.

Encountering one of these young pilgrims, Nicola asked her
where she was going. "To God," the girl replied. These brief
words, the banners and the songs and the trumpets, were all
that was needed to excite Nicola. The next day she marched
away with the girl, carrying a banner of her own, which I
reluctantly painted for her.

By the thousands the marchers reached the southern coast
and wandered about from one harbor to the next, seeking ships
to take them to the Holy Land. They lacked money but this
was no hindrance. Shipmasters gladly took them aboard, sailed
to infidel ports, and sold them, both girls and boys, in the
slave markets at Alexandria. Not one of the thousands of young
crusaders ever reached the city of Jerusalem.

Those who didn't sail — those who were still alive — were

left on the shores and wandered back to the north along the roads they had traveled. Without their crosses and banners and holy songs, they were coldly treated. Those among our citizens who once had pelted them with flowers now pelted them with stones. They mocked the youths as cowards and the ravished girls as rejected bawds.

Nicola returned on a wintry day — the first time in the memory of Aunt Sofia that seawater in some of the canals froze over. She looked much as she had when Bishop Pelagius found her on his doorstep.

I had long since finished Saint Augustine's *Confessions*, two books by Herodotus, essays by Plato and Thucydides, and a detailed history of Venice from the day of its founding to the present. I was halfway through a voluminous work by Maimonides, *Guide for the Perplexed*, a book written in Arabic and brought by Raul on one of his occasional journeys from Assisi, when Nicola returned to Venice. Dressed in a worn-out cloak and broken shoes, her eyes haunted and red from weeping, for days she was too exhausted to speak a word.

Aunt Sofia relaxed the rules and allowed us to talk during meals. She had a grand dinner with lentils and roasted ducks and served cups of a wine she had been saving for a happy occasion. Nicola's return was especially welcome to me, burdened as I was.

But in a few short months, Venice suffered a sudden and horrendous rout. The Fifth Crusade against the infidels, which had been talked about for a long time and which had already begun with a small foray against the Egyptian city of Damietta, burst upon us.

Crusaders came from hamlets, towns, cities, and provinces in Europe — princes and princesses, knights and priests, the strong and the feeble, villains and cutthroats. They pitched tents in San Marco Square, along the esplanade on the Grand Canal, and on the islands of the bay. They slept in alleys, in the holds of derelict ships. Gregorio made room in our warehouse for an English earl and his ten pikemen. Mother Sofia took in a French princess and her five ladies-in-waiting, shoving Nicola and me off to a dank hole in the far reaches of the monastery.

"Only for a week, my dear," she said when I told her that I couldn't work among bats, mice, and salamanders. "I can't refuse the handsome gift Princess Marianne has tendered us. The fleet has gathered. It will sail, I am told, within the month. Then you can return to your work."

But the fleet didn't sail in a month. Word came that Jean de Brienne of Champagne, son of Count Erard, who had assembled a fleet in Genoa and was supposed to be a leader in the crusade, had been replaced at the last moment by a cardinal from Rome. This caused confusion among the leaders in Venice, which was increased by the doge, who had made a bargain with the crusaders to put them safely ashore in the Holy Land.

When they insisted upon sailing to Egypt instead, to confront the sultan in his lair, the doge broke the bargain. Malik-al-Kamil, sultan of Egypt, was a business friend who favored Venetian ships above all others. The doge's ships carried silk and glassware to Egypt and returned with ivory, gold, and precious gems, making him and the merchants of Venice fabulously rich. Because of the risk to his friendship with Malik-al-Kamil, the doge demanded an additional sum, and after days of haggling the crusaders finally agreed to pay it.

Adding to the confusion, knights and priests and leading nobles were warring among themselves, seeking favors from the doge. Set into the walls of his palace were a dozen and more marble masks shaped in the form of lions' heads, each of the beasts having a wide slit for a mouth. If you wished to accuse someone — a relative, a rival in love, a beater of wives and children, usurers, givers of false promises, neighbors, a thief, a scoundrel — you wrote out a note of denunciation and slipped it into the appropriate mouth, unsigned.

On the other side of the slits, within the palace, sat an army of the commune's spies, ready and anxious to punish the accused. It was not a difficult task, since to escape punishment the accused must give proof of his innocence.

Whenever I passed this row of forbidding masks, their mouths worn thin by many notes through countless years, I was always impressed by the number at the scene. But now that the nobles and knights were quarreling among themselves for preference, the place was far busier than before. A long line of complainants reached from the palace to San Marco Square.

Hundreds grew discouraged at the delay, packed their belongings, and went home, including Princess Marianne. The day she left, Nicola and I moved back to our rooms and resumed work on the *Guide for the Perplexed*, burning candles well into the night, rising at dawn to make up for the hours lost.

It was shortly before nones, six days after we moved out of the doghole, when I was called to the door. My brother Rinaldo stood on the steps, blinking in the sun. He was dressed in the garb of a crusader, a red cross on the breast of his travel-stained tunic, armed with dagger and sword. Behind him stood three young men similarly garbed.

"We are here asking for help," he said with a courtly bow, as if I were some precious damsel and not his sister. "The streets overflow. We'll be swept into the sea with the next tide unless we find shelter."

I beckoned Aunt Sofia, who let them in but quartered them in the dank doghole in the far end of the monastery.

That evening, however, she had a special table prepared in the courtyard and asked them to partake of supper. She was keenly interested in the crusade. Indeed, during the past weeks as the hordes gathered in Venice, she had invited a chosen few to supper, notably Prince Rupert of Moravia and the Marquis de Tocqueville, who brought with him a brace of fat pigs and a goat as well as a retinue of ten.

Rinaldo and his noblemen friends appeared in the best of spirits, freshly bathed, with hair curled in ringlets. It was Friday, and usually on that day we ate cabbage and crusts, but on this occasion Aunt Sofia served eel, sea fish, and caramel custard. Hungry after the long journey, the men finished the food on their plates without speaking, but after the custard one of the noblemen said, "In Assisi there is a spate of rumors, concocted and passed along embellished."

"We've had a spring of rumors," Aunt Sofia said. "But word came Monday last that can be believed. It came from a fleet of pearlers fishing off the island of Crete. According to the captain, King Jean de Brienne, Leopoldo, duke of Austria, and William of Holland have sailed from the port of Acre with two hundred ships."

"Bound whither?" Rinaldo asked.

"To Damietta."

"Damietta?"

"A city at the mouth of the Nile River," Mother Sofia explained. She taught algebra and geography to the young nuns and to those of the older nuns who were ignorant. "Three of our sisters have made pilgrimages to the Holy Land, traveling through Damietta. If you wish to know more about this city, they will be most happy to inform you."

Rinaldo nodded, uninterested, and turned to me with the welcome news that the family was well. Not until we were alone after supper did he divulge the real news.

"Tomorrow, at last, you will be on your way home. Our caravan leaves the warehouse at noon. There'll be an escort, of course, and comforts. The weather is fine. You will be greeted warmly at home. Everyone has missed you. I trust that you missed them as much. Also, that you have learned a lesson or two."

I had learned nothing. Nothing except that I couldn't live without Francis Bernardone. I waited now for news of him, as I had waited many times before.

"There'll be an array of knights to greet you," Rinaldo said. "Since you're no longer a gawky child, your madness has come to an end." He paused. "And Bernardone the barefooted mendicant will not be there to tempt you further."

Where was he? Where? Could something have happened?

Was he dead? My throat tightened. Moments passed. I framed a lie and calmly said, "I have heard that Francis Bernardone is in the Holy Land. Mother Sofia spoke of this only yesterday."

"Little good he'll do in the Holy Land. Imagine, if you can, a weaponless crusader, facing the infidels with a begging bowl. But enough of the clown. I remind you, be at the warehouse no later than noon."

As he started away, suspicion caught my breath. Francis Bernardone was not in the Holy Land. He was here in the city of Venice. He was waiting, like thousands of others, for the fleet to sail. For what other reason would I be summoned home on a moment's notice? Why else would Rinaldo insist upon my being at the warehouse promptly at noon?

"It's not possible to leave tomorrow," I called after him. "There's a book to take to the bindery. And other things I need to do."

He returned to where I stood. "At noon tomorrow," he said, "you'll be at the warehouse, as your father wishes."

TWENTY-SIX

While we were making ready for bed that night, having said my prayers, I asked Nicola if she had thought of joining the new crusade. The nightgown she was half into fell to the floor and she stared at me with startled eyes.

"No," she cried, "not again!" She picked up her gown, slipped it over her head, and kept staring. "You're not, are you? Yes, you are, I can tell by your face, by your voice, by everything . . ."

"Who said I was going?"

"No one."

"Then don't worry."

She crawled into bed and disappeared under the blanket. After a long silence she mumbled, "I shouldn't tell you."

I pulled back the covers. "Tell me what?"

"One of the sisters, Sister Angela, saw him in San Marco today. Inside the church, on his knees, praying."

"Saw whom?"

"Francis Bernardone. But don't you dare follow him to Egypt. You'll be sick and die out there in the desert." She sat up in bed and began to shiver. "Promise you won't go."

"I promise," I said, to calm her.

Dreading tearful farewells, I left the monastery before dawn, as the bells rang for lauds, and quietly made my way to the warehouse. Arriving there well before noon, I was greeted warmly by Rinaldo, who was still in crusader's garb although he had come to Venice only to take me home. At midafternoon we were on our way in the wake of gondolas stacked with merchandise, and by nightfall we had reached the salt meadow, where the goods were unloaded and made ready to reload in the morning.

After supper I went to my tent — the same one I had used on the journey to Venice. It was pitched among the other tents, next to Rinaldo's. I got into bed and waited. Instead of hiding in the city and taking the chance of being caught, I deemed it best to go through this charade and thus put him off my track.

Near midnight, as the fog began to settle, I walked quietly out of the camp, through the meadow, and to the canal. I had to wait until dawn for a gondola. The problem then was where to hide in Venice.

"If you wished to go someplace where no one could find you, where would it be?" I asked the gondolier, an old man bent double by years of wielding an oar.

The man thought as he pushed the long black oar against the current.

We went under the Rialto bridge, then through the heart of the doge's fleet, stretched along the Grand Canal. The gondola was covered with a canopy and little could be seen of the men who crowded the ships, but I saw enough to tell me that the fleet was making ready to sail.

"I know a place, but don't expect too much," he said, turning into a narrow canal bordered on both sides by abandoned shacks.

The canal ended shortly on a mud flat. A derelict hulk lay keeled over at an angle, half sunk in mud. A seagull was sitting on the stump of a mast.

"When the tide is low," he warned me, "you can't go ashore because of the mud. This happens only twice each day, however. When the tide's high, you can tie a flag to the mast, a petticoat — anything will do — and I'll come and gather you up."

Not bothering to go aboard, I paid a week's rent and, wrapped in my heavy traveling cloak, was rowed to the San

Marco landing. San Marco's main door was blocked by a shouting mob, so I used the small door beyond it. The church was bursting with crusaders, kneeling on the stones, weapons at their sides, in the white tunics marked by red crosses.

I was certain that Francis was among them. He had to be. I searched their ranks for a modest robe. At last I found it before the altar, in the midst of resplendent figures clothed in churchly gold and lace.

The painted angels fluttered down from the vault and surrounded me. My head went round and round in giddy circles. I would have fallen had I not been held up by a solid wall of crusaders.

A sermon was given, which I didn't listen to. Then after another sermon, a long one, Francis came to the altar and raised his hands in a benediction. Speaking quietly but with passion, his eyes glowing, he said:

"My dear sons, so that you may fulfill the commandments of God, look to the health of your souls and see that there is peace and concord among you. Flee from envy, the beginning of the road to destruction. Be patient in tribulation, humble in success, and thus always in the battles that come be the victor. Be imitators of Christ in obedience and chastity. May God guard you always in the trying days ahead."

As the service ended I was swept away, out into the square, by a stampeding mob. I caught my breath and went back into the church and down the aisle. At the altar I called his name. He didn't recognize my voice. Shielding his eyes from the altar lamps, he glanced down at me.

"Ricca," I said.

He seemed puzzled, as though he had never heard the name before.

"Ricca di Montanaro," I cried.

I waited for an answer. None came. He turned away and for a time I lost sight of him. Then he was coming toward me, walking with the same lithesome step I remembered. Then he was beside me. Wordlessly, I fell to my knees at his feet.

"Ricca di Montanaro, of course, of course," he said. "You're not here for the pope's crusade?" His voice sounded reproving.

I jumped up. It was always this way. One minute I was fainting at his feet, the next moment I was angry with him.

"Why not?" I demanded.

"Judging from your letters, you are not much given to Christian thought," he said, so gently it angered me the more.

"In the old days," I reminded him, "you yourself were not much given to Christian thought. I recall those days and nights very well."

"You shouldn't," he said with a smile.

"Why? Because you are now a saint? Because people speak of you, I hear, as Saint Francis of Assisi? I also hear that Theophanes, the most famous painter in Venice, traveled all the way to Assisi to paint your picture."

His smile faded. He looked at me in a way that wrung my heart, like a child who has been wrongfully accused. I wanted to clasp him in my arms. And I would have done so had it not been for a pig that came down the aisle, chased by a gang of red-faced crusaders, then circled the walls and fled squealing from the church and into San Marco Square.

"Return to Assisi; you are needed there," Francis said. "Your dear friend Clare has done wonders but she needs help."

My dear friend Clare di Scifi. Dear, indeed!

"Dozens of girls and women, many you know, have joined her. Yet she's in need of workers. The task is great."

"You just said that my thoughts were too heathenish for me to join the crusade, yet now you ask me to join the Poor Clares. I am to take the oath of poverty. Beg for my bread. And so forth. And please don't tell me that all the thousands of crusaders milling around in Venice have Christian thoughts. Perhaps you are the only one."

"There's danger in Egypt," he said. "If you are captured, you'll be sold as a slave, or more likely given to the sultan as an ornament. If you are wounded, you may die for lack of care. If you die, and many have died, you'll not be buried in Christian ground."

I doubted that his concern was for my life or my soul. He was afraid that I planned to chase after him, afraid that I would hound his footsteps into Egypt.

"Why do you, this saint who goes around preaching the Lord's commandment about loving your neighbor, hurry off to fight people whom you don't know and who haven't harmed you?" I asked.

"I am not going to Damietta to fight. I go there to talk to the sultan of Egypt. If he will listen to me and become a Christian, the fighting that has lasted for more than a hundred years will come to an end."

"Being a Moslem, the sultan will never listen to you."

"We shall see."

He was ready to say more when shouts came from the square, followed by another rout, this one in pursuit of an unshorn lamb. The animal fled past me and up the steps to the altar. Instead of hastening away as the pig had done, it came up and stood beside Francis. He took the panting animal in his arms.

Quietly he calmed its fears and gave it back to the anxious owner who had appeared on the scene. Then he turned his thoughts elsewhere, upon me as I stood below him at the rail, trembling and fearful that by the power of his will I would be forced to stay in Venice.

I returned his gaze. I put on my cloak, pulled up the collar to hide all but my eyes, and fled. I ran the short distance to the Grand Canal, to where the doge's fleet lay moored.

TWENTY-SEVEN

S hips of all descriptions lay side by side along the canal,
farther than my eye could reach, bows and bowsprits
hanging over the street so that I had to duck my head at
every step. Among all these hundreds I surely could find passage, but my search lasted until dark and ended only by a
chance encounter with a black-hulled ship decorated at stern and
bow by red unicorns.

In the light of a ship's lantern I noticed a man standing on
deck, counting wine casks as they came aboard. I recognized
him at once as Leonardo di Gislerio, the well-known, bad-
tempered lord of Monte Sasso, a Perugian lately turned monk.

I informed him that I was seeking passage to Egypt and that
I had been sent to him by Francis Bernardone — a lie, of
course. He smiled and told me that this was the ship Bernardone
was sailing on, but that I had come too late.

"Alas, we're filled. Passengers are sleeping in the bilge, on
the deck, but you'll find a barque called the *Mermaid* farther
along, past a dozen ships or so. Painted white, her name on the
bow in gold letters. She's only for women."

He leaned over the rail and added, "You haven't had your
supper, young lady. You're hungry. Come, I'll see that you're
properly fed. You can't start out for Egypt on an empty stomach.
A cup of wine first."

He pointed to the boarding plank, but as he held out his bony
hand I moved away. Despite the glow of lanterns now that it
was night, all the ships looked the same. I moved from one to

the other and at last I heard a burst of a woman's laughter and made out the name *Mermaid* on the bow.

A young woman sat astride the rail. A giant of a man with rings in his ears held a lantern and a mirror while she braided her hair and tied it with ribbons. Without taking his eyes from her, he asked me why I was standing there agape. When I told him, he waited until the woman had piled her hair on her head, then disappeared.

The woman — from what I could see of her in the dim light she was no older than I — introduced herself as Rosanna. She asked my name and wanted to know where I had come from and how I had learned about the *Mermaid*. She spoke curtly in an unfriendly voice, as though I were an interloper.

"Who sent you here?" she said.

"Signor Gislerio."

"Who's Gislerio? What's he look like?"

"He's very tall, has a black beard, goes about in a black and white robe and bare feet."

"Bare feet?"

"He poses as a monk."

"How would a barefooted monk know about the *Mermaid*?"

I shrugged.

"He hasn't been here," she said. "And if he did come, Captain Vitale would never allow him and his bare feet on the ship. The captain is very particular. A nobleman from Paris came last night dressed in a monkey suit with a long green tail and a pink behind — the kind you wear at masquerades — and the captain refused him."

The laughter I heard when I was searching for the ship burst forth again. Two men came from below and disappeared in the night. It was then, as I listened to the laughter and the sound of men's footsteps moving away on the esplanade, that I realized the *Mermaid* was a brothel and Rosanna a harlot. I should have known this long before. At the moment Gislerio said that there were only women on the ship, I should have sensed it.

The laughter ceased. The giant came on deck, followed by a

man with a pale, bald head who looked like a clerk but was Emilio Vitale, captain of the *Mermaid*.

He held the lantern high so he could see me better and said, "You have a serious mien, an air about you that I find depressing — due to what, I don't know. But step aboard, we'll see where to put you. Rosanna, you do have an extra bed."

Rosanna gave him a sullen nod. Apparently she thought of me as a rival for the captain's favors.

"Take her below. Freshen her up a bit," Vitale said. "She looks frowzy. Escort her to the cabin. And do not dally."

I held my tongue. For hours I had traveled the esplanade and found nothing. It had taken the doge a year to assemble his ships. Months would likely pass before more ships were assembled for the perilous journey. From what I had heard, ships moved across the Mediterranean only in flocks like the swallows, twice each year, for protection from sea pirates.

I followed Rosanna through a tortuous passageway, past a large salon cut up into cubicles furnished with red drapes and couches, down a plunging stair into the ship's deep hold.

Rosanna's cabin was not much larger than a broom closet, with three narrow bunks, one above the other, and no window. It smelled of stale perfume and seawater that had been standing too long in the bowels of the ship. A flame in a pink bowl was smoking.

In the light she was a little older than I had taken her for, yet her voice was young and she was quite pretty. I shed my cloak, washed my forehead, and used some of her powder.

"Don't hurry," she said. "The captain's been drinking. When he drinks he forgets. He may even forget that he hired you."

She seemed less sullen now. I had the feeling that she was lonely and wanted someone to talk to.

"It would be a good thing if he does forget you're on the ship," she said. "In the morning we sail for Damietta. At least that's what I hear. Tonight will be hell. Having eaten their large suppers and swilled goblets of wine, the crusaders will descend upon us. This night until dawn, when the *Mermaid* sets to sea, the Devil himself will be loose on the ship."

She got up and emptied the bowl of water I had used into a hole in the floor.

"You're just starting out, I gather from your innocent looks," she said gaily. "You're far too young for tonight's frolic. Stay in the cabin. Should the captain ask, I'll tell him you're ill. Bar the door and don't open it to anyone except me. Do you understand?"

Before I could answer, again her mood changed and a cold light glinted in her eyes.

"Unless, of course, you wish to meet the Devil himself. Many of the women enjoy his company. Do you? Your innocent ways and demure looks may be deceiving. It would surprise me not at all to find you're a hellcat. We have a few of them on the ship. They're the most demure of the lot. A snowflake wouldn't melt on their lips. It's possible . . ."

I raised my hand to stop her, but she went on in this vein until breath failed her. I said, "Listen for a second. Say nothing and listen. All afternoon I spent searching for a ship. I didn't know that this one is a brothel. All I wanted was a ship."

Rosanna gasped. She hid her face and sobbed, then dried her eyes on her sleeve.

"I've been here hardly a week," she said. "I came from Lucca, near where you live."

"I know the town."

"I came because I had a vision in the night. There was lightning in the sky. The whole sky was lit up as when dawn is breaking. I saw Christ standing there. The tomb was behind Him and He was stretching out His arms, beckoning me to the Hill of the Sepulcher. My family was terribly angry. They did everything they possibly could to make me change my mind, but I ran off in the middle of the night and came here. Passage to the Holy Land costs more than my father made in a whole year. And I was without a *soldo*. That's why I'm here on this ship of harlots."

Her eyes blazed, daring me to condemn her. "I can tell what you're thinking."

"No," I said, "I am not condemning you. I am thinking about someone else, a girl who was born in Egypt, in Damietta where we're going. Her name was Mary and she had a vision like the one you had. She was poor also and the only way she could get to the Holy Land was by giving herself to the sailors on a ship bound for Jerusalem."

Rosanna was beside me on the bunk. She grasped my arm. "Did the people condemn her?"

"She was stoned."

"But did Christ condemn her?"

"No, He forgave her."

"Truly?"

"Truly. Christ told her to go and sin no more and she didn't. In time she became a saint, Saint Mary of Egypt."

The candle in the pink bowl was guttering. Rosanna reached over and trimmed the wick and we sat for a while in silence.

"You haven't told me where you are going," she said.

"To Damietta, in Egypt."

"Not to the Holy Land?"

"No."

"You seem determined to get to Damietta."

"I am."

"You have a purse. But tell me, if you were poor, like me, and the only way you could ever reach Damietta was by being a . . ." She searched for a word.

"I would do the same thing that you're doing," I said.

"Because you believe that Christ would forgive you, as He forgave Saint Mary of Egypt?"

"No — because I have to go."

"You would go, anyway?"

"Yes. Anyway!"

The ship rocked with the tide. The flame in the pink bowl swayed back and forth with the ship, yet the flame itself did not move. It remained upright and burned steadily.

166

TWENTY-EIGHT

T he night was a hell of shrieks and drunkenness as God turned His face while the Devil frolicked.

Well before the night began, Rosanna hid me away in a hole next to our cabin, a storage place stuffed with coils of frayed rope and tattered sails, lit by a slit of a window. She supplied me with a jug of water and a parcel of food she had stolen, and went off to tell the captain that I had fled the ship. For that reason, neither he nor the tattooed giant came looking.

I slept little, awakening fitfully to bedlam sounds. By dawn we were already in midstream, moving slowly seaward under oars and small sail. A body hurtled past my window, then a second body, then a third. They were crusaders, Rosanna told me later, thrown overboard by the giant, who was rounding up all those who had refused to leave the ship.

I was seasick for three days and during this time went undiscovered. Then, in a storm off the coast of Cyprus, sailors ran down to get sails, found me lying in the cubbyhole, and reported me to the captain, who threatened to have me tossed overboard but relented when I emptied my purse on the table and begged him to take all my money. Instead, he generously took only half, felt less angry, and left me alone.

The storm at Cyprus scattered the fleet. Eleven ships of the hundreds bound for Damietta were sunk in heavy seas or driven ashore. The *Mermaid* lost her rudder, but the captain managed to sail her safely to shore. We were on the island for more than a month while the ship was being repaired. There was a church nearby and twice each day I went there and prayed to the Virgin of the Sea.

She heard my prayers, for the first thing I saw when we sailed into Damietta, among all the dozens of ships, was Francis's black-hulled ship lying safely at anchor.

It was a sweltering noon. A coppery haze blown by a hot wind moved across the sea and the wide mouth of the Nile. We anchored close to the bank among other ships in a cove protected from the current.

None of the women went ashore except Rosanna and me. After I had helped her find a ship that was sailing to the Holy Land and given her money for her passage — Captain Vitale had cheated her out of what she had made — I trotted off toward the tents that stretched along the river between the cove and the city.

As I hurried along the path through the fields of towering grass and stunted plam trees, the sun beating down, wherever I looked — at the Nile shimmering like golden glass, so wide its farthest bank was hidden, at the colored pavilions and the white tents billowing in the wind — there was nothing that I knew.

Beyond the crusaders' encampment rose the high gray walls and the lofty minarets of Damietta. Not a sound came from the besieged city, though the war was now in its second year. Crescent flags flew from the parapets but I saw no signs of fighting.

Bewildered, I stopped at the first tent I came to. Smoke and the smell of food came through the flaps. Inside, tending an enormous iron pot, I found by chance a woman whose husband, Alberto, baked bread and sold it from house to house in Assisi.

"You are acquainted with Francis Bernardone, of course," I said to her. "Do you know where he is?"

"He comes once a day," she said. "In the morning or at night for supper."

"Where is he between times? Where might I find him?"

"He wanders about, preaching, tending the sick. You never know. He's sort of a clown, but most of the men like him and

168

the women love him. Myself, I think he's crazy, but not so crazy as my husband. Did you ever eat any of the bread he bakes? Yes? Well, the loaves with seeds in them, the caraway seeds — when he ran out of caraway he put mouse droppings in the dough. And he did other crazy things, too."

I remembered that her last name was Ubaldo and that everyone thought both the Ubaldos were strange. "You must be happy; you're in Africa now, far away from Alberto."

"Not far enough," she said. "We're having stewed lamb for supper. One of the young nobles — he's from Nîmes in France — he and his men captured a flock of sheep this morning on the other side of the river. They're Moslem sheep so I don't know how they'll taste."

She reached into the iron pot and forked out a steaming morsel. "Try it and tell me what you think."

The morsel was scalding hot, but having eaten little for days, I swallowed it.

"Can you taste Moslem?" she asked me.

"It's delicious, signora."

"Good. I tasted it myself and wasn't so sure."

She stepped back to get a better view of me. "How long have you been here?"

"Since noon today, and I'd like work."

"Have you tended table? By the look of your hands I should say you've never done much of anything. I have three helpers, but I can use another."

There were more than thirty thousand crusaders ranged before the walls of Damietta, she told me, all of them cooking for themselves.

"I only cook for the nobles," she explained. "Knights and priests and such. But there are near two hundred of them, counting our friend Bernardone, who shouldn't be counted because he eats like a sparrow.

"You never know what he'll eat. Usually something we haven't got. Last night he wanted an egg. Nothing else. Just an egg cooked for a long time. What kind of egg? Chicken, duck, crocodile — it didn't matter. We gave him what we had, a sea-gull egg. Don't let him bother you. Serve him the lamb stew and tell him he's lucky that it isn't horse, which I understand is highly prized among the Moslems. But don't wait upon him if you'd rather not."

She put me to work peeling a sackful of withered turnips. When I was through there was another sackful to peel. The long tables were filled, as I finished, with hungry men — marquises, dukes, counts, bishops, princes, Templars, and Hospitallers — so she gave me a great iron bowl of soup.

Dizzy from the heat, I stopped at the first table I came to and ladled it out. Moving along from place to place, I glanced about for Francis Bernardone. I searched everywhere in the tent, taking my time. He was not in sight, but at the head of the table I was serving I caught a glimpse of a man whose face was familiar.

I served two more crusaders and glanced again. He now was talking to a companion, his domed head turned in profile, his hawkish nose thrust out. I could be mistaken. Then I remembered Raul had told me that Pelagius was no longer a bishop but a cardinal-legate, that he had been sent to Damietta to speak for the pope himself.

Pelagius in Damietta, at my table, gave me a start. I did not wish to talk to him, to listen to the lecture I would receive, for he would surely know why I was here. I started for the kitchen, hoping to find someone to take my place.

I took one hurried step. My name sounded above all the clamoring voices. I thought of fleeing, pretending that I hadn't heard, but my name sounded again and a serving woman grasped my arm and pointed at the head of the table where Pelagius sat, waving his big eating spoon at me.

I walked slowly, and when I reached him he let me stand for a moment or two while he finished saying something to his companions. When at last he decided to speak to me, it was in a hearty tone, but in his eyes, which sometimes looked gray and sometimes green but always cold, lurked a glint of anger.

"How pleasing it is to have you with us in Damietta," he said, "heeding the pope's call for help against the infidel dogs. How courageous of you! How proud your father, my dear friend Davino di Montanaro, must feel!"

He knew that I had not come at the pope's call; he knew it well. His companion, a handsome youth in a steel cuirass, which was fast roasting him to death, rose to offer me his seat.

"Thanks be," I said, "but there are hungry warriors waiting for food."

"How thoughtful," Cardinal Pelagius remarked, fixing his gaze upon my shaking hands. "How noble of you!"

I made a small curtsy and was backing away as a man in full armor brushed me aside and spoke to the cardinal.

"Commander," he said, near speechless from excitement, "the infidels are preparing a machine to launch against us. A towering geremite. They are working at it now."

The cardinal, munching on a piece of Signora Ubaldo's tough bread, put it back on the table.

"What is your pleasure?" the messenger asked. "Shall we attack or wait until the machine is launched? Kindly give me orders, Captain Pelagius. My men are waiting on the river. On both sides of the Nile."

Captain Pelagius! My knees shook at the name. Cardinal Pelagius, Pope Innocent's legate, was now a captain, the high commander of the Fifth Crusade, giving orders to an army of thirty thousand men and women.

"How near finished is the geremite?" Pelagius asked.

"They could launch her in a week," the messenger said.

"Then we'll wait. Let the dogs put everything they have into the machine. Stack it high as the city walls. We'll attack the moment she's launched. Keep watch."

The messenger sped off with the orders.

"What do you have there?" Pelagius asked, eyeing the bowl I held in my arms.

"Soup," I said.

"Looks watery."

"It *is* watery."

"At your mother's table, thick soup was served, as I recall. Vegetables freshly gathered, larded with pork. What do you have in the kitchen?"

"Lamb."

"Stringy, this Egyptian lamb, and ill-flavored, but I'll try some of it, well roasted."

In the kitchen I repeated his orders and comments to Signora Ubaldo.

She shrugged. "I can't be blamed. I can only cook what I'm given to cook. If it's stringy Moslem lamb, then that's what he eats."

She carved off a double portion of the meat and set it on a platter. "The captain eats for two," she explained. "Sometimes four, it seems."

I was still shaking. My impulse was to flee. But where to? Cardinal-Legate Pelagius, friend of Pope Innocent, captain of the crusade, had the power to place me under lock and key, to send me back to Assisi.

Fearfully I picked up the food and, trying to smile, went in to serve him. He didn't look up as I set the plate before him, but he cut a piece of the lamb, tasted it, and nodded to show his approval.

"What do you intend to do while you're here in Egypt?" he asked. "Some of the women are in the army, half a thousand or more, dressed in full armor and carrying weapons. From what I have seen of them in a skirmish or two, they equal the men in bravery, if not in the skills of warfare. But you come unequipped."

"I can work as a translator," I answered. "As you know, Arabic is familiar to me. I've spoken it since I was seven and written it since I was ten. I could help when you talk to the Moslems."

"I never talk to the Moslems, but if I do talk it will be in Latin. If they don't understand Latin, then all the worse for them."

As if I weren't there, he placed his bowl to one side and set his knife and spoon and his companion's knife and spoon behind and in front of the bowl. I gathered from what he said to the young man that the bowl represented the city of Damietta and the rows of utensils the Christian army.

I curtsied and left, but as I made my way to the kitchen I felt his eyes fixed upon me.

TWENTY-NINE

That night I slept in the tent, as far from the kitchen fires as possible, for the night had not cooled much after the terrible heat of the day. I would have slept outside under the stars, save for the stream of carousing men that poured past the tent until the eastern sky was aglow.

Up early, I started the fires to show the signora that I was not helpless, chiefly to be ready when Francis arrived. What would he ask for? An egg? A small piece of fish? A morsel of the leftover lamb? Whatever it was, I would prepare it myself and stand over him to see that he ate it.

He didn't come to breakfast. No one came to breakfast.

At dawn, as the first light crossed the river, watchmen saw that moving down the Nile from Damietta were four great geremites, floats piled high with wood, straw, and brushwood mixed with tar. When they approached our ships, which were moored side by side from one bank of the Nile to the other, forming a solid wall between the city and the sea, the floats were set afire.

Watchmen had given the alarm with a call of trumpets. At once, Cardinal Pelagius had ordered everyone to make ready for an attack. A guard came for me and the rest of the women in the tent. All the women who were not in armor and prepared to fight were rounded up and hustled off to a quarry, where they were set to work gathering stones for the catapults.

Smoke trailed through the quarry all that day, hiding the

river. There were no sounds of fighting and we saw no fires until night came and the sky was lit with a sickly glow. I heard nothing of Francis Bernardone.

The battle ended that night with five of our ships having been burned to the water. The infidel Moslems were repelled, but angered by the loss, Pelagius had a full two dozen prisoners decapitated at dawn and the severed heads flung over the walls by catapult into the streets of Damietta.

But that night, late, three infidel spies were captured while attempting to ford the river. Jugs of the mysterious Greek fire and homing pigeons with secret papers tied to their legs, ready to fly, were found in their possessions. Enraged, the cardinal had the spies' arms and noses cut off, as well as their ears and lips. One of each spy's eyes was also gouged out. These bloody ghosts were then put on display near the Moslem walls so all their infidel friends might see them and take heed.

Breakfast was a sullen affair of threats and anger. I had given up all hope of seeing Francis that day when he appeared, delivered a short prayer thanking God that none of our crusaders had been killed in the foray, and sat down to eat.

"What would you like?" I asked him.

His eyes were closed, and after he opened them his lips were still moving in prayer. I repeated the question; only then did he recognize me.

"A piece of the barley cake Signora Ubaldo has baked," he said. "I have always liked her wares. That and a small cup of water, if you have it."

I brought Signora Ubaldo's barley cake and a small cup of water taken from the Nile and set them down in front of him. My hand was steadier than I thought it would be.

"I note a blister on your thumb," he said, "and in your eye a little of the fear that danger brings. You failed to take my advice."

"You're anxious to give me more advice, I can tell."

"Not anxious. Not even tempted. Girls of your age, I am slow to learn, do not make mistakes. They come to us full-blown, nymphs from the founts of heaven, shedding not foam but wisdom. Sister Clare is a precious exception."

Clare again. Now she was a precious exception.

I bit my tongue and asked if he liked the barley cake, which he was munching absent-mindedly. He didn't answer; he drank the cup of brackish water from the Nile as if it were wine and asked for another barley cake. When I brought two instead, he had left the table and was standing in front of the tent, gazing off toward the city of Damietta.

"I never pictured such a magical city," he said, "such a fairyland of spires and minarets. Little wonder that the sultan thinks of it as the most beautiful gem among all the gems of Egypt. It's a wonder to me how all this beauty could be created by people — and there are a hundred thousand of them behind those walls, it is said, misguided souls who worship at the feet of a false prophet. I wish that I could gather them all and explain how in the twinkling of an eye they could save themselves from damnation."

Eagerly, after a sudden thought, he began his little dance, his eyes upon the city whose streets were hidden by high gray walls but whose minarets and domes caught the morning sun.

"The sultan's word is law," I said, "or so I am told. Wouldn't it be better first to save him, then let him save his people?"

"The sultan's not in Damietta. He's in a pavilion leagues away to the south, somewhere near the banks of the Nile."

"And therefore easier to reach than if he were in Damietta, considering that Cardinal Pelagius has been trying for months to breach its walls."

I still had the barley cakes in my hand. He took them and fed the crumbs to a long-legged bird, which he addressed by an Egyptian name he had conjured up, that had wandered up from the river.

While he was talking to the bird, trumpeters rode by, announcing that the infidels had mutilated two crusaders they had taken prisoner weeks ago and thrown the severed parts over the walls into our encampment. Further enraged, Cardinal Pelagius had ordered that everyone halt whatever he was doing and prepare for an assault upon the city.

"If you do talk with him," I said, "remember, sir, that I speak the Arabic language and can translate anything you wish. If you talk in your Assisi dialect and the sultan understands Italian, he'll think you're making fun of him. He'll have your head cut off."

"I'll try to remember. I value my head but not nearly so much as my heart. But I'll remember."

"You always speak with your heart and not with your head," I told him, aware of my own heart beating. I left him with his face turned toward the city of a hundred minarets.

At dusk, messengers rode through the encampment and made known to all that Cardinal Pelagius had decided to attack Damietta within that week. He announced the attack at supper.

With a hand on the golden hilt of his sword, he addressed the captains, prelates, knights, and nobles, his voice trembling in rage, shouting when he spoke of Moslem brutalities, cooing like a dove as he related how much he had done peacefully to make the enemy relinquish the Holy Sepulcher, which was not rightfully theirs. As he spoke he was often so overcome with emotion that tears ran down his cheeks. At the end he issued six grave warnings:

"My first command, be it known: He that abandons the battle shall be tortured on the rack.

"Secondly, if he is a knight, he shall lose his arms and his horse and all his possessions. If an infantryman, his hand shall be cut off and he shall lose all his things. If a merchant or a woman, of those who are in the army, he shall lose a hand and all his things.

"Whoever, man or woman, shall be found without armor, unless he is sick or a child of those who look after the pavilions or gather stones, shall be excommunicated.

"He that turns back while going up the scaling ladders or on the cogs and other ships to make the assault shall lose his hand and all his things.

"All those who enter the city and find gold, silver, and all other things, alike shall put together all that they find in three or six houses that will be designated. If anyone steals, he shall lose his hand and the part of the booty that belongs to him.

"And those who have been ordered to swear shall swear to punish all those who do not observe the prescribed rules."

Frenzy gripped the crusaders. In the past, assaults upon Damietta were mere skirmishes except for the last battle, in which thirty of the Germans, thirty-two of the Hospitallers, and fifty Knights Templar had been captured and beheaded. The bishop of Belavio and his brother, the count of Belino, and the chamberlain of the king of France and his son had been killed. In all, more than a thousand Christians were taken prisoner and some four thousand fell.

The night after Pelagius announced the new attack, everyone was wild with fury. At last the infidel city would be overpowered and stripped of its treasures! The following day, however, with victory in sight, the fierce hatreds the crusaders had brought with them from home burst forth. Knights began to fight with the men on foot, nobles with commoners, commoners with serfs.

Pelagius put an end to these disorders. He banished six Roman nobles from the camp, decapitated a seventh, and after two days of hot consultations devised a battle plan by which one section of the army would defend the camp, another section would attack Damietta from the river, and the remainder of the army would strike by land.

All women without armor or a horse to ride, including myself and an Italian marquesa and her three servants, were put to work collecting stones for the catapults. By noon, despite the urgings of our overseer, I had little to show for my labor except a handful of blisters.

Late in the day, when the sea wind had died away and the heat was at its worst, a man came up the trail to the quarry carrying a bag and a walking staff. Something vaguely familiar about his striding walk caught my attention. I dropped the stone I held in my arms. The figure disappeared in the dancing heat.

For a moment I thought that I had seen an apparition. Then the man appeared again, and as he approached me I saw that it was Raul de los Santos. The overseer, a stout Venetian, challenged him at once, so not even a greeting passed between us.

"You carry a staff but not so much as a knife," the overseer shouted. "Two days ago a Spaniard, a spy, was caught selling bread to the enemy. He was attached to the tail of a horse and dragged through the camp. With your black eyes and swarthy skin, you remind me of him very much."

The overseer stood with his stout legs firmly planted, waiting and anxious to take offense at something.

"I *am* a Spaniard," Raul said, "but not a spy."

"Why then are you in Damietta, without armor, with nothing but a lean and suspicious look? You are not a crusader, most certainly. If not, what?"

I waited for Raul to say, pointing to me, "This girl standing before you is a runaway, to the great distress of her family. My name is Raul de los Santos and I am a tutor to this child. I have been sent by her father to take her home."

And this is what he did say, in his best, most believable voice, but it was far from the truth. Truthfully, he had come to Egypt to plead with me once again to forsake my mad pursuit of Francis Bernardone.

The overseer listened politely and then, despite my protestations, gave Raul into the keeping of a helper and had him marched to a filthy barricade where Christians and Moslems, prisoners alike, were kept under guard.

While the overseer was busy in another part of the quarry, I left and went to the camp. Cardinal Pelagius refused to see me but the man in charge of the barricade, a small Perugian dressed in armor, listened to me with a wandering eye.

"Where are you from?" he asked.

"Assisi," I said.

"And your friend?"

"Assisi also."

"A pretty town teetering on a cliff. Sometime it will fall, *swoosh*, into the valley and kill all the scoundrels who live there," he said, digging up old hatreds, and closed the gate in my face.

THIRTY

In the depths of the night, while he prayed on his knees for guidance, Francis was possessed by a vision. He saw clearly, as if it were written large on the door of his tent, that the Saracen infidel would be victorious in the battle to come.

At dawn he went through the camp, recounting the vision. Most of the leaders were impressed with what he told them, but the soldiers, who had visions of their own and feared the loss of the vast treasures that lay in store for them, pelted him with rocks, shouting that it was foolish to believe a ragged mendicant, cursing all those who did believe.

Cardinal Pelagius himself was one of the dissenters. Confronting Francis in the street, before a crowd of the leaders, he said, "Here we are ready to attack the infidel and you have a vision. Tell me, what does it propose?"

I had no idea of what had happened between the two men before I arrived in Damietta. Surely the cardinal must have been shocked to see Francis. He must have wondered how, despite the long list of heresies he had so carefully drawn up, the pope had given Francis the right to preach wherever he wished, even among the barbarians. And the shock that the cardinal had undergone was still upon him, expressed now by hostility that he was at no pains to disguise.

"Does your vision propose that while the sultan secretly calls upon all of his kingdom from Egypt to Syria, we sit and dream?"

"Neither to sit nor to dream. I should go and talk to the sultan face to face. I saw this clearly in the vision."

"The only talk he understands is the talk of catapults and sharp swords."

"You are playing a deadly game," Francis said. "You gather a big army. He gathers a bigger army. You gather one twice as big. Then you threaten him and he threatens you. You're playing leapfrog with the sultan and both of you will suddenly leap into the fire."

Pelagius scowled. "The sultan's camped beyond Damietta, far up the Nile, out of your reach."

"I'll find him," Francis said.

"You'll be captured and slain before you have gone halfway."

Sensing the anger beneath the cardinal's fear, I felt that he hoped Francis would depart at once.

A stout young man, Brother Illuminato, who had come to Egypt with Francis, said, " 'Tis foolhardy. If possibly you reach the sultan's palace, what pledge do you have from this stranger, whom no Christian has ever set eyes upon, that he won't decree your decollation?"

Brother Illuminato favored big words. What he meant by decollation was that Francis would have his head chopped off.

" 'Tis a wild thought," he persisted. "We'll all suffer decollation at the sultan's hands."

Francis was unmoved. "I understand your anxiety. It was I, Bernardone, who saw the vision. It was Bernardone who was commanded to go. And it is Bernardone who shall go."

Emboldened, I spoke. From my mouth came the words, "I'll go, too. You'll need someone to tell the sultan what you are saying — that is, what you are trying to say."

Francis, excited as a child, cocked his head and studied me for a moment.

"Of course, of course," he said. "We will go together and beard the lion. I'll speak to him and you'll make sense of my words."

At early dawn the following day, after the trail had cooled a little in the night, we started for the palace of Malik-al-Kamil.

It was located on the river, seven long leagues from Damietta. Francis and Brother Illuminato, Francis's shadow, insisted upon walking in their bare feet, but I chose to ride a shorn donkey. A donkey's coat, if long, can attract the sun and turn each hair into metal.

We skirted the besieged city and saw no one on the parapets nor at the loopholes. The gates we passed, five of the twenty-two, were closed and no guards stood beside them. At the last gate, tossed down from the parapet, lay the severed heads of five crusaders, their helmets still strapped to their chins.

It was time for food but no smoke rose from morning fires. Not a sound, not a voice, not the barking of a dog, came from beyond the massive walls.

Illuminato said, "The silence sits heavy upon me. My skin crawls with the silence. What do you make of it, Brother Francis?"

"The infidel prepares an attack."

"If that is the case, we should return and not be caught here in the wilderness."

"The more reason to press on," Francis said.

He had been moving at a steady gait; now he increased it to a trot. The Nile swirled past us. Hot rain began to fall out of a sweltering sky. We came upon sheep grazing in the green rushes. Francis took them for a sign straight from heaven.

"Place all your trust in God," he said, "for these words of the Gospel will be fulfilled in us: 'Remember, I am sending you out to be like sheep among wolves.'"

The rain ceased, the sky cleared. At a place where the river had overflowed, the wolves — a pack of black-bearded Moslem warriors carrying knives — surprised us. We were to be slaughtered, it seemed, before a word could be said.

Francis shouted to them, using the one Arabic word he knew, "*Soldan! Soldan!*" And I said that the sultan had invited us and we had accepted his invitation, and asked if they would be so kind as to escort us to his palace.

They took a long time to digest this information, meanwhile menacing us with deathly threats. But my story was plausible. What might happen to them, they wondered, if they did kill the sultan's guests?

A closer look at the two unarmed, barefooted pilgrims and the frightened girl on a donkey must have reassured them. With deep bows and false smiles they bade us follow them along the roaring Nile toward the palace of their chieftain, Malik-al-Kamil, supreme ruler of Syria and the vast lands of Egypt.

Brother Illuminato complained of the sun, which struck down upon us like a thousand burning spears.

It prompted Francis to repeat parts of a poem he was writing, singing them to the rhythm of his springing steps.

> "*All praise be yours, my Lord, through all that*
> *you have made.*
> *And first my lord Brother Sun,*
> *Who brings the day and light you give to us*
> *through him.*
> *How beautiful he is, how radiant in all his glory!*"

Somehow his words made the sun more bearable, though I still wished the sun wasn't so terribly hot.

The sultan's palace was not what I had imagined it would be, judging by the triple walls, the countless domes and lofty minarets of Damietta. Rising from an islet in the center of a small lake not far from the Nile, it was made of silk, a huge pavilion of rainbow hues, crowned by clusters of yellow flags.

A beribboned boat, rowed by six men cooked black by the sun, ferried us to the islet. Guards came out to meet us and led the way through a maze of trees and flowering bushes. A vast curtain swished open and we were led to the pavilion and, as cymbals clashed and lutes wailed, into the presence of Malik-al-Kamil.

THIRTY-ONE

He was seated upon a dais at some distance from us, down an aisle between two ranks of guards who were dressed in purple gowns and green turbans and armed with jeweled daggers. The aisle was paved with rich Sihouk rugs like those my grandfather brought back from the Fourth Crusade, so deep that I sank to my ankles.

Good manners suggested that I curtsy, as one would before any dignitary, but Francis approached within a few feet of the sultan, until he was stayed by guards, and stood staring at him, somewhat as if the man were Satan himself. The sultan returned Francis's stare but smiled at me, displaying dozens of white teeth. Swathed in silk, a winged turban on his head, a broad, curled beard flat on his chest, he was a strikingly handsome man.

"Speak," he said, settling his dark gaze upon Francis. "Or make a noise — squeak, groan, whimper, chortle, laugh. Do anything so that I may know you're alive, not a homeless ghost who has wandered about in the sun too long."

Covered with yellow dust, Francis did resemble a homeless ghost. Except for his eyes — they were alive. They burned in their sockets as he asked me to tell the sultan that we had come from a country far beyond the seas to save his sinful soul for Christ.

The sultan showed no surprise at being told that Francis was concerned about his soul. Politely, I left out the word "sinful."

"I thought it was the other way round," he said, again displaying a row of dazzling teeth. "I thought that you were messengers who longed to become Moslems."

When I translated these words Francis contained himself and said in a scarcely respectful tone, "Moslems we shall never become, but in truth we are messengers, come from God to save your soul. If you believe in Him we shall commit your soul to Him. And we will tell you truthfully that if you die according to your own law, you will be lost and God will not accept your soul. This is the reason we have come here. If you wish to listen to us and to understand us, we shall show you — let the wisest men of your land also come, if it would please you to call them — that your law is surely false."

The sultan listened intently to Francis, then to me.

"Christians," he said, "I am familiar with. I have been fighting against them for years. Fine enemies, these Christians. Skillful with the sword. Quick with the spear. Clever with the bow. Hard to kill, wrapped up as they are in their steel carapaces. Determined and unafraid of death. But about this soul business I am astounded, for I never suspected that these same Christian enemies possess souls."

"Souls we do possess," said Francis, "and I shall prove it."

The sultan turned to the men about him, all of whom had black beards and, from where I stood, looked quite alike except for one — the executioner (as I learned later), who was situated directly behind the sultan and held a scimitar in both hands across his chest.

"Speak," said the sultan. "My counselors will listen and tell me what they think. Then I will tell you what we both think. A fair bargain?"

"It is fair," Francis replied. "And if we cannot give you good arguments to show you that what we are saying is true — that is, that your own law is false — then have us decapitated."

The sultan slid his dark gaze over me from head to foot and winked both eyes, one after the other. "The young lady is far too pretty to decapitate," he observed. "Instead, if you lose

I'll add her to my chambers, which are poorly provisioned at this hour since thirty-two of my most beautiful women were lost in last year's plague."

He was having fun with me, I felt, but Francis was deadly serious. Therefore, when I translated the sultan's remarks, I cautioned him.

"Francis Bernardone," I said, "you're a fool. The sultan was born a Moslem. He will always be a Moslem. Nothing you can say will ever change him. Any more than he'll change you. And if there's an argument, who's to be the judge? Friend Francis, you're in danger. Please be content to explain to him the meaning of Christ's Passion and the Resurrection. If you must, you might add something about the inferno. But in God's name, do not threaten the sultan or madden him. You're in Egypt, not in Assisi."

Francis would not listen. He repeated the challenge in a bolder tone. I had to make his words sound more polite when I translated them.

The sultan took up the challenge. He called the priests and doctors to his side, more than a dozen of them, and they agreed at once on a decision. The sultan looked grave as he announced it, speaking slowly as though each word was painful to him.

"My advisers," he said, "remind me that I am the hope of the divine law and it is my duty to maintain it. Therefore they command me, in the name of God and of Mohammed, who gave us the law, to have you beheaded immediately. We will not hear what you wish to say. And if again someone comes burning to preach or to speak against the law, the law commands that his head also be cut off. So, therefore, we order, in the name of God, that your heads be cut off. The law commands it."

Francis heard the sultan's words in silence, his lips moving prayerfully. Brother Illuminato, starkly pale beneath his coating of dust, likewise prayed. Struck dumb, I could think of nothing to say. The executioner took a deep breath and elevated his chest.

Malik-al-Kamil's eyes were closed upon a thought. I wondered if he was recalling his great ancestor Saladin, whose sayings I had read. Possibly he was thinking of the time Saladin had asked a Jew, a scholar known for his wisdom, which of the three laws he held to be true, the Jewish or the Moslem or the Christian. The scholar had answered with the parable about three rings that were so very much alike that no one could tell true from false.

The sultan was silent for a time. He glanced upward at the swaying silk of the pavilion and then at Francis, who was still praying.

"My counselors have commanded me to have your head cut off, and at once," he said, "because the law commands it. But I shall nevertheless ignore this order and not slay you, for the reason that this would be poor recompense for your having come here at great risk of your life to save my soul."

Francis stopped praying when he heard this. He thanked the sultan breathlessly. I didn't hear all of his words but quickly made some up.

"Francis Bernardone embraces you as a brother," I said, "in the name of God who rules over us all."

I went on with my speech but was interrupted when Francis addressed the sultan again, this time more politely and in words that astounded me.

"I have heard that you are the incarnation of evil," he said. "The Devil himself, the sultan of an empire of Satanic imps. It makes me happy, therefore, to find these things to be false."

Francis was touched by the sultan's show of humanity, but this was not enough. In the spirit of love, fearing for the sultan's soul, he now made him an offer, so wildly dangerous that I was tempted to conceal it.

Reluctantly, against my better judgment, I said, "The humble messenger of God, Francis Bernardone, wishes to challenge you to a trial. You will have a large fire built on the riverbank and you will join hands with him and together the two of you will walk through the flames, over a carpet of burning coals."

The sultan winced at the thought and drew his slippered feet from view. He was an intelligent man, famed, I had heard, for his learning.

"I have a lively distaste for flames and burning coals," he said with a smile. "I inherited it from my father, who inherited it from his father. It goes far back into ancient times, this distaste. To Yusuf-al-Farasi, founder of the dynasty. It was Yusuf who undertook this trial to win the hand of Princess Zariti, the beautiful pearl of Egypt. All he got from it, I am sorry to relate, were blisters, for the princess wedded the servant who built the fire, with whom she was secretly in love."

There was, alas, still more for me to say. Fearfully, I said it. "If Francis Bernardone comes forth from the fire unscathed, you and your people will happily accept the power of Christ, the wisdom of God. Amen."

The sultan glanced at his huddled counselors, who had grown restless. "Happily we will accept God, because we already accept Him. But this matter of Christ . . ."

Francis took a deep breath, like a diver who is about to plunge into the water. He began to trace a circle with his joyful steps. I had seen all this before, but now he was possessed. A soul was within his grasp. The soul belonged to the man who could bring the war to an end with but a single word.

"This Christ matter needs thought," Malik-al-Kamil continued.

"Now, at this moment, is the time for thought," Francis said. "Death stalks our midst. God alone knows who will be taken. How tragic if the father of millions is to be killed before he embraces Christ! By this simple embrace he protects his people and saves his immortal soul."

The sultan parted his beard. Was he having doubts about the man dancing around before him, making whistling sounds, leaving toe marks on his fine Sihouk rugs? He examined the ring on his thumb; he cast his eyes on the executioner, who was muttering sounds of frustration.

"Ahmed," he said, "will you kindly keep disappointment to yourself? You're much too ambitious. In the past few days you've already dispatched a dozen."

"Only nine," Ahmed said in a thin voice. He was a thick-lipped, oily little man, hairy as an ape. "Not counting the two women, sire."

The sultan turned his attention to Francis. "You say that you have come to save my soul. How, kindly tell me, is this to be accomplished?"

"By acts of poverty, of love, and of chastity," Francis said.

"Poverty. What does poverty mean? Does it mean that I must give up my riches, my lands, my palaces, my libraries, my concubines, my slaves, everything, and become a shoeless monk, begging for my food and a place to lay my head?"

"That would be perfect poverty," Francis said.

The sultan blinked. "And perfect love. This sounds like the opium dream of an addled poet. Tell me about perfect love. How does this come about?"

"Simply. By loving your enemies."

"Huh!" was the sultan's reply, which I didn't translate. His minions, including the executioner, laughed.

"By loving your enemies," Francis said again.

"Impossible," the sultan said. "And you leave out the love of women. Why?"

Francis looked uncomfortable. He glanced at me but didn't answer.

"What you suggest by your silence," said the sultan, "is that I should never touch a woman. You wish to make me a eunuch. What nonsense! Tell me, poet, what would happen to the world if everyone took your advice? But don't bother to tell me. I will tell you. The world would come to an end, smash, and at once, during the lives of those now living."

Francis, to my great delight, still looked uncomfortable.

Three servants were swinging palm fans above the sultan's head, creating disturbing sounds; he ordered them to stop.

"And tell me also, poet of the lively eyes and twinkling feet, how your poverty and love and chastity are rewarded. You must have a heaven of some sort, hidden away somewhere in the clouds."

Francis was upset by this, but he said quietly, "Paradise is peopled by bands of angels and loving spirits."

"Who neither eat nor drink nor cohabit?" inquired the sultan. "How deadly! To dwell upon this heaven of yours makes my stomach turn over and over. Ours is far more inviting. Dates and olives and pomegranates, mountains of them. Rivers of milk and lakes of honey."

Francis's eyes brightened for a moment at the sound of food.

"Also, poet, do not forget the lovely, sloe-eyed women, aglow with precious oils and ointments, who inhabit our heaven. Who in no way are like those who, my spies report, are to be seen on the river not far below the walls of Damietta — a shipload of licentious creatures, unveiled, mocking, arrogant, impudent, bold of buttock, with eyes circled in black and hair tinted the gray of ashes."

I translated this long speech as best I could. Francis gaped, hummed a wordless tune, then stopped and faced the sultan.

"Why do you wish to repeat your life?" he asked. "From what you have said, your heaven is only an echo of the life you have now. Our heaven does not repeat the things we do here on earth. It is another world, a world of the spirit, nearer to God."

"I have spent many hours trying to get near to God, but He escapes me."

"If you have tried, then He has not escaped you."

The sultan frowned. "Enough of God," he said. "Tell me about this Christ of yours. From what I've heard, He's different from our Mohammed. Not so elegant and commanding. A ragged beggar, in fact."

"Yes. He wore a robe of a thousand patches. Every poor man He met gave Him a patch for His robe."

"And He was not so happy as our Mohammed. Indeed, a somewhat somber, black-visaged one, it seems."

"Remember that He carried upon His shoulders man's sufferings and humiliations."

"Who put them there?"

"God, His Father, put them there."

"Why on His shoulders?"

"To test His Son and to test us."

The sultan pushed back his green and purple turban. "My head grows dizzy," he said. "You wear a ragged robe, I see, and have bare feet. Is this the way your Christ went about?"

"Yes."

"In poverty, preaching poverty and, I am told, love, endless love for friend and enemy, for birds of the field, and for beasts of the forest. Tell me about this endless love, please, and about the need for poverty."

"They're both beyond is. Perhaps they are goals we pursue and cannot reach, were never meant to reach, this side of heaven. Yet we try. And in the trying we shed, as serpents shed their skin, some measure of greed and lust and selfishness."

Whispers ran through the restless ranks of the high priest and counselors. The cymbals and lutes and trumpets that had been quiet started up again and became a din that beat against the silken walls of the pavilion. Smiling, the sultan clapped his hands and whistled. He did everything except rise from his throne and dance.

Suddenly his smile faded. He arranged his flowered robe and gathered his followers. Without uttering another word to Francis or looking at him, he took his leave. Yet as I watched his stride down the aisle, I had the strong impression that in some way mysterious to me the two men had become friends.

THIRTY-TWO

F rancis and Brother Illuminato were hustled away by guards
and I was taken to a large silken tent a short distance from
the pavilion, inhabited as far as I could tell by the sultan's
numerous wives.

Within the tent, springing up like white mushrooms, was a
series of smaller tents separated from each other by plants
whose blooms were fashioned of wax and trees laden with
waxen fruit. Rivulets wound in and out through these small
gardens, gliding over golden sand, tumbling over miniature falls
made of precious stones. Turtles studded with jewels basked
on rocks and silver fish swam among turquoise lily pads.

The tent I was taken to was round and stuffed with pillows
of all colors. Fine rugs covered the floor. Furnishings were few.
Statues or paintings, I knew from my reading, were forbidden
by the Koran, the Moslem bible, and Moslems were warned
that when they died and appeared before Allah, if they had
furnished their homes with images of any kind, they must at
that instant either bring them to life before the judgment seat
or be banished to hell forever.

I sank into the bed. It was cool and soft; I felt as if I was
floating on scented foam. Through an opening in the roof I
could see the first star of evening and a rising moon, the same
star and the same moon that I had so often seen from my balcony at home.

A desperate calm settled upon me. I remembered that the
sultan had smiled when told he might be Satan himself. He was

amused rather than offended when Francis challenged him to a trial by fire. He seemed to admire Francis for having the courage to walk into the enemy's camp, boldly and uninvited. From all I had observed, he liked the barefooted pilgrim who danced like a clown and sang as he talked — liked him even as a friend.

But how long would this budding friendship last? An hour, a day? The sultan, I had heard, was moody, given to laughter and sudden fits of anger. Patient Francis thought of him as an infidel soul fluttering like one of the little birds he often talked to, ready to light upon his outstretched hand. What if the bird decided not to light and fluttered away to sit scheming in his great pavilion, turned into a hawk?

I fell asleep from exhaustion and awakened to the sound of lutes and the sultan's voice saying, "Night, not day, is a time for dreams, my pretty young Christian." Behind him were servants who laid down a velvet rug for me to step upon, who carried lamps smelling of musk to light the way.

He led me a short distance down a maze of paths to an enormous black barge, draped with flags and guarded by a phalanx of warriors armed with scimitars, and then to his quarters, which took up most of the bow.

Half of the quarters was decorated with palm trees in pots and shoals of black pillows. The other half was filled haphazardly with bound and unbound books, stacks of yellowing manuscripts, and two large brass lamps that gave off but a feeble glow.

Once seated, almost hidden in the billowing mound of pillows, I was passed a salver of confections. The sultan ate most of them, picking out the nuts and slices of citron and leaving the rest.

"I like this Bernardone," he said. "He's the first Christian among the many I have seen who reminds me at all of Christ. He even tempts me to compare Christ with Mohammed. The two men are much alike. Bernardone in his sackcloth and bare feet must be the first Christian since Christ. And from what I have seen of the Christians here in Egypt, he may well be the last, for they seem bent upon destroying the laws they profess so loudly, destroying themselves as well."

He was silent for a while. In the glimmering dark his eyes rested upon me.

"How long have you known this man?" he said.

"Since I was nine."

"Are you one of his acolytes or whatever they are called?"

"No."

"But you go about with him. You're with him?"

"I am now."

"You must like this man to follow him around."

"I do."

"Is it possible that you're in love with him?"

There was no need of an answer and apparently he didn't expect one, for he said at once, "Has he ever shown the least love for you? Not Christian love, mind you — he seems to love everyone, even us infidels — but the love of a man for a woman?"

I have never been sure about what happened to me next. It could have been the hour — the royal barge, the *Libelcio*, floating romantically on the lake; the sea wind, smelling of faraway places; the sound of cymbals in the distance; the misty stars crowding the night. It could have been that I was over-wrought after my long frustrations. Or a spell mysteriously cast by a man who had the gift of divination.

"Truthfully," I said, "never has there been a sign during the time I've known him. Nothing, though I have loved him with all my heart."

"And you love him now?"

"Now and forever."

"Knowing, as you must, that he's a man sworn only to God?"

"Yes."

"This could be his power over you. There are some who enjoy devoting their lives to the impossible, who prefer to fail at the impossible than to succeed at the possible. You may be one of these prideful people."

Prideful? How many times had the word been leveled at me! A hundred times? Since the day I was old enough to totter around in my mother's shoes, admiring myself in every one of the twenty-one mirrors in our room of mirrors.

"Francis will tire of his burden," I said. "It's heavy."

"He'll break holy vows for you? Do you really believe this?"

"Yes — fervently."

"If he doesn't, what then? You're very young. Are you prepared to spend your life wandering after him in silent adoration?"

"He'll tire of the burden."

"When? There were no signs of it today that I could see."

"You don't know him."

"Perhaps not, but I shall before many days have passed."

There was a disturbing note in his voice, the tone of a man who was used to giving commands and having them obeyed.

"Where is Francis now?" I said. "Is he safe?"

"Safe unless he decides not to be. He's an agile young man. Adventurous. Imagine walking through a fire to prove something."

A servant came to announce that his guests had arrived. Taking his time, the sultan rose, searched through a pile of manuscripts, and came out with a thin volume bound in golden boards.

"*Secrets of the Egyptian Dance*," he said, handing it to me with a bow. "A present to you from Malik-al-Kamil."

I spread the book on the rug and turned the sheets. There was much to read, sheet after sheet of illuminations, painted in garish colors.

"You'll find it of interest," he said. "We have a poor supply of oil for our lamps because of the siege, so you may wish to read by daylight."

"It's a wonderful gift, sir. I'll take it with me and read it when I get back to Damietta."

I met his gaze. He showed his dazzling teeth in a gentle, fatherly smile. For some reason a chill raced through me.

"I suggest that you read the book tomorrow morning," he said, "for tomorrow you will take your first lesson."

"Lesson in what?"

"In the charming dances of Egypt. Those first danced by the daughter of the beautiful Queen Nefertiti."

"But I am not a dancer."

"More reason for you to take lessons."

"And horribly awkward," I said, aware now that I was destined to take a place in the sultan's harem.

"Not awkward," he assured me, smiling his dazzling smile again. "Though you are somewhat tall and lacking in the matter of flesh."

Two servants came to announce at the same time, in the same words, that his guests had arrived and were waiting in the garden.

"Tomorrow," the sultan said, escorting me to the boarding plank and waving farewell.

I would have waved back, though I shook in every limb, had not a distraction taken place before my eyes.

Men were lowering an object into a boat, obviously a body wrapped in a winding sheet. As I watched, the boat crossed the lake and the body was carried toward the river. If it was one of the sultan's people it would be buried, not thrown into the Nile. The Moslems, I had heard, wrapped food in these windings, along with secret messages, which floated on the current into the beleaguered city of Damietta and there were fished out.

This scene further upset me and I carried it to dinner. After a meal in the company of the sultan's several wives, I tried to read the *Secrets of the Egyptian Dance* back in my tent among the mountains of scented pillows, by a feeble light that gave off the smell of jasmine, and fell uneasily asleep to the far-off sound of the Nile rushing toward the sea.

THIRTY-THREE

T he next morning, after a breakfast in the company of six of the sultan's wives which dawdled along from dried dates and fresh pomegranates to turtle eggs and lamb couscous, all of which I was much too frightened to touch, I was given over to an instructress, a small woman with large Egyptian eyes who looked like an overstuffed doll.

"My name is Aimee Yusuf," she said. "You have read the book?"

"No, I have not. I was much too exhausted for frivolity." Then, seeing tears well up in her eyes at my harsh words, I added, "But I'll read it today."

"Do, please. There you'll find the arts that enthralled the sultan. It will be a guide for you."

"For what?" I asked, still not believing that I was fated to become an odalisque in the harem of Malik-al-Kamil. It was a dream. No, not a dream. I was awake and living in a nightmare. "What am I supposed to do?"

"What the sultan has asked you to do."

"But I am not a dancer."

"The sultan thinks that you will become a dancer. His thoughts are very strong. What he thinks comes to pass."

Eunuchs removed my hose and gown and took them away, even my shoes, leaving me half naked.

"Shoes make sounds that spoil the notes of the lute and tambouri," she explained. "Besides, with shoes you cannot grip the earth, the marble floor, the soft carpet, whatever you dance upon. It is necessary to do so, for otherwise it is not a woman dancing but a woman struggling."

She stood off and studied me. "You're too tall and too thin," she announced, echoing the sultan's words. "We can do little with this tallness, I am afraid. For the thinness, I have a special oil — it comes from the coconut and does magical things. In a dozen days you'll be plump as a pigeon."

While I gritted my teeth, she showed me how to stand, not stiff-legged but with one knee bent, arms raised and clasped above my head.

No one had ever complimented me on my dancing and I had never thought of myself as graceful. It was not difficult, therefore, to be awkward, to appear all arms and legs as I took the first position of the stomach dance.

As awkwardly as I could, I went through this exercise a hundred times, sweating in the searing heat, bewildered, frightened out of my senses, until Aimee was forced to say, "From what I've seen this morning, you Christian girls must have your thoughts fixed only upon yourselves, upon food, the state of your health, whatever. Those of our faith are quite different. We dance for pleasure, to display the curve of an ankle, the shape of a breast, to woo the beholder, to please God and celebrate those things He has so generously given us."

She sent me back to my tent with the suggestion that I not return until the book had been read. I spent the rest of the day with it, torn between thoughts of what would happen if I did learn to dance and what would happen if I didn't learn.

The lessons lasted for eight days and on the ninth day the sultan came to see what my teacher had done for me.

Smiling, clapping his hands as I danced, he said, "You have learned much, and in such a very short time. It pleases me. It is a miracle. You remind me of the Persian girl — I have forgotten her name — who was so light, so graceful, she could dance on the bottom of a drinking glass."

He sighed at this memory and called the teacher to his side. "There's an occasion tonight," he told her. "It begins with the moon. With this one, whom you have taught so well. On our little Christian, use colors sparingly so as not to conceal her natural beauty. She's quite blond; therefore do not employ henna, and only small touches of kohl."

I was taken to the tent where the sultan's wives were bathed and was left to a bevy of servants. At times there were two women and two eunuchs working on me at once. They handled my body carefully like some precious figurine, yet it's a wonder that any of me was left.

When a slender moon came out of a cloudless sky, I was swathed in veils, borne away on a litter to the deck of the royal barge, and set down in the center of a miniature glade. As in the gardens around the sultan's tent, palms lined a stream that wound here and there, and men stripped to the waist were toiling at a wheel, dipping water from the lake to feed it.

At the far end of the glade, Malik-al-Kamil sat in a nest of colored pillows. Behind him stood Ahmed, the ugly executioner. The sultan welcomed me with a remark in Latin but my throat was too tight to form so much as a single word in reply.

"As you may know," he said, "you are here to dance. Let me explain. It is not for my pleasure, unfortunately. For me you would be able to conjure up but a little fire. None, I am afraid. The dance is for our friend, the Christ-enthralled Bernardone."

I stared.

"We can't challenge him, not openly, of course. It would put him on his guard. Forewarned, he would gaze at the moon, the stars, the lake, not at you. Or close his eyes and set his mind on holy matters."

A burst of light, the truth, struck me. All of the truth, at once in a blinding light. Malik-al-Kamil, the sultan of Egypt, was insane. *Pazzo! Pazzo! Pazzo!*

"You have loved this Bernardone from childhood, which is a miracle I can't explain. But during these long years he has never shown the smallest sign of love for you. Now, at last, you have a chance to see if he can be tempted to lay aside these curious vows he has taken. If he ever intends to show a sign of love. If he's capable of one, which I doubt. Certainly you don't wish to trail along for the rest of your life after someone who aspires to sainthood. Or do you?"

"No," I cried. "No!"

"We'll soon learn whether he's a man or not. First, a word of wisdom. Think little, dance from the heart. Masked, you'll not be recognized until you wish to be. You're simply a dancer I have chosen from many to entertain him. Your name is . . . Let's see. Will Zahira do?"

The wind caught my flimsy veils. They changed color as it whipped them about.

"Do you like the name Zahira? It sounds romantic."

When I didn't answer, he said, "Are you frightened? I hope not. Perhaps you wish to go back to Damietta and continue on the path you've pursued since childhood, worshiping Bernardone from afar? It's not too late. I grant you a safe journey. You can go now, though against my judgment. But speak. The river of time flows fast, faster than the Nile — the past into the present, the present into the future, the future into infinity. And all this, my friend, while you take one long breath."

"What music will I dance to?" I asked breathlessly.

"The same as you danced to when you were learning. And played by the same musicians."

Servants hid me away in a thicket beside the gurgling stream. Francis appeared, unfortunately with Brother Illuminato, and they were given places on either side of the sultan.

Tambouri and lutes began to play, so softly I could scarce hear them above the noise of the river. My Egyptian name was called twice. It sounded lively the way the sultan called it out, alive and commanding. I ran out of the thicket, catching a corner of a veil on a small thorn, and stood in his presence. In the torchlight I blinked and my knees shook.

The music changed its rhythm and grew louder. Taking a breath of the hot night wind and then another, forgetting most of what I had learned, I began a slow circle, my arms raised and beckoning, my eyes fixed gravely upon the sultan.

If only I had read more carefully the dancing book the sultan had given me. If only I had listened to my teacher and not wasted precious time. If I had not deliberately tried to look awkward, to be awkward. And if I had not succeeded in being awkward, graceless, unprovocative, leaden-handed, big of foot!

I dropped the first two veils at his feet. Clasping them to his breast, he cried out in his booming voice. "Good!"

The next two veils I strewed around the circle at the feet of imaginary guests. The fifth veil I unloosed before Brother Illuminato. Fluttering like a bird, it lit across his bony knees. He frowned, snatched it away, and hid it.

I hadn't looked at Francis. I did so now as I started the next circle. His eyes shone forth from their caverns. He was watching. It meant nothing at the moment, this shining. His eyes always shone.

I made two circles of the carpet before I writhed out of the sixth veil and dropped it at his feet. He did not touch it. He did not move. The torch flames, shifting in the wind, gave off an uncertain light, yet I was sure that his gaze moved away from me and sought the sky, as if he were asking for God's help.

"Good," Malik-al-Kamil said again. "The statue crumbles. It totters. It casts about for a rescuing hand. Excellent."

But at that moment, as I stood close to Francis, I saw his gaze leave the sky and fix itself upon me. It was penetrating, steady, and cold. I dropped my arms and stood still. In panic, I remembered a story that Brother Illuminato, in one of his worshipful moods, bragging about Francis, had told me.

Years ago, soon after the pope had given Francis permission to speak, the two men were in Syria. It was a cold day so they stopped at a house to warm themselves. There lying in bed was a naked woman who asked Francis, he being the more handsome, to join her.

Francis was surprised but not shocked, Brother Illuminato said. He looked at the woman in pity, troubled that she was so brazen. But when she rose from the bed to grasp him in her arms, he drew back, saying that already a more comfortable bed awaited them in a different room.

In this room, where a large brazier burned, he stripped off his clothes and threw himself upon the coals, asking her to come join him on the sumptuous bed. The woman clutched her throat in horror and did not move, but watched him lying there happily, untouched by the flames. So appalled was she by the sight that she repented of her sins and through the help of Francis became holy in grace and thereafter did much good.

I had not believed this story then and I did not believe it now. Francis talked to the birds and beasts because he loved them. And they talked to Francis because they loved him. But I didn't believe that he could lie unharmed on a bed of burning coals.

I danced away from the gaze he had leveled upon me, thinking of the tale of the Syrian woman. Fearful that he would build a fire there on the deck, take me by the hand, and bid me lie there with him, I danced in front of the sultan.

At my distress, Malik-al-Kamil said, "I hear a crumbling sound in Jericho. Do not grow faint."

I circled back to where Francis sat, so close to him that I could feel his breath upon my flesh, and took off the mask that hid my face. Brother Illuminato gasped. He reached out a hand, then withdrew it as though scorched and began to weep.

Francis did not move. He looked away, raised his gaze to the heavens, started to speak, and stopped. Hidden among the palm trees, the musicians paused. From far off toward the city of Damietta came the call of trumpets. The dark waters of the lake held a net of swarming stars. The drums began to beat once more, louder now, and the wild tambouri joined them.

"The eyes of the statue," Malik-al-Kamil said, "waver between heaven and earth. And since they do waver, please continue. Rid yourself of the last, the seventh veil, which hides the supreme mystery, life's beckoning secrets, the very fountain of life."

The veil made whispering sounds as it fell. Lowering his gaze from the heavens, Francis glanced at it, then at me. His eyes had changed. They were no longer cold. For some reason, a gentle light shone in them.

"Before the Lord," he said in his gentlest voice, the voice he used with birds in the meadow, "you are committing a sinful act."

Was he again in Syria, admonishing the Syrian woman, about to command her to forsake her lustful ways, to find happiness not in his arms but in the arms of Christ?

"The statue speaks," Malik-al-Kamil said. "What does it say? The words have a promising sound."

"That I am a sinner before the Lord."

"Before the Lord? Allah be praised! Tell him why you are dancing. Tell him you are dancing for him. Not the Lord."

Straightening myself, in a voice to match the gentle voice Francis had used, I said, "I am dancing for you, Francis Bernardone. And not as a sinner, but as a woman who loves you."

He looked away into the night, at the waning moon. There was a long silence, so deep that my ears clamored with a host of deafening sounds. Francis looked at me again. It was a terrible moment. Before he uttered a word I saw the answer in his eyes.

Malik-al-Kamil saw it too. A half-smile parted his lips. "This one," he said, "as I have feared, is not a man but a holy man. How clever of me, don't you think, to discover this? And how fortunate for you that I have done so. Holy men should be worshiped from afar. They make poor lovers and impossible mates."

"I am not deaf to your words," Francis said to me. "But still they disguise a sinful act. In the name of our Lord, I beg you to repent. And do not wait. Repent now and the Lord will forgive you."

He watched, waiting patiently for me to fall upon my knees and ask forgiveness. I did not move. Years of devotion had come to this. An awful scene rose up before me. It was from a passage I had copied from the Bible long ago:

> *And when the daughter of the said Herodias came in and danced, and pleased Herod and them that sat with him, the king said unto the damsel, Ask of me whatsoever thou wilt and I will give it thee. And he sware unto her, Whatsoever thou shalt ask of me, I will give it thee, unto the half of my kingdom.*
>
> *And she went forth and said unto her mother, What shall I ask? And she said, the head of John the Baptist. And she came in straightway with haste unto the king, and asked, saying, I will that thou give me by and by in a charger the head of John the Baptist.*
>
> *And the king was exceedingly sorry; yet for his oath's sake and for their sakes which sat with him, he would not reject her. And immediately the king sent an executioner, and commanded his head to be brought; and he went and beheaded him in the prison. And brought his head in a charger, and gave it to the damsel . . .*

I saw the head of John the Baptist on the bloodstained charger. For an awful moment I wished with all my soul that it was the head of Francis Bernardone.

THIRTY-FOUR

I covered myself and fled, though Francis called me back and sent Brother Illuminato trailing my footsteps, pleading in his singsong voice, reminding me how the Syrian woman had repented of her sin and been forgiven. He followed along to my tent and stood outside, yammering away.

At last, when he saw that the talk of repentance failed to move me, he said, "Without you, the men cannot converse. And they have many important things to converse about."

"About the state of their souls?" I asked. "Which is greater, the Bible or the Koran, Moslems or Christians? And is the God they worship the same God or are there two different gods? Let them make signs to each other, jabber like monkeys in a tree. Francis has the power to talk to birds and beasts; perhaps God will give him the power to talk to Malik-al-Kamil."

I hid myself in the pillows, but he stuck his head through the curtains.

"Why did Brother Francis come to Damietta?" he asked.

"I don't have even one idea why Brother Francis came to Damietta."

"Oh yes, oh yes, you have. You know how the battle goes. You have seen corpses floating in the river. And the severed heads of Christian warriors lying outside the gates. You've heard the cries of the wounded and the moans of the dying. You told Brother Francis — I heard you tell him — that you could not sleep for the terrible sounds and the awful smells. And you know that he has come here to talk to the sultan about peace, because he told you not once but twice, and in my hearing. I beg you to come before you commit another sin."

"I'll come if you just quit talking about sin," I said, getting into my clothes.

Braziers were still aglow on the royal barge and the tambouri were whining sweetly and the two men still sat in the garden among the palm trees. They were making gestures, urgent noises, trying to say something to each other. And though nothing was being said that made sense to them or to me, somehow across the gulf of hatred between Christians and Moslems they had silently joined hands and become friends.

Francis welcomed me with one of his rare smiles and no sign of anger. Indeed, I believe that he had forgotten that I had danced unveiled, as he had forgotten the scene on the steps of the bishop's palace. He was thinking, no doubt, of the awful destruction Pelagius was determined to unloose upon the city of Damietta. As for myself, I greeted him with a smile, though I was still the sullen daughter of Herodias.

The sultan rose from his pillows and bowed. "You have come at a good time," he said. "The deaf are leading the deaf. We make strange sounds, like burros braying. Tell the holy man this: although my counselors think me foolish, I am prepared to strike a bargain. I offer Cardinal Pelagius a truce of thirty years. The cession of all Palestine to the Christians. Money for the cost of repairs to the walls of Jerusalem. A gift, a free gift, of a goodly piece of the True Cross, and twenty Moslem nobles as hostages besides."

Francis threw up his hands. He leaped to his feet and clapped his hands.

"I'll go now with the wonderful news," he shouted. "The Lord has sent Sister Moon to light our way. Come, Brother Illuminato, come, Ricca, we'll travel in the cool of the night and reach camp tomorrow. Praise the Lord and Sister Moon."

The sultan sent men to have three of his Arabians saddled, but at the last moment Francis decided that he wished to travel on foot. There was much jabbering about this, the sultan distressed at the needless loss of time. A compromise was finally agreed upon. Sleepy burros were brought to the lake, one for Brother Illuminato and one for me. Francis and the sultan clasped each other and exchanged vows, so warm that I didn't need to translate.

As we started off, the sultan said to me, "Our Francis, with scarcely a change of countenance, has passed an awesome test. So be it! And you, dear friend, though trembling and a trifle pale, have also passed a test. Now at last you possess the key that unlocks the door to womanhood."

"Key?" I asked sullenly. "What key?"

"Tears are the key. Tears."

His words lifted my spirits but little.

Walking in the lead when we reached land, forcing the donkeys to move faster than they wished to, Francis was silent, wrapped in his dream of peace. I nursed my anger and said nothing to disturb him.

But at noon, when we neared the Christian camp, an argument occurred. The guardhouse where I had last seen Raul was within sight and I started off toward it, suddenly worried about what had happened to him.

"Wait!" Francis shouted. "I need you when I talk to Cardinal Pelagius. He will never believe me when I say that the sultan has made him a marvelous offer of peace. He will think I am lying. I need you as a witness. You were there and heard everything."

"Brother Illuminato was there also," I said.

"But he understood only what I said, not what Malik-al-Kamil said."

I held back, my worry about Raul increasing.

"Come," Francis urged me. "Whatever your present concerns may be, they can't outweigh the sultan's message. The lives of thousands depend upon how Cardinal Pelagius receives the news."

Reluctantly I went along and we found the cardinal at his bath. A tent had been set on the riverbank for his convenience and he was just emerging from the water, pale as a flounder's belly except for his hands and face, which were burned red by wind and sun.

Francis went into the tent while Cardinal Pelagius was being dressed and at once hot words came tumbling out. The cardinal, despite the pope's acceptance, still thought of Francis as one not to be trusted, one who had somehow escaped the net but would be caught one fine day and exposed as a heretic.

"Preposterous!" the cardinal shouted.

"The truth," Francis said quietly.

"I've heard that the sultan is a slave to opium. Did you perchance acquire the habit while you were his guest?"

"I carry a true message and I'll prove it as soon as you're dressed."

The two were silent for a time. Francis paced up and down in his bare feet, while the cardinal, in a bad temper, upbraided the servant who was curling his locks. Still not speaking to each other, they came out, Pelagius shining in a brocaded gown.

He gave me a suspicious look. "You were present at these sessions. You were the means by which these two men talked. Did the sultan say that he was ready to lay down his arms, surrender the whole of Jerusalem, and sign a thirty-year truce? Could there be confusion about this?"

"None."

"You heard him clearly?"

"Clearly."

Pelagius nodded, seemingly impressed by the truth of the sultan's offer. But that night at supper, when everyone in the camp had heard the news, he stood up and said:

"I have given close thought to the plea for peace which has come to me this day from the clever king of the Saracens. The very same king, when a baker demanded money from a beggar who had wandered into his kitchen to smell his baking bread, ruled that the baker should be paid by the sound of money. A subtle man and a perfidious foe."

"A scoundrel," said Anselmo di Luni, the provost of

Sant'Omaro and the leader of eighty knights. Brave Andrea da Pisa rose to his feet and shouted, "Sly fox!" Lord Viccari struck the table with his fist, saying, "But can we trust this Francis Bernardone and his acolyte? Do they bring the truth?"

Pelagius frowned. "They know full well that they dare not lie to me about such a serious matter. Furthermore, on the face of it, the sultan's offer is understandable. The great devil of the Saracens begs at our door now that he's at the brink of defeat. What else can he do except lay down his arms and sue for peace? But he shall not have peace. He shall have a knife instead."

THIRTY-FIVE

B y messengers on fast horses every warrior in the camp —
and there were more than thirty thousand — was called
to arms that night. All of the hundreds without arms —
men, women, and children — were likewise called upon. With
other prisoners, Raul was freed from the guardhouse and sta-
tioned below the river gate, and I and all the women who had
worked in the quarry were sent there to feed stones to the
catapults.

The battle for Damietta began at dawn. First, the great iron
chain, which stretched from bank to bank across the Nile,
guarding the city from attack by sea and river, was cut. Floats
were brought up and fastened against the massive river wall.
Ladders were raised and six crusaders from Pisa scaled the
wall and reached the walkway. But there they were attacked by
a band of Saracens, who killed them and tossed their severed
heads down upon us.

Toward evening, clouds raced in from the sea. Lightning
flashed and a deluge of hot rain swept our ranks. Fighting
ceased until the next morning, when, under a cloudless sky and
stifling heat, the catapults whirred and stones thudded against
the tower. Two men were sent up with jugs of Greek fire — a
lethal mixture of oil and secret flammables.

They lost their lives in the conflagration, but at noontime
seven Florentines, carrying the commune's red and white
banner, reached the highest ramparts and found the loopholes
deserted. They were much disturbed, however, by an ominous

211

wave of silence that came up from the city, as if the infidels were about to make an attack upon us from a different place.

It was then that Cardinal Pelagius decided to use his most powerful weapon, the floating fortress. To the sounds of trumpets it was moved by oar and sail to the river gate and secured there by grapple hooks. From its loftiest decks, reaching to the high walkway that encircled the gate, a horde of warriors poured forth.

They met only small resistance. In a short time the massive gate that stood between the sea and the city was breached. Cardinal Pelagius, sensing victory, sent heralds to the thousands who were waiting on the riverbank, all armed for a general assault, among them Raul with a knife he had stolen and I with a club.

Heralds repeated the orders the cardinal had already drawn up — the severe penalties for cowardice and treachery — and added to the list his instructions for the occupation of the city once the enemy had been defeated.

Certain places in Damietta were parceled out to various knights and noblemen, to churchmen and to churches. For instance, the Church of Rome was given the strongest of the many fortresses, the beautiful Tower of Babel, so high and majestic it was visible from far out to sea. The northern part of the city was promised to Archbishop Gabrieli, the southern part to the king of Jerusalem, Jean de Briênne. Even the wives of the warriors were assigned generous shares of the booty.

Two of the city's twenty gates were broken down by mid-afternoon and the Christians, Raul and I among them, entered Damietta. There was no one in the winding street we came to except a stray dog, dragging a shriveled pup clamped to one of its teats, that slunk away as we approached.

The street wound into a square strewn with starving people too weak to raise their heads. They followed us with their eyes but said nothing. On the far side of the square, in front of a mosque, naked children lay about, their arms and legs contorted, their shriveled bodies gnawed by dogs.

Beyond the mosque a great field stretched away between rows of palm trees. It was furrowed as if ready to sow with wheat, but as we passed, following the glittering army, I saw that it was not a wheat field but a cemetery. The heavy rain during the night had uncovered the shallow graves and the dead were emerging by the thousands. The only defender of the city was the awful stench that drifted down upon us.

In the central square and mosque of Damietta, at the far end of the field, Cardinal Pelagius assembled his warriors, congratulated them upon their brilliant victory, and reminded them of the strict rules he had set down for the division of property.

Yet no sooner had he gathered his retinue and set off for the mosque to pray than the soldiers broke rank and began to plunder those parts of the city that had not been assigned to the nobles, the prelates, and the Church.

Raul and I were following after the cardinal and were about to enter the mosque when a rabble of warriors blocked our way. They had rifled the houses around the mosque and were piling up their booty, shouting a ditty at Francis, who was coming toward us:

> *"Look what all of us have found!*
> *It was Bernardone who preached defeat!*
> *Miserable clown from that doghole, Assisi!*
> *Let us build a fire and roast the hound!"*

Francis turned and, facing his tormentors, made the sign of the cross, made it slowly, twice over.

He was shaken and breathless when he reached us. I had never seen his eyes dull before. They were deep in their sockets, lost, as though hiding from the awful sights that lay around us.

The rabble had returned to their loot, but I feared that when they were through parceling it out they would again turn their spite upon the man who had tried to deprive them of these riches.

"This is not a safe place," I said. "The mosque is open."

213

Francis agreed. "Let's go and pray to God and ask His pardon for this unpardonable sin. I had visions of a Christian defeat and what it would mean, but never a vision of a Christian victory. I have looked into the depths of hell. Doors open on empty houses, women and children dead on the doorsteps. The men gone. The women and children dead, without a drop of blood in their bodies."

"I have wondered about the crusades," Raul said. "About this fifth one especially. Because the other four mostly served to feed ambitious prelates, to enrich the already wealthy, to enable the nobles to display their skills, to titillate the bored and absolve the sinners."

"Horror!" Francis said, looking beyond us at the furrowed cemetery. "In the name of Christ, His Son, the Christians have preached love and I have preached love. And this is the answer."

He brushed his eyes. For a moment he seemed blinded and I thought that he would fall on the stones. I took him by the arm and led him, like a child, into the mosque. Raul and I left him there on his knees.

It was cool under the soaring dome, among pillars of black and white marble. It smelled of cedar and sandalwood, a relief from the sweet, awful smell of putrefaction that engulfed the city.

"This mosque is famous for its library," Raul said. "Next to those in Cairo and Alexandria, it's the most famous in Egypt. It has, I have heard, the original manuscript of Maimonides' medical essays on Hippocrates and Galen. What treasures!"

The mosque was filled with Christians, some praying, most of them gawking at the magnificence and planning how best to dismantle it. There were no infidels around to ask about the library, but we found it behind a door banded with gold and marked in Arabic.

There were three large rooms stacked halfway to the ceilings with scrolls, connected by long corridors, which were also stacked with scrolls. The place had the musty smell of forgotten times. Since there was no one in any of the three rooms to aid us, it took a long time to locate the works of Maimonides.

Raul handed me his essay on Hippocrates. It was a small scroll, not illuminated, written on glossy vellum in the twists and turns and fishhooks of Arabic script.

"I have always wanted to handle this," Raul said. "I have coveted it. We'll take Maimonides, the most brilliant man of his time, back to Assisi with us and make an illuminated copy on the finest of vellum."

Raul held the book like a casket of jewels. He had forgotten where he was. That in the city, starved to submission by hunger and disease, there might still be one or two living men who were willing to die to protect this treasure.

"We can return the book when the crusade is over," I said, struck by a twinge of conscience.

"By that time there'll be no library here, nothing except a pile of ashes."

"There were fires burning behind the mosque as we came in," I said.

"Christian armies always burn what they cannot carry away. Fires burned in Constantinople and Jerusalem and Beirut. They have burned everywhere armies have set foot, in all of the past crusades. And they'll burn here in the name of Jesus Christ, though this is one of the great libraries of the world. For the crusaders are not heedless. They set their fires with deliberation, knowing that the scrolls collected through the ages are the works of infidels. Not knowing — and worse, not caring — that they hold the most brilliant thoughts of our day."

"There are thousands of scrolls," I said. "What can we take?"

"All of Maimonides." He picked out one of his scrolls and began to paraphrase the Spanish Jew who lived and wrote in Egypt, professing to be a Moslem in order to save his life. "Maimonides asks, did God create the world in time, or is the universe of matter, as the Greeks thought, eternal? Maimonides says here that reason is baffled. We can prove neither the eternity nor the creation of the world. Therefore, let us cling to our fathers' traditional belief in its creation."

Through the dome above us, set with yellow glass, was the reflection of the flaming sky. And I suddenly detected the smell of Greek fire.

Raul went on. "Adam, Maimonides says, is pure spirit. Eve is pure, passive matter, the cause of all evil."

"I have heard enough about Adam and Eve and evil," I said. "And I smell smoke. We could burn up at any moment."

"But evil is the mere negation of good," Raul continued. "God allows man the freedom of will. Man often chooses evil. God permits him to do so, even foresees the choice, but does not try to determine it."

"There's a fire," I said, gathering up a bundle of manuscripts.

The light that filtered through the aperture was now a deeper shade of red. We were in the third room at the far end of the three long corridors. As we left, I heard the faintest of sounds behind us. Rats had been scurrying around in the shelves while we talked, but the sound was more secretive than rats make.

I turned apprehensively to see a tall man with a white beard that came to his waist; he was dressed in a white robe and a white turban. Too thin to be human, he was a collection of bones and hair moving lightly toward us, more wraith than living being. In a shriveled hand and wrapped about his wrist was a heavy gold chain.

I spoke to him in Arabic, greeting him as a keeper of scrolls, saying that those we were taking we would return. He made no reply. He kept on moving toward us, cautiously, as if he were on a high rope and feared to tumble.

He was speaking rapidly in a thin voice, words that I didn't understand. When he was quite near he bowed three times, and then as he rose from the last bow he raised the knotted chain. The small effort proved too much for him. With a groan he took a step and died at our feet.

Carrying torches, crusaders swept past us. They went to the

last of the rooms and set it ablaze, and then moved back toward us along the corridors from room to room with their torches. The leader, a knight in armor, came out of the smoke and snatched one of the scrolls from my arms.

"Look," he said to his companions. "These Arabs never learned to write. Their scrawlings look like drunken worms dipped into ink and set loose to wander around the page."

He turned to me. "What are you doing with these Arab lies?" he asked. "You're not an infidel, are you?"

There was much in his face that I didn't like. "We've been with the cardinal. The scrolls are souvenirs we're taking home to Assisi."

"To infect people with the babblings of the devil."

"As souvenirs."

He dropped the scroll — it was one by Maimonides — and set it afire. "You can take the ashes home as a souvenir," he said.

We ran into the palm-lined square in front of the mosque. It was crowded with crusaders and piled with loot. Fights had broken out. Threats and curses and shouts of joy rose above the crackling of the flames.

Making our way through the swirling smoke, we came upon Francis. He was on his knees, his gaze upon the burning mosque. We spoke to him twice. He didn't look at us or answer. Suddenly he began striking his head against the stones.

The beautiful mosque burned all that day; then, fearing that the thousands of unburied bodies would bring on a plague, Cardinal Pelagius burned them and set fires in the streets to cleanse the polluted air.

Christian losses were only thirty-six dead, a hundred and ten wounded. Few infidels were killed because there were only a few left to kill — no more than three thousand women and children and old men out of the eighty thousand that once had lived in Damietta. The women were not molested, since they were unappealing, but the children were rounded up and sold into slavery.

For two days Pelagius feared that Kamil, who had a small army with him on the river, would send it against us. But we soon heard that the sultan was in deep mourning.

When word of Damietta's fall had reached him in the night, he ordered silently, by gesture, that the messengers of the awful news have their heads removed, which was done at once. After hours of sadness he arose, drew the sword that he carried at his side, and severed his beard and braids and the long tail of his favorite horse. Those of his court did likewise.

The day after the Christian victory, Francis disappeared from camp. Brother Illuminato thought that he might be hiding in one of the mosques that was not ablaze. He was gone for more than a week, and when he returned he had little to say. He kept passing a hand over his haunted eyes, as if to brush away a nightmare from which he had not fully awakened. And when Pelagius asked him to speak at a victory feast, seemingly in an effort to humble him further, Francis refused.

"It is not a victory you celebrate," he told the cardinal. "It is a defeat and a humiliation."

"What would you have me do — sit and wring my hands?" the cardinal asked.

"Yes, sit, but do not wring your hands. Instead, ponder, knowing that the city of Jerusalem is not worth the lives of the thousands who starved to death in Damietta, not worth the death of the least among them, the lamb in the field, the dog in the street."

The meeting between the two men took place in the dining tent during the feast of victory. At Francis's words, the crowd jeered and banged on the table with their knives. Someone shouted, "Heretic!" Buonaguisa dei Buonaguisi, the brave Florentine who had raised the red and white flag of his commune upon Damietta's tallest barbican, mumbled a threat. The cardinal glared, his face drenched with the hatred that had prompted his letter to the pope so long before.

Francis waited until it was quiet. "I can't forget the furrowed fields sown with bodies, not with wheat," he said. "Nor the dead children held in the arms of their dead mothers." He had not touched his food, but he rose and left the table. At the tent door he said, "I will never forget these horrors and neither should you, Cardinal Pelagius."

The next day at dawn he left Damietta. Raul and I would have gone with him had not the boat, a leaky tub, been bound for Syria. We stood on the bank, waiting for the boat to anchor. A wind from the sea flapped Francis's tattered robe around his knees.

Brother Illuminato said, "And to think that the bridge was nearly complete."

"What bridge?" Francis asked.

"The bridge between the sultan and you. The bridge called love, whose stone pillars are Christ, our Lord and Redeemer."

Francis smiled. "Once long ago Brother Illuminato was a builder of bridges," he explained. "The builder of the pretty little bridge below Assisi and two big ugly bridges near Perugia and a half a dozen middling ones in other places. He's built so many bridges that he thinks and speaks and dreams only of bridges. Love is a bridge but it's not made of stones. It's made of the dew on the rose, the flaming bush, the shy smiles of children, birds in the meadow, a fall of snow on a winter day. And more, more."

Expecting Francis to go on with his poem, naming the signs of God's love, I waited for him to finish so I could ask him if Damietta was also a sign of God's love. But he was silent for a while; then he broke into his little dance, stepping lightly from side to side, clapping his hands above his head. Finally, he took a leap, as if he were about to leap through heaven's door. But he fell back to earth. He frowned and picked himself up and made the sign of the cross.

Our parting was awkward. Francis put a hand on my forehead. As he blessed me without words, tears sprang to his haunted eyes. The wind had shifted from the sea. It now blew in gusts from the smoldering city. We held our noses. The boat-men had trouble with the current and cursed us instead of the river.

The boat pulled to the shore as close as it could, but the two men had to wade. Francis was so thin that he looked like a stork striding through the water. In silence Raul and I watched them clamber aboard and the boat slip away on the current. A flight of silver gulls flew low above the water, following in the boat's wake, following him whom I no longer followed. The sun was bright in a cloudless sky. It sparkled on the river and turned the ruined walls of Damietta to gold. I turned away from every-thing. I closed my eyes and wept.

THIRTY-SIX

R aul and I learned very soon that we should have em-
barked on the leaky tub bound for Syria and, once there,
taken our chances on finding a ship sailing to Ostia or
Ancona or Venice. For on that day Cardinal Pelagius issued an
order prohibiting all vessels of whatever size from leaving the
port of Damietta.

His reason was simple. Every ship in the harbor was crammed
with loot. The looters, fearing that the sultan might rally his
forces and seize their treasures, were anxious to leave the fallen
city.

The loot-laden ships did not sail. The crusaders did not leave
the camp. And the sultan did not attack. Instead, after weeks
of mourning, he changed from the friendly man I had known
and dispatched heralds to the four corners of his kingdom,
announcing what whoever brought him a Christian head would
be given a purse filled with the purest gold.

Obsessed, Pelagius saw a chance to strike a last, crushing
blow. Drums beat, trumpets roused the camp. Crusaders, dreaming of home, fearing the loss of their treasures, reluctantly
heeded his call. In less than a month an army of thousands
was in pursuit of the sultan. Fortunately, Raul and I remained
in camp, assigned to care for those who had been wounded
during the two-year battle for Damietta and those who were
yet to come from the battle in the south.

Weeks passed and no wounded came. Then, in the midst of a
wild sandstorm, a lone horseman rode into camp to report

disaster. The Christian army had been trapped on the Nile, near the moated city of Tanis, trapped by the sultan and the clever use of a river in flood. The Christians suddenly found themselves caught between the Nile and a deep lake, in swift-running water. All would have perished had not the sultan, overcome by a generous mood (some said that he called out the name of Francis Bernardone as his men rescued the floundering crusaders), saved them. Thus ended the Fifth Crusade.

That night, defying the order of Cardinal Pelagius, ships sailed out of the harbor. Raul and I sailed two days later, bound for Venice with an honest-looking bark and a dishonest captain, who put us ashore at Kefallinía in Greece and told us we were now in Ancona, not far from Assisi, and bade us Godspeed as he headed back to Damietta. The great flock of swallows, moving north for the spring, that had roosted on our masts since the day we left Damietta knew more than we did. They wisely flew on, while we were stranded in Greece for two long months.

At last we found a ship, crossed the Mare Adriaticus, and landed on the beach at Ancona, just over the mountain from Assisi. Though we were held up on the way from Ancona and robbed of everything we owned except the scroll of essays by Maimonides, which after a short examination the brigands deemed worthless, we arrived home in midsummer.

The city held a grand festival for their crusading hero and heroine. My father prevailed upon the commune to declare two days of celebration instead of one. Church bells rang. Smoke curled up blue from busy ovens. There were three parades, three masses in the cathedral, and a concert of minstrels in San Rufino Square. Assisi loved festivals even more than they loved us.

On the last night of the celebration, while Raul and I were on the balcony watching the crowded square, a minstrel was tuning up his lute. He was directly below us, his face upturned. Thinking of Francis and the nights he had sung beneath the balcony, I let a lingering sigh escape me.

Raul said, "I see that you haven't forgotten."

Sailing home from Damietta, I had not mentioned Francis's name once. Indeed, one night in the harbor at Kefallinía while we were waiting for a ship, and the breeze was scented with oranges, I had taken Raul's hand and kissed his cheek, feeling that when I was wedded it would be to him, my valued tutor and dear friend since childhood, so kind and darkly handsome.

"You haven't forgotten, have you?" he said.

"No," I said, speaking the truth.

"You still think that one of these days you will have him back."

"Not back, because I never had him."

"But you moon."

I kissed Raul again, the second time since the night in Cyprus, but he didn't return the kiss. There was no response from him, not a word, nothing.

"And I don't moon," I said. "I never mooned. I was in love with Francis Bernardone but I never mooned."

"Your heart bled; is that better?"

"Yes."

"And now it doesn't?"

"Yes."

The lutist's voice rose around us in a plaintive song. Raul was leaning against a column. He looked very much like the column, cold and stiff and remote.

He said, "After all that happened in Damietta, it will be difficult for you to settle down in the scriptorium."

"I start in the morning. But I'll need your help. I've peeked at Maimonides. His Arabic is quite difficult and his ideas are somewhat beyond me. He writes about Plato and Aristotle a lot. I'll need your help, Raul. Shall we start early or late in the morning? Early, I hope."

"Early."

"At dawn?"

"At dawn. Because at noon or soon after, I leave for Córdoba."

I drew a breath. "Why Córdoba, pray tell?"

"To see if I can find the first essays Maimonides wrote. He was born in Córdoba, you know, and wrote there before the Christians drove him out with the rest of the Jews."

"But we have a scroll of his essays here. The one we brought from Damietta."

"Afterward I'll go to Morocco. Maimonides lived there for a while. Some of his essays are in the library at Fez."

"But all this will take you weeks and weeks. How long *will* it take?"

Standing against the pillar, like an actor about to make a speech, he didn't answer.

"I don't know how I will ever manage without you," I said.

"You will," he said. "You've become very good at copying and an artist at illumination. I have nothing more to teach you."

"In the morning you'll show me how to work with Maimonides. He can be very prolix. He'll take me all winter. By summer you'll be home."

Raul turned his back and said over his shoulder in the voice he used when imparting some detail about the art of illumination or Arabic, "As much as it distresses me, I must tell you that I'll be gone longer than next summer."

I was silent for a while, planning how best to calm his anger or salve his hurt feelings or whatever it was that suddenly had come over him.

The bells of San Rufino rang out, and one by one, sheep following their shepherd, other churches joined in. I had always liked the sound of bells, especially the merry bells of the smaller churches, but at this moment they all had a discordant ring.

I didn't plan it, but suddenly hot tears welled up in my eyes and ran down my cheeks. They must have glistened in the torchlight for Raul stepped forward and wiped them away.

"How old are you?" he asked.

"Too old to cry," I said.

He was standing so close now I expected him to take me in his arms. Instead, he cleared his throat.

"You wait breathlessly for more of the remarks I made before you left for Venice. But those accomplished little. More, if I wished to bother, would accomplish even less. You're a heedless girl, Ricca di Montanaro, heedless of all save your own large pleasures and small pains. You wince, you weep —"

He broke off in midsentence, before he was fairly launched on the list of my shortcomings. "Enough," he added and took a step toward the iron-banded door.

There was a sound to his voice that I had never heard before. I stepped in front of him to bar his way.

"Wait and we'll talk about everything," I cried. "You can't go running off and leave me here for months and months. What will I ever do?"

"Now that Francis has left, I don't know what you'll do. And it may surprise you to know that I don't care."

I was speechless. His back was toward the torchlight streaming up from the square, where revelers danced. His face was hidden from me. I didn't need to see it. In desperation I flung my arms wide, across the doorway.

"I don't believe you," I cried. "You're lying. You do care. I can tell. You have always cared!"

He escaped my arms and went quickly through the door. He paused at the stairs and said in the quietest of voices, "And what's more, Ricca di Montanaro, I'll not be back in a few months or in a year. In truth, I shall never come back."

I listened to his footsteps on the stairs as they slowly faded away and were lost in an awful silence.

THIRTY-SEVEN

I saw Francis only once again, a few months before his death. It was at Porziuncola on a day of blue skies and birds singing in the fields and trees blossoming, a day like those he especially loved and wrote poems about. But as he faced the crowded church, holding flowers in his hand, he was far from joyous.

Brother Illuminato had warned me that Francis was changed. "Don't expect too much of him," he had said. "For months now, through part of the winter, he's lived alone at La Verna, high in the clouds, starving to bring himself closer to God."

I knew La Verna only from a distance; I had looked up at it from the plain as I rode by. A harsh cliff surrounded on all sides by a mountain, crested by perpetual clouds and swept by violent winds, it was the home of falcons and wild beasts. I had always shuddered to see it soaring far above me.

"Francis went there seeking God," Illuminato said. "Whether he found Him I don't know. He has never told me, but he came down from the mountain in a quiet mood. You will find him very weak and distraught."

Despite this warning, I was shocked by the man I saw at the altar holding a bunch of spring flowers. He was pale and thin — this I had expected — but I had not thought to find him nearly blind, groping for the lectern when he began to talk.

From time to time I'd heard that doctors were treating his eyes with burning irons. The signs of this treatment, in scars and furrowed flesh, wrung my heart. They said that he had contracted an eye disease in Syria, known for its diseases, but I knew the truth. The blindness had come upon him that morning in Damietta when he looked out at its broken walls and burning mosques, the streets peopled with the dead and dying, when he realized that all this had been done by Christians in the name of Christ.

He spoke briefly to those who had gathered, ending his talk with a benediction, in a voice that smoldered with fire.

"Lord, make us an instrument of Thy peace," he said. "Where there is hatred, let us sow love; where there is injury, pardon; where there is doubt, faith; where there is darkness, light; and where there is sadness, joy."

Worshipers ran forward to crowd around him and touch his robe. Fearful of old memories, I didn't join them, but when I returned to Assisi I went to San Rufino and prayed for his soul and for mine also.

There were many rumors during the next few weeks. The city was saddened by them. People wept openly in the streets, and the churches were filled. Some of the rumors were true. The truest: Francis was dying.

The doctors strove mightily, trying to restore his wasted body and his sight also, because he kept asking to see the sun and the moon and the stars. They heated an iron in the fire and drew it out, shining hot. Before they used it on his eyes, Francis stirred himself and sang a hymn in praise of Brother Fire, asking him to be kind and courteous in this hour of need.

Days passed in the quiet city. Word came that Francis wished to be moved from the bishop's fine palace where he lay. He asked that they build him a hut of straw and timber at Porziuncola, and though many feared that if this were done, if he were left alone, he would be snatched from the hut by those who were envious of Assisi, the hut was built and he was taken there.

Beyond Valecchi, the dreadful village that furnished Assisi

with all its executioners, at the crossing of two narrow roads, Francis asked that his bed be set down. There, though he was blind, he raised his eyes and blessed the place of his birth.

Word raced through the city that he was dead. But other news came: Francis was alive and had asked the brothers who were with him to remove his clothes and his bandages and place him upon the earth. Weeping when they saw his ruined face and body, they dressed him again in cloak and hood.

Days went by. Then word came that Francis was dead and that at the moment of his death an exaltation of larks had been seen above the hut where he lay. There was an exaltation in Assisi, too. People wept but also raised their voices, joyful that Francis had been released from his earthly ills. There were those, however, who were secretly glad to be rid of him, among them my father and Rinaldo. My mother remained in her rooms until the day of the burial.

It was a sparkling day with a breath of winter in the October air. Leagues long, the cortege moved away from the hut at Porziuncola to the sound of bells and trumpets, up the winding road to Assisi, and through the big gate to the church of San Giorgio.

After the service, while my mother lay weeping on the stones before the altar, I sought out Clare di Scifi. I found her on the church steps waiting for me. She was dressed in the white and black garments of the Poor Clares, which, severe though they were, did nothing to dim her beauty; indeed, they seemed to enhance it.

I smiled and kissed her because we were rivals no longer, and we talked for a while about how well behaved were those who had come from other places, even the people from the jealous town of Perugia. When we ran out of chatter, in the midst of the silence that fell between us, Clare said:

"You've loved Francis Bernardone for years."

"How do you know so much?" I asked.

"It's not a secret. It's a scandal. Everyone knows that you

228

have been in love with him since the day you disrobed on the cathedral steps."

"Long before that," I said. "I was born in love with him."

Clare started to smile.

"It is possible," I said.

She shook her head. "I can imagine you loving Christ when you were born because He is divine and divine love is everlasting. It exists always, from the beginning to the end."

"Human love is divine also," I said. "I heard Francis say so, once in Porziuncola. I remember the hour and the day and the month."

"And the year, of course."

"I remember him saying, 'O Master, grant that I may not so much seek to be consoled as to console, to be understood as to understand, to be loved as to love. Love is . . .'"

Trumpets drowned out my words and a chorus of bells rang forth. As Francis was borne away, we followed him.

Clare said, "When he took his vows, during all of the days since that time, when you were breathlessly pursuing him, did you ever say to yourself, 'Ricca di Montanaro, you are committing a dreadful sin'?"

"No, why should I?"

"But now that he is dead, what do you say to yourself?"

"I say that sometime he will be a saint, though this is the least of all that he would wish for himself. And that you will be a saint also — Saint Clare of Assisi. And that never, never, in this life or afterward, will I become a saint."

"You feel little."

"Little and seldom."

"Not a shred of contrition for all your lustful striving."

I shook my head and was silent. I had no intention of letting Clare know how I thought or felt.

We were on foot, trudging along in the mud, hopping over puddles because rain had fallen in the night. We came to the bottom of the hill, to the crossing of the two narrow roads. It was here that Francis had asked those who were carrying him to put him down so that he might look back, though he couldn't see, and bless the city of his birth.

Suddenly to me he was there again, kneeling in the mud, his arms outstretched, his blind eyes fixed upon the gray walls of Assisi. Myself blinded, I thought of the thousands of outcasts he had taken into his arms and of the multitude yet to come whom he would comfort.

Clare was in a wheat field, wandering about. She came back with a wildflower called footsteps-of-spring that somehow had bloomed beyond its time, and she gave it to me.

The trumpets were quiet now. The only sound I heard was the singing of larks. Then from beyond a sharp bend I heard a bell.

We came upon the man suddenly. He was in the middle of the road, not ten strides away, walking slowly with a leper's bell held in both his hands. He started as he saw us and shambled off toward a clump of trees, the iron bell still ringing.

I overtook him though he tried to flee. His face was thin and scarred. I held out the four-petaled flower Clare had given to me. He glanced at it for a moment. Then he took the flower and held it to his twisted lips and thanked me with his eyes.